Influences in MB

(Rudolfo Anaya)

Allegorical — spiritual journey
of Johnny Flynn

Esme — Ultima

Scottish "Be Happy While You Are Living
for you're a long Time dead"

The Crossing

A Novel

"When love is trapped in the maelstrom between then and now, the crossing cannot be made."

"Run from fate and he will catch you.
Hide and he will find you.
Turn on him and he will cower."

Ashby Jones

The Crossing

A Novel

Addison & Highsmith

Addison & Highsmith Publishers

Las Vegas ◊ Oxford ◊ Palm Beach

Published in the United States of America by
Histria Books
7181 N. Hualapai Way, Ste. 130-86
Las Vegas, NV 89166 USA
HistriaBooks.com

Addison & Highsmith is an imprint of Histria Books. Titles published under the imprints of Histria Books are distributed worldwide.

Library of Congress Control Number: 2021931159

ISBN 978-1-59211-089-6 (hardcover)

To my Family
for your unwavering love and support

Chapter 1

Roughly a mile from the Statue of Liberty, Johnny Flynn stood trembling on the bridge of the ship called *The Pestilence*. His hands were rope-bound at the wrists and a rucksack filled with heavy stones was strapped to his back. His executioner, seaman Bile, named for the Celtic god of Hell by Johnny's long-gone friend and fellow prisoner, Seamus, had tried in vain to kill Johnny every day on this voyage from Ireland, and now he would have his way. The vessel from which Bile would send Johnny to his death was the recently recovered, ancient famine ship found in the Bay of Kinsale. The ship still contained the skeletons of the three hundred dead who'd tried to escape the Great Famine by taking passage to America but whose journey had been ended by typhus, cholera, and tuberculosis. In hopes of hiding their humiliation, the Irish had returned *The Pestilence* to its parting pier unannounced and mothballed in what soon became a drying, wooded alcove south of Kinsale, leaving the three hundred bodies to rot in the hold.

The ship was discovered by a group of young Irish campers shortly after the Treaty with the victorious Brits was signed, ending the War of Independence. Soon thereafter, in the fall of 1921, the Rebels filled the arid tributary with fresh water, freeing the ship and setting it on a crossing to America to test its sea-worthiness. The next step in purging their embarrassment for the deaths was to cleanse the ship's hold of the bones and restore its ability to make money for the Emerald Isle.

Johnny, having been declared a traitor to the Irish cause when it was discovered he'd once served on the firing squad that executed James Connolly, the cherished signatory and contributing author of the Proclamation, was given a deceptively free passage to America — along with Seamus, a declared deserter — for his work in the hold. But the cavernous hold was thought to be a death-trap, as it was commonly believed that the hulls of famine ships were infested with disease. The members of the Kinsale Court secretly informed the Rebels in charge of the vessel that if Johnny and Seamus somehow survived dying from disease, they were to be drowned for their treachery before they reached America.

In the torch-lit hull they chipped away at the skeletons with spades and crowbars, prying them from the wooden bunks and the floors, the walls, shelves, and each other until after three weeks in the contagion the skeletons seemed to come alive. Occasionally, they caught themselves making friends with the dead, asking about their passages, jobs and children and even inviting the phantoms to go with them topside before being fed to the sharks. There the illusions joined them for meagre lunches of salt water, bacon, and black bread. All the while they watched the sharks swarming behind the ship in anticipation of the bones being tossed overboard.

As Bile blared orders behind him on the bridge, Johnny fought for distraction and a last-minute sense of peace. During the crossing, fate's metaphorical existence had spread through his senses, causing him to assign it a grand and more inclusive control over life's events. Johnny had drawn the conclusion from Bile and his reign over goodness, that fate, more broadly defined, governed one's destiny and butchered one's hopes when they became too inspiring. It had been the case with Nora, the love of Johnny's life, and the hopes he'd had when the journey to America began, and during the crossing, the role of fate had embedded itself in his mind and soul for the remainder of his life, which was about to be cut vastly short.

Johnny wasn't blindfolded because Bile wanted him to die in regret, looking out at what might have been. "I've killed many a man," Bile told him as he filled Johnny's rucksack with the stones, "and I can tell you this, more than one has begged me to blind him before he left this earth. I asked each of them why, and, in one way or another, they all said the same thing: 'My eyes are tethered to my heart and my heart to the past. I do not want to die looking at what might have been.' I granted their requests, but you, Johnny Flynn, are the exception."

Johnny tried to set his eyes on Liberty to see if she might be reaching out to him. She did not reply but remained a distant, formless blur whose green complexion had been masked by the winter's ochre sunset. He thought he heard the faraway sound of a church bell. Was it Sunday? He'd lost all track of time, bound as he'd been for a fortnight in the hull where Bile had kept him unfed and constantly awake, hoping Johnny would die from the strain and if not, to ensure that Johnny would be too weak to survive his plunge into the sea. As the ship was about to pull into Hudson Harbor, Bile had given him a choice, to die by gunshot or by drowning. Johnny had chosen the latter because while an extra minute drowning would barely add to his mortality, it might add at least a chance for one last memory of Nora or one throbbing pulse of his heart. Maybe it would only allow for just a brief, ghostly silence, impossible to separate from death itself.

Whatever the extra moment might offer, Johnny would take it. He'd faced the brevity of gunfire many times on the battlefield fighting for the Rebels against the British whose army he had once belonged to. And he'd faced the barrel again at the hands of Nora, who discovered what she'd never suspected, that Johnny had served on her father's firing squad. She made Johnny's treachery known to their brigade commander, and when O'Neill issued the order to execute Johnny, she'd volunteered to be his executioner. Moreover, she'd insisted that she alone take him to the site of his death, an untrammeled bluff overlooking the harbor of Kinsale.

"Up on the plank, you feckin' traitor!" Bile barked.

With the stones shifting in his rucksack, Johnny struggled to climb onto the gangplank.

"Move, goddamn you! You should have died on board, like your friend, Seamus! 'Twud'uv been my pleasure to feed you to the sharks along with him."

The ship's staff, all former Volunteers, who like Johnny had offered to serve the rebel cause and vowed never to quit, cheered as Johnny edged toward the tip of the plank. With Bile's horrid breath in his nostrils, he inched toward the end of the board trapped in the brief but deafening span between life and death. Nora's voice settled on its resilience. "I love you," she said. His fear, dread, and near-by hysteria fused into a glowing image of her face as she raised the pistol to his temple. Tears streamed from her fierce eyes when she jerked the gun from his skull at the last possible second, stepped away, and quickly mounted her horse to gallop off into Nevermore.

Johnny's legs began to shake so hard the plank quivered.

"Get on with it! You're wasting God's time!" Bile shouted.

Johnny slipped into the plank's rhythm. He flexed his legs, pressed down on the plank with all his might and took the deepest breath he could possibly muster. But before he could release it, on the plank's sharp rebound, Bile shoved him into the air.

Unable to control his form, he jerked his knees to his chest just before the frigid water opened to swallow him. As he sank, his heartbeat thudded against his ribs while the quickness of the cold sent a numbing pain into his arms. His ears shrieked as the light disappeared. Water surged through his nostrils down his throat causing him to swallow convulsively. Cascading deeper, he felt as though he was tumbling through an empty well. His rucksack led the fall.

When he hit bottom, he thought his back had shattered and he grimaced, swallowing even more water. Instinctively, he began to kick and paddle his arms. Astonished at how easily he rose, he suddenly realized the rucksack had split open. The straps were still about his shoulders but the load was much lighter. In one motion he lifted a leg to shove a boot between his wrists and jam it into the leather bands. At first, he thought the rope had ripped off his skin like a pair of gloves but his hands had slipped through the binding.

Instantly, a rousing paradox sprung from his melancholy and surged through him. There had to be light once more, land anew and another morning!

He doubled over and rammed his legs against death's pull. Forcing his breath out in little puffs, he sank after each rise but went slightly higher each time. He kept telling himself that he would not die. He'd come to America to escape death.

When the sky's orange dome broke through the darkness, he shot his arms frantically above his head and with all his might thrust them to his side again and again. At last, he surfaced into the blessed glare of evening sunlight. He caught a glimpse of *The Pestilence*, its stern barely visible as it disappeared behind the Lady into her shadow. And then his body gave out.

Breathless, he tried to call out for Nora, using the Irish name for freedom bequeathed to her by her father — *Sarosa*. He couldn't choke out the word. Just when he thought he was about to go under for good, so close and so far from the harbor, something bumped into his skull. He reached up and grabbed onto a loose, floating oar. While it couldn't support his weight for more than a moment, it briefly kept him from going under.

Blinking away the brackish water, he caught sight of a rowboat moving toward him with two men moving, swapping their lone oar back and forth. He seized his oar with both hands and held on as they drew closer. Clutching his rucksack, they dragged him over the side of the boat and laid him on the bottom between two large kegs.

"My God, let's get this sack off you," one said. "Two stones inside? They threw you off, did they?

"Thank you," Johnny rasped, barely able to move and unwilling to answer. "God, thank you."

A man with a scared face leaned closer. "You sound Irish. Well then, God may have had something to do with saving you, mate." The man pointed to Liberty. "After all, how could something that large have made it across the Pond without His help?"

"Where... where are..." Johnny couldn't finish.

"We're headed to Hell's Kitchen," the voice answered. "They call it Satan's playground, though some say God's been seen there having a drink or two. We're the Swamp Angels, rum-runners who keep Him supplied."

Johnny could not feel his lips move as he attempted to smile. He looked up at the sky, bound for America at last. The boat inherited the flow of the water and so too did he.

He struggled to remove a small cross from his pocket. It was made of the finger bones of the baby twins whose skeletons he'd pried from their mother's ossified grasp. As if memories were flowing through the bones, they were warm to the touch. Before following Bile's order to throw the skeletons away, when he was searched before boarding the ship, he'd slipped the tiny bones into his shirt pocket and later knotted them with a bootlace. The tiny fingers clasped each other in the shape of a cross. He'd sworn to keep it with him always, as a reminder that forgiveness for killing another, regardless of the side one was on, stood forever apart from the seeker. And for those who had served on a firing squad, though justifications could be had, not even with love as powerful as he and Nora had shared, could forgiveness be found.

"My name's Seth, mate, and the young insect by me we call Locust. What's yours?"

"Johnny," he whispered.

"And your last name?"

"Johnny," he replied and closed his eyes. If he had no full name, maybe he would not be pursued in this new world. Maybe he could find a new beginning, a purpose which could not be taken from him, neither by his guilt nor his longing for Nora.

Chapter 2

The Swamp Angels hired Johnny to run whisky to the pubs. They gave him a prime spot, Hailey's on West Twenty-fifth Street, a speakeasy that dazzled him with its rebellion and joy. From the first day after he moved into the tiny tenement the Angels had found for him, he became awash in the Christmas season. It had eluded him for years, and he felt a shock of happiness and gratitude — except for when he feared being found out for the turncoat he'd been declared, and except for Nora's relentless presence in his heart.

The peculiar American law called Prohibition had just been enacted. Alcohol was illegal. But Hailey's was filled with citizens who with jazz in their souls and whiskey in their glasses were enthusiastically attempting to overthrow the recently imposed law. Johnny found spirits especially high deep in Hell's Kitchen where rebellion had become the rite of the night and guilt the rite of the morning. But layered within those transient states, he saw victims of both then and now: the mangled veterans of the World War, the homeless, disease-ridden immigrants and the bones of the dead afloat in the cemetery of the sewers.

Set between the joyful and the bereaved were the warlords, the gangs and gangsters from whom sex, murder, torture, and affliction could be purchased for prices spelled out on menu-like scrolls, had for a quarter. These thugs cared for nothing beyond governing the fate of their victims while relishing in the shock of their detestable surprises. Little did they know that fate, the self-ascribed master of fortune, controlled many of the outcomes customarily attributed to God and instinct, and governed them as well.

In the Kitchen, fate was God's taxi driver, obedient and loyal while in His presence. But when he dropped The Almighty off at Hailey's, fate was at play. Joyous at being left alone in the swirling presence of randomness, he could not help himself. He had to distribute the gifts of disappointment and sorrow, which is to say, he fed on the hopes of those who celebrated, those convinced there is more to life than regret.

Chapter 3

Despite the freezing December cold, the sties in Johnny's eyes had begun to burn as though ants had invaded his eyeballs. Swiping at them and sweating, he approached the entrance to the sewer on the corner of Ninety-fourth and Death Avenue, an interchangeable epithet given both Tenth and Eleventh Avenues, so-named because of the many poor and befuddled vagrants who mistook its newly laid train tracks for a bedframe and the lonely sound of the neighborhood's old tram to be a begging call from God to take solace and rest for the night.

At the nearby pier, the Swamp Angels had filled his cart with ten-gallon kegs of rum for Hailey's. Though trash and bones cluttered the drearily cobbled tunnel, Johnny always delivered his allotment through the vast cavern to avoid being robbed or arrested. Even though the public rage against Prohibition had lowered the cops' enthusiasm for arresting rumrunners, the law had caused the demand for whisky to soar. While the pirate gangs were cheerfully willing to meet the rising demand, the supply of Caribbean rum came to the Bay just twice a month, pitting the rival gangs against one another to eliminate the scarcity.

The closer Johnny got to the tunnel opening, the stronger became his urge to disappear into it. He was about to pivot the cart around the stone bolster above the entrance ramp when a massive figure sprang from behind the wall and grabbed him by shoulder. Seizing the cart's handle, Johnny spun and gasped, stunned at the sight of Bile, grinning at him.

Bile's face had not changed. It still possessed the brutal, rutted surface which spoke of too many years in battle and a life of cruelty, aging him far beyond Johnny's twenty-eight years. Double layers of brown teeth were embedded in his gums like randomly scattered gravestones. His bulging eyes blazed over gouty cheeks. His highly tanned, salty temple slid from a bald head to rest above eyes frozen in hate.

Speechless, Johnny stared into them.

Bile's lips cracked into an unexpected smile. "By God, Johnny Flynn, it's you at last, the deserter, the one who got away — or until now thought he had." He jerked a pistol from the black trench coat and jammed it into Johnny's ribs.

"Ahhhh!" Johnny clutched his side.

"You can't escape fate, you lying traitor! Get down the ramp. Ireland shall finally have its revenge!"

Johnny's heart pounded. Bile, a former Black and Tan expelled from the British Army for torturing prisoners while fighting on the Continent, had been captured by the Irish Republican Army in a battle outside Kinsale. Spared execution, he was given conditional passage to America with the proviso he would stand merciless guard over Johnny and Seamus as they toiled to scrub clean the ship's hold of the skeletons. Bile pledged to the court that they would either die from disease caught from the infected remains of the dead or, if not, be drowned before reaching America.

Seamus, who'd become Johnny's friend, wasn't even allowed to die from the cholera he'd caught. On that stormy day, while taking a basket of bones from the hold to the stern in order to feed the sharks, Seamus slipped on the rain-drenched deck, slid the length of the ship as it rose on a turbulent wave and smashed headfirst into the railing that spanned the stern. Bile ran to the bow of *The Pestilence*, lifted Seamus from the deck, and threw him overboard to the delight of the white-tip sharks.

An instantaneous demand to avenge Seamus poured through Johnny as Bile pressed the gun between his ribs.

"Flynn, by the time we saw them pull you from the Hudson, the ship was in water too shallow to turn and chase you. They blamed me for not loading your rucksack with enough stones and said I wouldn't be allowed to return to Ireland until I saw to your death. I took an oath, swearing to my mates and God himself I would correct my mistake and by Christ, I'm about to!" He shoved Johnny toward the opening. "I'll take your head back in my rucksack to show I kept my promise!"

Johnny would be dead in seconds if he didn't act. Back when he'd stood guard over the Rebel leaders of The Rising who were waiting their execution, Patrick Pearse had prolonged his life, at least for a few minutes, by asking Johnny for time to kiss the childhood cross his mother had sent him.

"Please, give me a moment," Johnny begged, quickly reaching under Bile's grip for his shirt pocket and pressing down to show him the outline of a small cross. "Please, before I go, may I kiss my cross. I made it from the bones of two children in the hold, cradled in their mother's arms."

When Bile dropped his eyes to stare at the image and its memory, Johnny kneed him squarely between his legs, rammed an arm under Bile's armpit, pivoted and flipped him over his hip. Bile tumbled down the ramp to the cobbled floor of the sewer. The gun clattered on the stones. Johnny shoved the cart down the ramp. At the sight of the cart hurtling toward him, Bile screamed.

The cart's steel-banded wheels smashed into his chin and hips, caromed off the tunnel's stone walls and wobbled to a halt. Johnny rushed down the ramp, grabbed the pistol and dropped to his knees in front of Bile as blood poured from his nose.

"You fucking bastard! You threw Seamus overboard and wouldn't even let me *try* to help him." Johnny buried the tip of the gun in Bile's ear.

Bile jerked his head back and squealed. His eyelids fluttered. Johnny yanked the gun from his ear and pressed the barrel against Bile's lips. He leaned over until they were eye-to-eye. "We named you Bile because he was the god of Hell. We were afraid of you. You starved us, beat us and laughed with every lash. You appeared from nowhere to stamp out our hope of coming to America and replace it with fear. And you never fought for Ireland — you fought against it. Now Seamus has *his* revenge!"

"Don't, don't! Please don't!" The plea ground into a snarl. Bile grimaced as the gun trembled against his lips.

"Don't worry," Johnny said. "I'm not going to shoot you — there's no need. But I'm staying in your sight until you're gone. I'll be the last thing you see on planet Earth."

Bile squeezed his eyes shut.

"Open your fucking eyes!" Johnny shouted. "I'm your escort to Hell."

"Help me."

"Did I hear you say, *help me*?" Johnny inched so close Bile's breath made him wince. "Can't you see I *am* helping, helping God rid the world of Satan's shit?"

"I'm glad I killed the scrawny bastard," Bile muttered. His eyebrows drooped toward his eyes. His body sank into itself. He was dead.

Johnny cocked the gun. He was about to fire a bullet through Bile's skull just to make sure he was gone, when he remembered what the priests attending the executions at Kilmainham jail had stated as Gospel: each executed rebel had to receive the *coup de grace* before they could be anointed with the oils of sanctimony. The anointment guaranteed the victim's soul had been set free to find its way to heaven.

"Your fucking soul's staying right here," Johnny whispered into Bile's ear. "I've only got rum and a handful of sludge to anoint you with and I won't be wasting either."

The harshness of his words filled Johnny with a strange sense of victory, similar to those he'd often felt in battle, on those especially brutal occasions when revenge had served to convince him that might did indeed make right — as when his column bombed Angel's, the Tans' favorite bar in Bandon, and a dozen murderous Tans were cast flaming through the pub's huge glass window. They'd damn well gotten what they'd deserved, and Johnny and his men were better off for having delivered it. That night they celebrated by counting the dead and raising the count to cheers after every round.

If there was such a thing a thing as an afterlife, Johnny hoped Seamus would be smiling down on him. Maybe, together with apostles, he was in heaven's tavern, hoisting a glass. He emptied the cartridge, sprinkled the bullets over Bile's body and threw the pistol into the darkness. When the clatter settled, the silence released a deep and welcoming sense of relief. Johnny grabbed the cart and set off in a rush, feeling a glow he'd not experienced since the evening on the O'Briens' porch with Nora. She'd told him that the rain pouring down softly on the tin roof sounded like her father's favorite Beethoven symphony, *Dead Heroes*, written to honor the ghosts of slain martyrs escorted back to the safety of Valhalla. She'd looked at him and whispered, her voice barely above the rain's patter, "I love you, Johnny Flynn."

She said it for the first time on the porch that night, and for the last time on the bluff above Kinsale just before she lowered the pistol from his temple.

Thunder rumbled overhead, reverberating like a bass drum along the walls of the sewer. Rain began dripping through the manholes. The tunnel took on the tightening darkness of a grotto. Every day at roughly this time, whether in the sewers or on the streets, melancholy's compression settled around him. With every sundown, even as the holiday lights were coming on, loneliness pierced his heart and hope vanished. When it came on, he had to beeline it to Hailey's where he could lose himself in poteen, which took him away from the reality of the past into the realm of fantasy where he could be alone, but not lonely, and settle into the familiar self he couldn't otherwise recognize.

Clinging to the good deed he'd just carried out and trying his best to delay the past from invading him, he shoved the cart with all his might, released his hands and ran to keep up with it.

"I'm coming!" he called out, plowing ahead so furiously the wheels banging the stones created a continuous unbroken noise. At last, he surfaced on the corner of Twenty-sixth Street and Tenth Avenue, just a short block from Hailey's. Light snowflakes greeted him. He hurried to Hailey's, veered from the street up the hidden path that ran through the pub's small garden.

As soon as he parked the cart by the spindly storage shed, the thick green prison door Hailey had bought in an auction on Blackwell's Island opened, and Hailey stepped outside, puffing the cold. The roar of jazz and the clamor of patrons accompanied him. Though it was early, even for a Saturday, the night was in full swing.

"Where you been, lad? We're on fire in here." The snow settled on Hailey's thick white hair and on his huge shoulders draped with a green bartender's apron.

"Sorry, but I had a bit of a delay on the way down, a turn of fate, if you will," Johnny said.

"Have to do with your eyes?"

More with Bile's, Johnny thought. "Want the kegs in the basement?"

"We don't have time, lad. Just roll them into the shed and throw a canvass over them. We've still got part of last night's backup in the cellar. I've saved your space at the bar. Eoin's already opened a bottle of our best poteen, but go slowly, three glasses at most, for our new singer for the Christmas season starts tonight. I think I told you about her. Her body's a bit off, but my God can she sing. She'll be on at eight."

Relieved to be within reach of the poteen, Johnny unlatched the kegs and rolled them into the shed, covered them with the torn canvass, and after pinching at his eyes hurried into the din.

Chapter 4

Barely an hour into the evening, Johnny had already drunk Hailey's three-glass allotment, downing it fast in hopes of slipping quickly into the soothing territory of forgetfulness. His fourth glass of poteen, the scarce and powerful Irish moonshine brought ashore by only one pirate ship, sat eye-level before him as he slumped against the bar. The reflection of Christmas lights floated in the whisky's purple hue, the mystical color giving him a sense that the netherworld was well on its way to his aid. The memory of Bile's grimacing request, to be left alive, faded from guilt to pleasure and gradually disappeared altogether.

Fastened to the Irish tricolors tacked to the wall above the cash register were the baseball bats gifted to Hailey by former Yankee relief pitcher, Lefty O'Doul. To Johnny's smarting eyes the overlaid bats formed a blurry, misshapen cross in the form of an "X", which strangely prompted him to wonder if such a shape would have made it more comfortable for the crucified Jesus than the upright "T". He welcomed the idiocy, because it meant his mind was beginning to drift from port.

He looked down the counter trying to make out the simple but unforgettable words of Sir Walter Scott that Hailey had etched into the wood for the veterans. But the letters flowed in a muddled rivulet down the long, shiny stream of the bar. It mattered not, for the words were locked in his memory. He shook his head, took a deep breath and hoisted his glass to Seamus, "Soldier rest, thy warfare o'er."

The Irish War of Independence, the war he'd fought with the rebels to win — but he himself had ultimately lost — was over. While a relief, it was beyond him why Michael Collins, such a firebrand rebel leader, had agreed to a Treaty allowing the British to govern Ireland, but his disappointment gradually succumbed to the swelling sound of customers who'd begun to dance and shout to Hailey's scratchy, vinyl recordings of jazz greats as they joyously celebrated the upcoming holidays and raged against the absurdity of Prohibition.

Johnny found himself staring at a host of swirling faces gleeful with the glorious trickery of a speakeasy which gave them a brief hideaway in a make-believe world of joy and bliss. A blend of businessmen, flappers, veterans, and hookers fused indistinguishably with policemen in disguise, gangsters and thugs all masked by the eerily colorful haze of Christmas lights. Were they all trying to hide from something, someone, evading what was for what they hoped would come? If, so, they, like he, had come to the right place.

The poteen had taken seed and was gathering harvest in his head. The lone foreign being who stared back at him from the mirror by the cash register attested to that. His once fine-looking face now resembled those of the prisoners in Kilmainham, paled and furrowed by the mold that had gathered on the wet stone walls of their cells. Greasy and disheveled, his dark hair seemed to cast a shadow over a skull that housed the unshakable memories of Nora. Losing her made him feel he'd been weathered by a God grown weary of filling people's hearts with hope. Instead, He'd hired fate to be His go-between.

Johnny glanced away from the mirror but could barely distinguish the patrons. The ever-present swarm of lice in the hull of *The Pestilence* had feasted on his lids and rims leaving small, but blistering sores that had started to burn more each day. Squinting to partly drain them, he reached for his glass but it stood closer than his eyes suggested and he knocked it over.

"Fuck," he mumbled. "Another!" he blurted out. His voice vanished into the racket.

He was about to shout again when, like a call to arms, the blast of a trumpet erupted from the elephantine silver speakers set on the tiny stage. A saxophone growled through the din, followed immediately by the piercingly high note of a flute. For several beats the sounds drifted down the corridors of their registers where they seemed to gather in secrecy before bursting into a thunderous crescendo that overwhelmed the background noise. The frequencies reverberated between Johnny's ribs like an electric shock. Grabbing onto the counter he settled the seat and lunged for his overturned glass, grabbing it by the stem. Sensing a victory of sorts, he peered down the bar. There in one whirling motion, Hailey and Eoin, his young Italian helper with an Irish name, were frantically filling glasses, ringing the cash register and slapping change on the counter.

Johnny waved his glass. "Down here, mates!"

Hailey glanced at him, shook his head and continued to serve the customers. Eoin took no notice.

Johnny shoved his glass toward the rafters, "Another, Goddamnit!"

"Wait your blessed turn!" Hailey shouted.

Relieved he'd at least been acknowledged, Johnny settled back onto the stool. That terrible day on the bluffs returned but this time he had trouble telling if it was a memory or the same day somehow brought forward in time. With her eyes full of tears, Nora pressed the barrel of her Mauser against his temple and cocked the hammer. Johnny froze.

"Don't you think you've had enough, lad?"

Johnny drew back almost falling off the stool. At first, he thought a deflated soccer ball had sprung up before him. He squinted but barely recognized Hailey's sea-green eyes peeking out from the sweaty folds of his cheeks.

"Mate, maybe 'twud be wise to call it a night with the booze." Hailey's tone suggested the words were more a demand than counsel. "We're taking a break after this record to introduce the singer. Stay steady lad, so you can enjoy her."

Johnny thought hiring a singer for the Christmas season was a stupid idea because no one wanted to listen to someone praising God when the most important thing on everyone's mind was overturning Prohibition. He tipped his glass toward Hailey. "In that case make it a double."

"Look here, lad, given what you've had already, a double could well kill you. It's poteen you're drinking."

Johnny's face became a vacant smile. "But it's been a while since the last round, and I got some catching up to do."

Hailey rolled his eyes, ballooned his cheeks and reached under the counter for the bottle. "Promise me now, this here's the last one. You gotta get hold of yourself. Once the lass is done singing, I'll be back to check on you. You can stay out in the shed, if you feel you can't make it home," he said, pouring the glass half full.

"Come on, Paddy, to the brim. After all, I'm your favorite rumrunner. And if that's not enough, you should be proud of me. I killed a Tan today."

Hailey looked alarmed and quickly scanned the room. "Quiet, you drunken arse. If there're coppers in here, a lie like that could turn us in for a Christmas dole." He sighed and went back to the pour. "Here then, to the brim for your labor. But not one drop more." He topped off the glass and stuck the bottle under the counter as the record ended. "Got to go now. You stay put."

Johnny watched Hailey shove his way through the crowd, then drained the tumbler and stretched over the counter to fetch the bottle. Grinning to himself, he rounded off the glass yet again and took a swallow so large it caught in his throat before the torrid but gratifying burn scathed his chest. Pleased with what he knew to be forthcoming, he set the bottle on the counter and tried to settle in. Breathing deeply to cool his throat, he planted his elbows on the bar to steady himself.

"I killed a Tan today," he heard himself say, as if in the meter of a rhyme, to jest with Hailey. Bile's plea to live returned on the confession, followed by his statement of gratitude that he'd killed Seamus. Johnny watched Bile's chest surrender to the afterlife and attempted to smile, but the smile did not come. Nor had it ever come in battle, not even when watching an enemy die. It kept its distance because in war such memory had no guilt to revive it. Why then had this one returned? "The son-of-a bitch deserved it," he said, pointing to the mirror.

It didn't take long before the memory, along with all awareness and rationale, flushed from his brain. He smiled at the vacuum, welcoming the whisky's most treasured gift, the vivid distortions of time set in a calm and caring kindness: his pram on the cobbles of Cork; the crippled, elderly spy who helped him find his way on the streets of Bandon just before he led the attack on Angel's, the Tans favorite watering hole; James Connolly's nurse in the Royal Castle, Nurse Meeks, who'd helped him find where Nora lived, and Dahl, his cherished, dying friend, who wrapped in Johnny's arms and unaware Nora had just shown up in the doorway, asked Johnny if she knew he'd been on her father's firing squad.

Hailey's voice rumbled over the microphone drawing Johnny's eyes toward the stage. A lime-colored mist rose around the small, raised platform. A strangely shaped figure, which in the haze seemed more like a specter than a human, drifted toward Hailey. The image appeared off-center, set into misaligned halves like a poorly assembled Lady of Liberty. Squinting, Johnny leaned toward the stage. Reaching for the loudspeaker, the now willowy figure came together for a second before appearing to slip apart.

"Ladies and gentlemen," Hailey growled, "for your holiday enjoyment I would like to introduce Esme, a lady with only one name but with a voice so intoxicating you'll not need another to remember her by." He turned to the figure and continued his welcome, but the sharply rising sound of enthusiasm silenced him.

A soft, tender voice emerged from the vapor. Tremulous at first, it gradually strengthened until every note seemed to anticipate a crescendo. Johnny couldn't distinguish the words of the Gaelic song she sang, savoring only the rise and fall of her Irish pitch as it modulated mystically between the notes. The quiet resonance of a chorale began to cradle her voice. He looked for the back-ground singers, but there were none. He wondered if anyone else heard them or if somehow the poteen had brought the chorus together only in his head. He had to get closer. Swilling down what remained in the glass, he spun away from the counter and felt the stool tip forward. He grabbed at the air but too late to catch himself.

Just as he smacked against the wood, poteen's familiar flight from regret and melancholy flooded over him. The comfort held even when he felt the crossbones of the twins claw into his chest. The pain seemed so far away, the embarrassment idle, the worry about any disease they might have borne, as barren as the day he separated them from their mother's arms. The music stopped but the melody sauntered on in his head.

"Is he all right?"

Even in his frail happiness, Johnny could tell it was the singer's voice.

"Just another fallen comrade, lass. Nothing to mind," Someone yelled. "Back to the song!"

"To the song, girl! To the song!" became a chant that mended the awkward break.

Esme's voice resurfaced. Johnny tried to latch onto the words but he could only make out the rise and fall of the notes. He attempted to crawl toward the stage. Shoes, heels and stocking feet bumped his head. A drink splashed on his back. Once he grabbed a woman's toes, but her shriek remained far above him.

Abruptly, Hailey's unmistakable mass squatted in front of him. "Get up, Johnny! I can't allow it. My God, there's blood all over your shirt."

He grabbed Johnny and brought him to his knees, dragged him back-wards and rested him slumping against the garden door. "I'm going to leave you here until she's done," Hailey said. "Then I'll come for you and make room in the shanty. I don't want you moving, not a smidgeon or so help me, I'll tell the Angels to find me another runner! Do you hear me, Johnny?"

Johnny awoke to silence. The speakeasy had closed. He could barely lift his head. Except for a slight glow in the mirrors the barroom was dark. His head dropped to his chest, and he went back to sleep, until a pair of hands clasped his cheeks. A beam of light, stark like a freshly struck match, flared before his eyes. He tried to shake free but Hailey's huge, spongy hands tightened about his face.

"Steady there, lad. 'Tis but candlelight. She's trying to help you."

"Who…?"

"Shhhh… Johnny. Esme, the singer."

"Open his shirt, please."

Something cool poured over Johnny's chest. The scratches seared. Before he could clutch his chest, a warm and soft towel was stuffed into his shirt. Fingers poked softly into the corners of his eyes and squeezed at the lids. The light became a blur trapped in a green aura.

"Try to keep your eyes open. I'm not a Cumann and must be careful."

The shortened word for the rebels' nursing corps came through to Johnny. Briefly he wondered if the voice belonged to Shannon, the Cumann na mBan who'd brought him back from the dead after a Black and Tan had taken a rifle stock to his head. She'd laid him on a cot and placed him in a shallow grave, hoping he would come out of it but not expecting him to. He'd awakened, certain he'd passed on.

"Am I dead?" he mumbled now as then, as though death itself were a repeated source of coherence.

"You're close," Esme replied.

He grimaced as her nails dug into the buboes, pinching and draining them. At last, she released her grip to let his eyes close. He blinked but could not see through the glaze of mucus. The fragrance of lilacs crept into his nose.

"Hailey, they're infected, badly," she said. He needs sage and turmeric within a few days, or he could lose his sight altogether. If he's able to walk tomorrow, send him to The Woebegone early in the evening. I've got both treatments there for the children. If he can't make it, I'll bring them to you tomorrow night when the show is done."

Her words had assembled but rushed away when Hailey opened the door.

"Shannon?"

"No lad, I've told you, this is Esme. It's time to get him outside. I'll tell him what you said when he wakes, hopefully sometime this week."

Hailey brought Johnny to his feet, lugged him out to the storage shed where he laid him on the gritty floor beside the kegs and tucked an old, shredded raincoat around him. Using a small fire log for a pillow, he propped up his head, pulled a piece of thick canvass from the whisky barrows and covered him twice over.

"The Woebegone," Hailey said, as though reminding himself.

As the words receded Johnny deciphered what little remained, *Woe*, and then his world went dark.

Chapter 5

The sound of rain beating loudly on the shed's tin roof wakened him. The rain came in bursts, at times shaking the rickety coop. The crusts on his eyes were so thick he could barely tell if it was night or day. He tensed as the cold rain started to drip between the slits in the roof. Shivering, he started to roll onto his side but forced himself to lie still, so the rain could collect on his eyelids. He waited as the water ran down his cheeks and then pressed gently against the residue. Relieved to find it softening, he relaxed and slid his eyes back into the rain.

Hailey's blurred image struggled into focus. He crouched beside Johnny and gently shook him by the shoulder. "Your eyes look like almond shells. Here, let me get you inside for a hot towel."

"Just a minute," Johnny said, picking away at his eyes until Hailey's jowls took shape.

"Can you see in the least, lad?"

"In the least." Johnny pushed himself up onto his elbows. Grimacing at the scalding pain over his heart, he edged upright against one of the kegs and pulled the bloodied towel from inside his shirt. He used a clean edge to remove the muck remaining in his eyes. It took a few seconds for him to separate Hailey's umbrella from the grey sky. Shifting his eyes from side-to-side he searched for the sun but it appeared to have taken asylum. "What time is it? Hell, what day is it?" he asked, flustered.

"We're closing in on mid-day Sunday, lad. Can you see any better now that you've cleaned them?"

"A little. Sleeping out here might've made them worse."

"Wasn't the cold, Johnny. They're infected and badly so."

"It's just lice. I caught them on the crossing. They'll heal in time."

Hailey's cheeks inflated before sagging again and he sighed. "Johnny, last night you were as drunk as a man can get and live to regret it. I've never seen you like that before. I tried to warn you beforehand. Do you remember *anything*?"

"The jazz. I remember the jazz... and the noise and later on a voice, and then, this... this weird mist settling over the stage. He felt for his shirt pocket and winced. "Feels like somebody raked me with a pitchfork."

"I don't know about any mist but you fell off the barstool and hit smack on the floor. You tried to crawl to the stage. You got lots of laughs and hoots, I can assure you that."

Johnny glanced at his shirt pocket. The dry bloodstains were visible even against the dark blue wool. He traced the outline of the crossbones. Relieved they had held together, he thought of how they had saved him from Bile's attempt to kill him.

"Thank you for helping me."

"I didn't do any more than drag you out here, Johnny. T'was Esme, the singer, who took care of you. But for her I don't know what we'd have done. I had no idea you were bleeding, but she knew the minute she laid eyes on you. You do remember her, mate, the singer? Esme by name?"

Johnny hesitated. "Her voice, sort of, and something about her body, the way it shifted in this green... but mainly I remember her voice."

"It could resurrect the dead, and indeed, she may have saved you from the grave. When she finished singing, she took a seat at the bar and asked if the 'eejit lying by the door,' — is how she put it — was still alive. 'That's blood on his shirt!' she said all of a sudden and ran over to douse your chest with rum. Said it would slow the bleeding to a standstill. As it turned out, she was right. Somehow she knew."

"Is she a nurse during the day?"

"Not in the true sense of the word, but in her own way, yes. You have any idea what she said about your eyes?"

Johnny was distracted by the hieroglyphics dancing across his vision. "What's that?"

"I asked if you remember what she said about your eyes?"

"She's a singer, not a nurse. You said so yourself. So why should I care?"

"Johnny, you *are* a feckin' idiot. Listen to me. Those bumps in the corners of your eyes and on your lids are filled with infection. They're not lice, Johnny. Sties are what she called them. They're infected, badly she said. She's seen it often at this place called The Woebegone where she sings most nights. When I told her about your crossing she said she wasn't at all surprised your eyes were in such a state. She's seen the same in many who've come over on the old coffin ships. To make sure, she went so far as to dip her fingers into this little sack she carries and scrape out some of the gunk with her fingernails. She held it to the light. It was dark yellow with some blood mixed in. That's infection, lad. Then she dipped her fingers back into the sack to make sure it didn't spread to her. She said you needed these spices, white sage and turmeric, to get rid of it — and the sooner the better."

"Did she say where I could get them, what drug store?"

Hailey shook his head. "They're not legal drugs, at least not yet. I got the idea they're something like hash. I guess they get smuggled up from Mexico."

"She's from Mexico?"

"No, Johnny! Didn't you notice her brogue? She's as Irish as we are. She came to America about two years ago when the Brits were ushering the war-worn weak and feeble offshore. Thinning the population, so they could take over the land — you must have seen that? Anyway, she showed me her pass from Ellis. She had no one to meet her but back then the authorities were a bit easier on letting women enter without a relative to claim them. After she told them her story, they let her through. The young woman's a cripple, lad."

"A cripple?"

"Her hip and left leg, if I have it right. She and her Da were put to a gun dance by the Tans. She was hit in the foot and then her old man went down. They put a gun to his head. When she tried to stop them, this Tan shattered her hip with the butt of his rifle. She had to let it mend on its own, with the help of a friend, who, thankfully, *was* a nurse and latched it into a brace she made from a horse's rein. Esme has to bathe in ice to keep the pain at bay. Bless her heart, when she sings she takes a few sips of poteen to keep it under control." Hailey smiled. "Just so you know, she keeps a flask in her garter for when it really acts up."

"The Tans, the fucking Tans. Once outside Bandon we went to this house where an old man and his wife... were put through the same..."

Hailey laid him back against the keg. "It's okay, mate. You don't have to go into it."

Johnny could feel the rage return with overwhelming force. He found himself on the lawn just outside the elderly couple's house. A dozen or more pigs lay slaughtered on the far side of a barbed wire fence. He'd been sent to gather intelligence from Ezra, the woman's husband who'd spied for the Rebels. The old man lay pale white on the lawn while a dozen or more pigs were oinking crazily on the far side of a barbed wire fence. The woman stopped shoveling his grave when Johnny appeared.

Johnny's voice followed hers when she told him what happened. He spoke in a hurry, yet with sympathy, as though he might be able to help the woman when the story ended.

"While they were shooting the ground around his bare feet, a Tan grabbed hold of her and said her husband's fluttering feet was the funniest sight he'd ever seen, and if she didn't join in the laughter, they would kill the rest of their pigs for good measure. She tried to fake a laugh but it couldn't stifle her pleas for them to stop. So, when Ezra fell, they slapped her to the ground, shot the pigs and rode off howling."

The stubborn need for retribution seethed inside Johnny. A voice he could only recognize as the old woman's shoved his own voice aside. " 'Were they before me now, I would kill each one and rejoice!' "

Hailey's startled face came into view.

"Sorry," Johnny said, wincing. "Sometimes, I just... I just want to square things, you know, to make the bastards pay somehow. They often put people through the gun dance. It was like a game they enjoyed playing."

"The sons-of-bitches. I can't imagine what the likes of you and Esme have been through. And even for an old timer like me, I've had those same feelings of wanting to square things since I was a wee one. They don't disappear or fade into idleness. If only reprisal were closer to our fingertips and not a thousand miles away." He sighed. "But Esme seems to have found peace in helping poor, afflicted children sing. We could all learn from her."

"I do remember her voice ," Johnny said. "Not the words so much but the silence between them, even with all the screaming."

"Goodness, they wouldn't let her leave the stage. After she started losing her voice, she told them she was done for the night but would be back next Saturday. But even so, when she went to the bar they wouldn't leave her alone. Eoin had to force them back to give her some breathing room."

"What's that she said I needed?"

"Sage, white sage, and turmeric. She has a supply at The Woebegone. Remember, the old theater where she sings? Apparently, she uses the stuff to treat ailments of all sorts but mainly those of the children she teaches who can't afford doctors. It's over on Thirty-fifth between Ninth and Tenth Avenues." Hailey stood and took Johnny's arm to help him to his feet. "Here, lad, let's get you inside. You can wash up in the basin downstairs while I make you some toast and eggs. My shirts are a wallop too large for you but at least they're clean. You're in no shape to run any whisky today."

"They don't run on Sundays anymore, even leading up to Christmas. The pirates need time to go to church and give thanks for Prohibition."

"You can stay out here, or in the basement, if you think finding your way home's going to be a problem."

"We'll see," Johnny said, pausing as the unintended play on words made them both chuckle.

Hailey walked him inside and filled a tumbler with ice to cool the burning in his eyes. Within minutes he'd cooked a bevy of eggs, a rash of bacon and given Johnny so many cups of black coffee he thought his heart was going to sprint out of his chest.

When they finished eating, Johnny pitched-in to help clean up the night's mess and prepare for Sunday evening when the crowds would return to forget the night before. His chest ached as he scrubbed the traces of blood off the floor. He remembered being adrift on the wood unaware of any pain or blood. He'd heard a woman scream but couldn't remember why and everyone laughing as Hailey dragged him to the door.

Hailey's boots reappeared in front of him. "I forgot to tell you, lad. Before you woke, the Angels came to pick up your cart since you hadn't returned it," Hailey said. "I told them you'd taken ill for the while, and it would be fine to take it. Forgive me, it wasn't me place to do so, but I thought it best."

Johnny smiled. "You helped bring me back from the dead, so please feel free to at least lie on my behalf."

Hailey laughed quietly. "The floor's shining, Johnny. You've tithed generously." He glanced at the clock on the wall behind the stage. "The hour's closing in on three. If you're stopping at The Woebegone, I'd suggest you be on your way. She starts with the kids at four on Sundays. You might want to get there beforehand."

Chapter 6

Invigorated by the coffee and eager to find The Woebegone before the burning made its way through the ice, Johnny hurried to Death Avenue and headed north. He did his best to dodge the vagrants who'd gone to sleep in the nearing sunset. Some had taken fate up on his offer to bed them safely by the train tracks where the train's rumble assured them that they would sleep better than ever .

The veterans and their shadows were often easier to identify due to their missing limbs and frayed combat boots or soiled uniforms with military belt buckles they kept polished with spit and unyielding pride. Johnny once spotted an Irish vet with a bayonet fixed to his hip and a stained British flag draped over his shoulders like a shawl. Anger crept back into his heart as he thought of the dead Rebel whose stiff body the Tans had stretched over a stone outside Dublin's Royal Castle to serve as a card table for those who enjoyed playing the card game, twenty-five.

Something about the way veterans wandered also separated them from others living on the streets. They seemed eternally caught in battle, occasionally darting behind phone poles or cars to dodge the bullets that splattered their eardrums or shuffling down their foxhole alleyways, searching to see if their buddies had survived the last round of gunfire. Johnny knew their confusion and remorse well, for he shared their world, a world unto themselves where life played out in fear, pain and regret, a world where the desire for retribution ate at them incessantly.

The veterans weren't alone in their despair. The poor from all backgrounds and cultures haunted the streets and the curbs as their silhouettes smoked, cried, jabbered, and tensed when a cop passed by. The fortunate among them found pavilion in the few unbarred entrances to stores and eateries where they readied to scramble inside, if the police actually showed. The worst-off lay immobile, freezing in the cold, their memories troubled. All prayed for the law to keep its distance.

And for the most part it did, except at month's end when the city's coffers needed filling. Occasionally, as many as three or four police cars would skid to a stop at an intersection where the poor had gathered to share a stolen bottle of whisky or a filched pack of cigarettes or had come together to protect one another as they relieved themselves. The cops would jump out and arrest anyone for anything, for drinking, peeing or puking, whatever they could label as disturbing the peace or indecent behavior, especially any blacks who wore homemade, wooden shoes or sat shivering, half-naked under a soiled blanket. Any coins or bottles, the cops would keep for themselves, but they were more lucratively reimbursed by the city with a perk for each person they threw into a cell. It was called the Mayor's Allowance and permitted the commissioners to boast in the newspapers that the city was being stalwart in its effort to rid the streets of those who disregarded Prohibition. However, there were times when Johnny had seen the cops in tears dragging them out, for many of the officers were veterans themselves, still trapped in the angst of war.

As the clouds darkened, Johnny had trouble differentiating the bodies from toppled carts, busted kegs and countless trash baskets put out for the never-appearing garbage men. With each step he worried about tumbling over someone or being struck by a vagrant with a damaged mind who mistook him for a monster.

When he reached the corner of Eleventh Avenue and Thirtieth Street, he could barely see through what had become a deep fog closeting the rain. A salty wave of air shifted around the tops of his boots. The curb began to move like an unstoppable undertow, and for a moment he felt the pitch of the ocean's swells while on *The Pestilence*. The wind blew harder, sweeping the rain across the street on a slant, tilting his world even more. A cab hissed by with the flat and lonely sound of rubber peeling from the wet street.

Without warning, lightning split the sky. Startled, he glanced up to see the shadow of something hurtling toward him. His mouth opened to yell but before he could utter a sound the object had already smashed against his shoulder and bounced into the gutter. More in shock than pain, Johnny slumped into a crouch and spotted the raven a yard away, its black feathers glistening in the rain. He reached out the way his mother did the day a sparrow struck his pram and fell to the ground. She held the little thing in her hand and rubbed its chest. Magically, it had sprung to life and with a glimmer of gratitude in its eyes, flown away. And to Johnny's astonishment, she'd explained that birds were very easily shocked and often taken for dead when all they needed was a touch, - a touch of hope, she added.

Johnny bent down, carefully picked up the raven and held it in his palm. He touched its chest and felt its tiny heart racing. He stroked its chest. A wing sprung open, spinning the bird into the street and back into the wind, miraculously defying its destiny. He watched it disappear into the fog and rubbed his shoulder. Maybe that was what he'd been sensing ever since he was pulled from the Hudson: the pulse of danger thick in the air. Had Bile been the only one after him or were there others? Is that what he felt? Steadying as he braced, he tried to see through the smoky veil to get his bearings.

He jumped as a car sputtered by, narrowly missing him. A man with a beard on only one side of his face leaned out of the passenger window. "You drunk motherfucker!" he shouted as the car disappeared into the boundaries of Johnny's terror-stricken eyes.

Nearing the end of the street, he tripped over a dark and stubby figure sitting on the curb. Coming to his knees, he tried to see what or who he'd fallen over but the figure had curled into an unrecognizable, moaning shadow. It seemed too small to be a person and too limbless to be an animal. Johnny wiped his eyes with a sleeve but nothing changed.

When a towering black man grabbed his arms and yanked him to his feet, Johnny stiffened and was about to try and break away when he froze at the sight of a painting of Cuchulain, the legendary, mythic hero embedded in every Irish history book. The flat alabaster eyes stared down at him from above the door of what appeared to be an old theater. The painting lacked color except for the red blood on the raven's beak and the young warrior's shoulder. The blood had been retouched so brightly the treasured figure seemed no longer a myth but a cartoon that had fallen subject to a child's crayon.

The black man had let go and was squatting beside the bowed figure. His hands were on a set of shoulders Johnny imagined but couldn't see. "You okay, Dillon?" the man said.

Johnny watched as the fellow bent into the darkness and lifted a stocky young boy, maybe nine or ten years old, whose legs ended at his knees. He held the boy at arm's length, inspecting him. "Answer me, son."

"Yes, Daddy. He tripped over my shoulder," the boy rasped through a severe under bite. He turned his huge, gentle eyes to Johnny. "I'm sorry, sir, I didn't see you coming."

"No, lad, I'm the one who's sorry," Johnny said. "I should've been more careful. It's just that my eyes are... no matter, I should have been more careful."

The boy's father brought Dillon to his chest and raised his elbows so the youngster could slip his legs under them. Dillon's eyes remained on Johnny. "Daddy sat me on the curb so I could make sure my nubs were on tight before we went inside. The stage gets slippery sometimes, when the sage settles on it. I should've sat in the light over on the steps."

Dillon's dad held the boy firmly with a hand supporting the back of his head as though he was about to be laid into a cradle. "I love you, son." He looked at Johnny. "My name's Joshua and this little scoundrel's my boy, Dillon. You looking for a pub? I'm asking 'cause here on Sundays you can't get a drink 'til nightfall. On Holy Day it's a place for misbegotten, impaired children like my boy here. No need to go inside unless you're one of us. By that I don't mean you have to be a Negro, just a fellow with woes he can't handle on his own."

Johnny smiled. "That would be me."

Joshua removed his hand from Dillon's neck and sat him on his shoulders. Dillon leaned against his dad's head and wrapped his arms around his neck. His legs stuck straight out. The ends were blunted with dark nubs latched to his thighs with leather belts.

Johnny glanced above the door searching for a name. "Is this place called, *The Woebegone?*"

Joshua's smile widened to reveal his missing front teeth. He nodded and reached into the pocket of his raincoat, pulled out a box of stick matches and a pack of Camels. He stuck two cigarettes into the gap between his teeth and lit them both. The brief flame highlighted the auburn tone in his skin. As his eyes scanned Johnny's face, he inhaled so deeply a good third of both cigarettes became ashes.

"Woebegone's the nickname," he said, "but the real name is The Raven."

"The Raven? I just…" Johnny caught himself.

"They changed the name when this young Irish woman started here a while back and began teaching blind, deaf and crippled children how to put their woes behind them by learning to sing and make music."

"By any chance would the singer's name be, Esme?"

Joshua grinned. "It would be, and she's a lot more than a singer. She's the only reason we come here. She's got a way with people you ain't never seen. She knows me better than I know myself." He glanced at his watch which was tied around his wrist with a shoestring. "She comes on for the kids in a few minutes. How come you know her?"

"I heard her sing last night, down at Hailey's, this pub on Twenty-fifth. She told me I needed some kind of drugs for my eyes. She said to meet her here."

Joshua peered into his eyes. "Jesus, brother. Now that you brought it up, looks like you got worms creeping out of 'em. Lean more into the light. Damn, man, the right one's dark yellow with blood veins running all through it. You got impetigo or something? I heard a lot of them from Ireland has it."

Johnny felt his face warm. "She said they were sties."

"I had them too, Daddy," Dillon said.

"Yes, you did, son. When we first come up from the South, Dillon went to a school run by Irish immigrants." Joshua said to Johnny. "It was the only school what would take him in, 'cause he couldn't walk properly and was black as well. He got sties in his ears. Caught them from his second-grade teacher, Mrs. Schultz, an old Irish woman who brought typhus ashore when she come here, but she seen Esme and got cured. Dillon went deaf for a while, but Mrs. Schultz sent us to Esme and he ain't deaf any longer. She even made him a set of nubs."

Johnny glanced at the boy's legs.

"I lost my legs when we lived down South," Dillon said. "There was this flood under our house and I fell off the porch into it...."

Joshua's lips tightened. "Let's just say you was in the wrong place at the wrong time."

Dillon's head began to shake violently. Instinctively Joshua reached up and squeezed his cheeks, stilling the motion and forcing Dillon's mouth into long oval. He winced and his legs tightened against Joshua's ribs.

"Sorry, son, but I thought we weren't going to talk about it no more. Anyway, time's awasting. We got to get you down front."

Joshua pulled the door open, and they were greeted by a cloud of thick, white smoke. At first Johnny assumed it was nothing more than a pent-up haze from a room filled with smokers and tried to brush it away but it lingered. Gradually the pleasant smell opened his nostrils and seeped into his throat. His vision widened slightly. "What is this?"

"Esme's potion coming at you. White sage," Joshua said, glancing over his shoulder as he leaned into the doorway. "It's pretty crowded in there, and I wouldn't trust them eyes of yours to find a seat. Put your hand on Dillon's shoulder and we'll help you."

As they edged inside Johnny realized he'd stepped into a small theater terraced into twenty wide rows or so, each with a dozen tables. He glanced at the wall surprised he could make out the writing. Names had been burned into the wood in deep charcoaled letters. He'd seen it before, on the posts at the pier. Late one night, rumrunners from a cattle ship had taken branding irons and etched the names of their families, alive and dead, on the posts. They were still in business charging a nickel per letter and a nickel more if the customer wanted the figures in cursive.

There were dozens of names on the walls with dates marking the births and deaths of the bearers. In rural Ireland such memorials appeared on deserted stones, obelisks, even on the floors of castles, but until he came to America he'd never seen them scorched in wood.

Joshua stopped at the back row and pointed toward the far end. "There's an empty table down there. Can you find your way?"

"No, you take it, you and Dillon," Johnny said. "I can sit on the steps."

"We gotta go down front with the other kids and their parents. Dillon ain't on tonight. He's just learning to play the orange crate 'cause we can't afford a drum, but we have to be on stage." He looked at his watch. "She's about to start. Want me to let her know you're here? By the way what's your name?"

"Johnny."

"Your last name?"

"I don't know if she'll recognize it. Just tell her I'm the drunk from Hailey's, and thank you, mate."

"I bet I'm the first black man in history ever been called 'mate' by an Irishman."

Chapter 7

Johnny cautiously wedged past tables plumed with smoke rising from what appeared to be stones set like cradles in the middle of each. Patrons mostly sat leaning over the bowls, staring at one another while breathing deeply and smiling, as if the smoke were as natural as their breath. When he reached the table, he realized what he thought to be stones were actually flared conch shells, each filled with three short stacks of grey, straw-like leaves wrapped tight with twine. Stick matches on a piece of finely grated sandpaper lay next to the shell.

He slipped into the chair and started to light the bundles when a line of multicolored stage lanterns flared, casting holiday halos into the mist. The auras reminded him of those of the angel's lamps carried by the priests in Dublin's Kilmainham jail when called upon to anoint the souls of those Johnny had stood guard over before they were executed. Once shot, the coup de grace was administered, freeing their spirits to wing their way to heaven. Bile entered Johnny's mind. Thankfully, his soul was locked in hell.

The haloes hovered over the row of children packed on a bench at stage right. Joshua sat among them with Dillon wrapped in his lap. The first notes of "Molly Malone" came floating through the room as if given birth by the cloud of sage. Even with the night before still blotting his memory, Johnny knew the voice belonged to the woman he'd come to find. It drifted over him leaving the same silent spaces he'd noticed at Hailey's, and then, unlike the night before, it echoed from the walls an octave higher.

From deep on the smoky stage, Esme appeared. Her face, hidden behind waves of golden-brown hair, began to glow as she moved toward the children. She wore a loosely cut, yet shapely, green dress glittering with gemstones whose reflections blinked the closer she got to them. Her body, as Hailey said, did appear strangely misaligned, but as the cloud thinned, the distortion seemed to enhance her magnetism.

She opened her arms to the children and held the falsetto longer than Johnny could ever hold his breath. Her voice caressed every niche in him. She closed her fists and flung her arms out so far in welcoming the children she had to stutter-step to find her balance, yet her voice never wavered from the crescendo. Her strangely shaped body moved about the stage loosening Johnny's memory, allowing him to see the ghostly green mist rising between the speakers at the pub.

When the song ended those who could stand came to their feet and cheered. Those unable to do so clapped and shouted. Esme bowed and moved to center stage where she motioned for a child to come forward.

A young boy skinny as a twig, dressed in knickers and a green wool sweater stood and walked over to her. Esme smiled, kissed his forehead and stepped back to open her palms. The youngster did not take his eyes from her. As her fingers began to move, he nodded eagerly. Her hands rose and lowered slowly, inviting his voice to join hers. Together they eased into the opening lines of "The Irish Dream."

Johnny soon realized that she was coaxing the boy's voice with sign language. She carried the high notes with her raised hands and commanding alto, and he gave it support with rolling, lower tones. Their voices blended. The words of the song wafted between the notes as the melody flowed past. The song ended in a room bearing not the faintest whisper, until the spell collapsed and shouts of "Blenny! Blenny! Blenny!" erupted in joy.

Joshua stood and held Dillon high in the air. The boy clapped and kicked his stubs wildly.

Esme clapped as well and motioned for another child to come forth. A gleaming porcelain girl, wearing a ragged yellow dress, came to her feet with help from the children beside her. Esme took the girl's hand and escorted her to Blenny where they hugged. Johnny knew by the way the girl caressed the air in order to keep her footing that she was blind. Esme turned her by the shoulders to face the audience and placed the mike in front of her.

"I'm Debbie," the girl said. "I sing to see."

Johnny's heart instantly drew him into the past where joy had sprung from only the most unsuspecting moments, such as in James Connolly's hospital room at the Royal Castle when the signatory received word that General Maxfield had finally given permission for his execution, permission Connelly had craved, feeling it would serve to bring more support to the rebellion against British rule. Johnny had never seen such joy written on a person's face. Tears dripped from the old man's dark eyes. His prayers had been answered.

Esme stooped in front of Debbie and brushed the child's light hair from her face. She smiled as Esme whispered to her and then she began to sing, "It Came Upon the Midnight Clear." Within seconds the girl's voice registered, though just slightly behind Esme's. Yet after three or four notes she caught up with her mentor and their voices blended. After a refrain Esme motioned to Blenny to join them. As the lad nestled up next to the girl, Esme slowly knelt to give them the stage while she whispered and signed the lyrics.

The children finished the song softly, soulfully, like fawns being fed. When the applause settled, the entire row of children stood. Some were blind or headed there, others deaf, and still others trapped in unseen difficulties. Two children stood shakily on crutches — each had but one leg. A young girl was missing a hand and a toddler, whose sex Johnny could not discern, stood at attention. The child's bald head was covered with scars.

The underlying empathy for the wounded in his own flying columns, as well as for the enemy his men had slain, poured over Johnny. He felt his fellow soldier's pain as Dahl lay dying in his arms. Unaware that Nora was entering the room, he asked Johnny if she knew that he'd been on her father's firing squad. Johnny had never adjusted to the moment nor its memory which was as torch-lit as the moment itself. All along he'd so carefully tried to bury the truth deep under his love for her, telling himself that if she never knew, it may as well have never happened. After all, her father had prayed to die before a British firing squad, saying on the eve of his execution that his death was the grandest contribution he could make to the cause of independence. Johnny had convinced himself he'd done no wrong by serving on James' firing squad. He hadn't so much as killed James as he'd helped fulfill his deepest held wish.

Shouts of "Esme!" and the names of the various children resounded amid the applause.

Johnny had become momentarily lost between the past and present and had to search for her. His eyes found her slowly backing away from the audience to turn the clapping over to the children who bowed over and over again. When the ovation ended the parents hurried to the stage to hug them and help them down. As if the glow from the lanterns had somehow been perfectly timed, the flames flickered and went out leaving only shimmering red wicks to light the stage with their hems.

Joshua disappeared around the side of the curtain with Dillon saddled to his hip but soon returned to the aisle to make his way toward Johnny. Dillon reached out for his shoulder. Johnny hugged him awkwardly and was about to lift him from his dad when Joshua stepped back.

"Stay put, son." Joshua looked at Johnny. "By the way, she did remember you."

"Did she grimace?"

"Not at all. When I told her you were here for the sage, her eyes smiled. She wants to be of help. A healer, that's what she is. She believes in giving and refuses to receive. She says it's because something greater than herself gave her life, and she owes repayment to the source. She'll be along soon."

"She made them for me, out of old tractor tires," Dillon said lifting his legs. "I had a hard time crawling before my caps. She taught me how to walk."

Johnny ran his fingers over one of the caps. The treads were a couple of inches deep, reminding him of the softeners he and his men had strapped over their knees so they could crawl noiselessly along the railroad tracks in pursuit of the reprehensible Judge Gaggins who, without a moment's thought, sentenced anyone suspected of being a rebel to death by hanging. They found him in a hotel outside Kilkenny with the biggest mistake of his life, his "whore" for the night, Nora, who as an undercover Irish rebel, stood naked before him for one insulting moment and then blew his brains out with her gun.

"Dillon and me got to get home," Joshua said. "School in the morning. Then I go to the pool hall to clean the floors and rack tables until school's done. Then, I go fetch him and bring him back to the hall so he can do his homework while I do more cleaning and racking. All the luck to you, mate."

"Bye, Johnny," Dillon said.

Hearing Dillon say his name warmed him. There was something curiously loving about a child calling an adult by his first name, a sound that carried Johnny back into his knickers and helped him lace his shoes and kept the cobbles bouncing gently below the memory.

He waved as they left.

Chapter 8

The theater continued to empty, though slowly, with parents turning to chat with one another, pointing to the stage, clasping hands, and talking excitedly about the kids, while along the stage, workers had begun to clip the fading wicks. Though most of the sage had drifted out with the exiting audience, the stalks, still smoldering in their shells, gave off a haze whose glow rose in a thin pink cloud.

Esme appeared from the darkness carrying a lit candle and somehow, a glass of what Johnny guessed to be poteen in each hand. As she made her way up the aisle, he couldn't believe she was the same person who'd been on stage moments ago as a lass in a brightly bejeweled dress, someone's date, raw and windblown. But now she was a woman. How old he couldn't tell — in her late twenties perhaps but still trapped in that state of eternal youth reserved for old photographs.

Moving in a perpetual but curiously off-center motion, she seemed layered into two perfectly cut halves, obliquely set, one higher than the other. She appeared in danger of tilting over, a toy doll on the edge of a shelf about to be wind-struck. Her long, gold streaks of hair narrowed her face. The neck of her now red, velvet dress, marred with several blemishes, dipped down to her breasts which were partially hidden by her falling hair. Taken altogether, the dress, the light from her candle, and the way she moved accentuated her otherworldliness.

She turned down his row wobbling in high heels as if she hadn't had time to put them on properly. As she eased past the tables toward him, balancing the drinks, her breasts flexed as her shoulders moved. She placed the glasses on the table, slipped into the seat across from him, and lit the stalks with her candle. The smoke curled from the shell and drifted toward him, gradually forcing its way into his eyes. She blew out the candle and waved the smoke toward him, then with a few swishes coaxed it her way. Closing her eyes, she tilted her head back to inhale deeply, further sculpting her high cheek bones.

Her beauty was vastly different than Nora's. Esme's seemed governed by an eerie, changing light, while Nora's beauty defied any lighting at all. It came out in her fierceness and determination which resided in an impenetrable solitude and never changed. Her stark attractiveness appeared the same, whether in battle or around a campfire, in sunlight or in darkness. But Esme's perplexing attractiveness seemed to change with the moment's hues. And yet both women possessed an inherent look of indifference, as though their beauty meant nothing to either of them. Both seemed alone in their own world and pleased to be so.

Johnny thought that maybe his faulty eyes prevented him from seeing Esme as she really was. Maybe the reflection of the burning stalks on their shells cast an unnatural radiance over her skin, or maybe she was simply as she appeared, two persons in one, each stunning in its own way. And then again, maybe his impressions were twisted by the enduring remnants of last night's poteen. Regardless, she was captivating.

"If I had to guess," she said, pushing a glass to his side of the table. "I'd say you might enjoy a taste."

He smiled, pinched the stem and tipped his glass to her. "Thought you'd never ask."

Short of clinking his glass, she took a sip of the whisky. "Ireland's finest gift to mankind," she said, keeping the glass close to her lips.

He couldn't help but notice what appeared to be two yellow sunspots shaped in a figure eight just above the velvet edging her breast.

"The symbol of infinity, the never-ending cycle of things past. Maybe your eyes are fine after all," she said, smiling and causing his cheeks to warm. "Here, lean over the wands and pry your eyelids open." She looked closely into each eye. "The sties are somewhat larger than last night. What do you say we get on with the treatment? Lean closer to the shell and try not to blink for as long as possible."

She stood and lifted the far side of her dress, removing her flask and a small, thinly veiled sack tucked into the garter. She quickly dropped her dress and placed the flask on the table before opening the pouch for him to see the brownish-orange powder.

"Turmeric," she said. "It combines with sage to fight infection. The American medics used it in Germany to help cure bugs of all types." She opened the sack. "The first time won't be easy but if it works, the next time won't cause as much burning. Wet your finger, dip it into the powder and spread it over the sties."

The turmeric was soft to the touch, but as he daubed it on his lids, the tiny granules scratched the sores, and discharge began to work its way into the corners. He winced, opening his eyes to see only a yellow pall. When he started to wipe the turmeric away, she grabbed his wrist.

"No, don't use your fingers, it'll make things worse." She reached for a clean napkin on the next table and handed it to him. "Don't wipe them. Blot them and tell me when the burning starts to die down."

As he touched the cloth to his eyes, the buttery film masking his vision gradually began to fade. The smoldering wands came more clearly into view. His gaze across the table became a stare trapped by her deep blue whiskey eyes, the color of the dark azure horizon when nightfall settled onto *The Pestilence*, the only time of day when he and Seamus were allowed topside.

"How are they?"

"I can't believe it," he said, unable to look away.

"Better?"

He caught himself. He'd meant the color of her eyes. "Much better."

"It'll last for a while, an hour or two at most, and that's when you must treat them again. Start with the sage followed by the turmeric." She drew the string around the sack and placed it close to his glass. "There's enough for a day or so, maybe two at most. We used it up on the tables tonight. I won't be back until Wednesday, but I have plenty where I work, in a second-hand store called Rags-To-Riches just a few blocks east on Forty-fifth. If you can come by tomorrow, I'll give you a better supply."

"I've got to work tomorrow but I'll do my best."

A cold draft rushed over him. "We found it!" a voice shouted. "Daddy and me found it!"

They flinched and turned to see Dillon on Joshua's shoulders leaning through the open door.

"Sorry, folks," Joshua said. "We didn't mean to scare you, but wanted to say, hi, as long as you were still here. We almost made it home before Dillon realized he'd lost one of his caps. It must've come off right when we left, when he was bouncing around clapping and kicking. We found it outside the door." Joshua held up the round black object. Straps dangled from the sides. Dillon stuck out his leg for his dad to bind them. "Got to get him to bed now. School tomorrow and Blimey's early. Hope to see you folks soon."

All four voices blended into a goodbye.

"Thank goodness they found it," Esme said as the door closed behind them.

"Joshua told me you made the nubs?"

"A small thing really, considering what he'd been through — actually what they'd both been through, not to mention Dillon's poor Ma."

"You gave the boy back his legs. That's how Dillon saw it. I'd call that a lot more than small."

"He just meant that I helped him walk with what he had left... after they..." Esme cleared her throat. Her eyes scanned the room as if searching for permission to continue. "After they came up from the South..." She took a deep breath. Her fingers tightened as she brought the glass to her mouth. She bit her bottom lip and tapped the table with her free hand. "Hailey said you fought for the Rebels, so I'm sure you've had your fill of horror..."

"It's all right. You can tell me."

She took another swallow, set her glass down and let her breath out slowly. "What happened in Hell was this: they're from a small mill town down South, aptly named Malville. They lived on the edge of a Negro cemetery in a shanty built on stilts. The town's judge, a man named Aiken, ordered a ravine dug between the cemetery and the road in front of their house. Based on the 'best southern research', the judge ruled if something weren't done to separate the black graves from the road, the germs from the buried blacks would sooner or later eat through their saw-board coffins and find their way over the road to the white part of town. He ordered the tributary dug to reroute water from a stream along the Mal River, where the poison dyes from the town's mill were dumped. The trench passed right in front of their house."

Johnny could feel the anxiety building in his chest.

Esme paused and took a large swallow of poteen. "I'm sorry, Johnny. I just have to get it out."

"Then do."

"One of the backhoes digging the trench ran into the stilts and part of their house collapsed. Dillon and his mommy, Sally, were home after school having a snack out on the porch. When it gave way, they fell. The driver of the backhoe — Joshua said he was a member of the Ku Klux Klan — plowed them under. Thank God, later that day, after they'd let the water flow through, Joshua found Dillon washed up on the road, barely alive, but alive! Dillon's legs were crushed below his knees. They never found Sally." Esme paused. Her eyes were glazed over. "But that's not the end."

Esme's trembling voice toughened as though she was determined to finish the story. "Dillon's eyes and fingernails, as well as his tongue, all turned blue. Joshua rushed him to the only hospital in town, but before the white doctors would touch a black child turning blue, they called the judge to get permission. Aiken wanted to know if Dillon was infected. They said without question he was. The bigoted fools didn't stop to even consider that the blue might have been the color of the dye!

"Aiken ordered them to amputate his legs far enough above the knees so the germs couldn't 'jump the gap between them and anyone who might take notice' — as Joshua quoted him. Within the hour Dillon had stumps for legs and Aiken banished them from the South."

Johnny could barely speak. "Makes me want to go down there and kill the bastard. How in God's name did they make it up here?" His words lingered in the smoke while Esme collected herself.

"Kindness. That's how. The hobos living by the railroad tracks got wind of what happened and passed the story up the tracks past the Mason-Dixon line. The homeless stood in front of trains to slow them down so Joshua could jump into the empty freight cars. Then they'd lift Dillon into his arms. They fed Dillon at every resting place and bathed him. They treated his wounds with this gas they sniffed and drank called Sterno. That's how the two of them made it to New York. It was a miracle."

Her eyes began to flicker as if they were reviewing a thousand frames of an infinitely tragic film. "About a year ago, they heard about The Woebegone from Dillon's first teacher and came to spend an evening. I used to take Dillon with me when I bathed in the Hudson to oust his pain. In time I figured out how to make the nubs. When I saw him wearing them for the first time, I came apart."

She looked away and stretched her legs out on the floor while layering the folds of her dress over her canted leg. She slipped off her red heels. The toes of her good foot gripped the floor like a cat's paw. The toes of her damaged foot were knitted together. She placed her glass on the table and leaned back. Her head swung lazily to the side as she picked up one of the wands. She placed it between her lips like a thick cigar and inhaled, letting the smoke out slowly. As it hovered around her nose, she leaned forward and drew it into her nostrils, then placed it in the shell. "Please, tell no one, Johnny."

"It will stay with me. I promise."

Her eyes skimmed over the table. She raised the flask. "So saith Falstaff." She searched his face and waited.

The toast sailed past him, though he thought he recognized the name, *Falstaff.* "Shakespeare?"

Esme's lips settled into a smile. "The Bard, indeed! Falstaff, the most highly revered drunk in literature. It takes one to know one," she said, leaning over for her shoes. "Remember now, Rags-to-Riches, the second-hand store on Forty-fifth. You'll see a manikin out front dressed in a tarnished red velvet dress."

"It's late," Johnny said. "Would you like me to walk you home?"

"Goodness no! We'd just end up drunk in the Hudson. 'The fairest stars in all the heavens will see me home.' "

"Romeo and Juliet," he blurted out.

She looked back over her shoulder. "Who knew, but this Irishman across from me ?"

"I'd best be going."

Her smile widened. "So must we all at one time or another but not to worry. The past and the present are one in the same. We, you and I, are breathing the same air Caesar breathed. Good night, Johnny."

Chapter 9

Across the street from The Woebegone, Johnny was standing under the raised awning of Mule's Smoke Shop waiting for Esme to appear. She'd just told him she needed no help in finding her way home, but he knew that the effects of poteen would sooner or later leave her stranded, unable to decipher the names of the streets.

The rain had stopped, leaving a cold, thick mist to fill the street. He wiped his eyes with the chilling air and then blew into his palms to warm them. The sage and turmeric seemed to be working, so much so he thought he could see the disappointment in Cuchulain's eyes in the painting above the doorway, that very moment when the eternal hero realized he'd been defeated for the first and final time. Yet he'd found the strength to bind himself to the stone in order to remain upright in the face of death.

Why did the legend end with death and despair? In every battle Cuchulain, the iconic warrior, had taken up the fight against huge odds and won, sparing his foes nothing short of ravaging defeat. Why had a raven been sent to peck at his shoulder so that his rapidly approaching fate could be witnessed by his enemy? Was it to show the world that the unassailable conqueror had been deprived of retribution? Was the gruesome ending the work of a jealous writer or simply an attempt to make the point that given time, fate will eventually overcome what one believes is their destiny and render them helpless?

Fate, thought Johnny, Satan's debauched ally — or was he God's — who somehow exerted such influence over one's expectations, turning hope into disappointment and giving the victims an escape in calling such turns in their lives, the will of God. He'd seen it happen so often in war.

"What are you doing here?" Esme said, startled. She grabbed at her smudge-streaked, yellow raincoat and jerked the sides together. A dark-checkered beret covered her left eye and made her look like Blackbeard in hiding.

Johnny steadied himself against her sudden, odd appearance. "I thought maybe... I thought maybe I should follow, you know, at a distance."

She raised the beret and looked at him curiously. "I told you inside I did not want or need your help. Has the infection entered your ears?"

When he stepped off the sidewalk toward her, she pushed against the air with both hands. Her face was flushed, her lips were dry and her eyes struggled to stay kind. Johnny stopped. He knew she'd just had more poteen.

"You're very kind, Johnny, but it's not necessary. I've been here long enough to know the streets. Besides, there's something you should know, something I've been told by others and happen to agree with. It will give you solace." She burrowed her eyes into his. "I've been called an apparition, someone God failed to piece together properly, and for His confusion I ended up benefitting in a way the good Father hadn't imagined, as did Isaac when he could not tell who his true son was."

Johnny had no idea if she was joking or citing a Bible story, something only those who made it a habit of going to church would understand. But Hell's Kitchen probably appeared somewhere in the Old Testament as a precinct of the Inferno. "Thugs don't care in the slightest if you're a ghost or carry a Bible or if..."

Her damaged leg wobbled but she kept her eyes tight on him. "Or what? A cripple? Is that what you were about to say?"

"No, no, by no means. I just meant, even if they do see you as you've described, you might have trouble defending yourself or even running from them. That's all I meant."

"That's not what you meant." She paused. "I told you once, no thank you for your offer. I've told you twice now. I've faced thugs before."

He couldn't help himself. "They left you alone because they thought you were an apparition?"

"If you're being sarcastic, let me take a moment out of yet another of my drunken evenings to explain something to you."

Johnny raised his hand and backed away. "That's okay. I'll be gone. I understand."

"It sounds as if you don't. I became an apparition through hearing what another whispered… and if you don't believe me, best *you* hear what I have to say."

"That's all right, I'll be on my way. I got it."

"My mother died thirty minutes before I was born."

The softness of her eerie comment halted him.

"I'm sorry but…"

"When her soul began to pass from this world, she spoke to the spirits hovering over us, the faeries. Entombed in her dying body, I heard her last words, 'Take care of my daughter,' she begged in a lisp that caused the walls of her womb to quiver. 'Please bring her into this world as an apparition so you might make sure she knows her life's mission — to show others how to cradle the gift of love.' The last beats of her heart faded like those of a distant bagpipe, dire and foreboding, yet uplifting. In the stillness the faeries entered her womb and escorted me into my father's hands." The words faded.

Johnny watched as she searched down the street as if looking for her voice. He opened his mouth to ask how a baby could have possibly understood her mother's words and then realized it would do no more than stir her anger. Perhaps the story was made up by her father in an attempt to share his love for her mother. The story was hers to believe, not his to discredit.

She slipped the flask into the raincoat. "Twice before, I've been threatened by gangs and both times upon hearing my story and taking notice of my body they backed away without a word. I'm not what I appear to be — I'm what I become once the story is told. And what I then become I have been since the moment they escorted me into the daylight."

Johnny couldn't help wondering if he'd been listening to the voice of madness or simply that of an infant clinging to its long-held, childhood myths, such as that of Cuchulain. "I'm sorry," he said, immediately realizing she might take the apology to mean he was attempting to express sorrow for her mother's misfortune, but that's not what he meant. He meant he was sorry for his doubts about her strength on the streets.

"There's nothing to feel sorry for," she replied. "Only I should feel sorry for once again breaking a pledge I made to my mother years ago at her graveside, that I would never tell anyone what she said to the faeries. Until now I've only told strangers to save myself from danger. With you... I'm not sure why, it just came out." She rolled her eyes. "And to think the man with whom I went beyond my pledge would be another Irish drunk with sores in his eyes, which no doubt prevented him from seeing the truth." She put her hands together in prayer. "Mother forgive me."

Johnny expected a smile but she lowered her hands and rushed away. Turning north onto Tenth Avenue, she moved faster. He was about to leave for his apartment when a chilling premonition came to him. One's deepest beliefs, regardless of how pure and convincing they might seem, were fate's spoils. He could not let her go alone. If something happened to her, he wouldn't be able to forgive himself.

He'd keep his distance. She'd never know he was following, unless trouble hit, in which case she'd be grateful he had. He ran to the corner. More than a block away she crossed the avenue and disappeared down a side street. Now he was free to pick up his pace. As he approached the side street, someone yelled in an Irish brogue, "You there, lass! Slow your gait, I've got a bod the size of a langer. Come to your Da!"

Laughter filled the narrow street as Johnny rounded the corner expecting to find her surrounded by a gang of thugs. She was nowhere in sight. Had they grabbed her and dragged her into an alley? His foot struck something hard and grating. Slabs of broken keg slid to the curb. Fighting to stay upright, he zig-zagged through the reflections of streetlamps in the windows of the closed shops. When he reached Ninth Avenue, he saw her besieged by a U-shaped wall of silhouettes, grabbing at their crotches and taunting her.

In an instant, before a shout could clear his throat, the scene before him was obliterated by a bolt of razor-sharp light more blinding than lightning it-self. The dull brick walls of the buildings sprang to life as the shouts of vagrants erupted. The store windows shot the glaring reflection back into the street. A lamppost, bent like a crane's neck, was suddenly uprooted from the concrete and slammed down onto the curb sending piercing strobes of light into every niche.

Johnny could clearly make out the clover-leafed, leather jackets of the Go-phers, the notorious rival gang of the Angels whose cruelty knew no end. Still encasing Esme, they'd been rendered speechless by the light.

Esme removed the raincoat and let it fall to the street. Johnny saw she had changed back into the tight-fitting bejeweled dress she'd worn on stage. In the weakening bursts of light, the gold and silver trinkets on the dress blinked like fireflies. She leaned to the side, stretching her upper hip so high it seemed to disconnect from her legs. Then she slowly shifted in the opposite direction, lowering the raised hip to reassemble and again disassemble the halves of her body like a carnival freak.

In shock, Johnny watched the gang back away. He stood fast, not wanting to destroy whatever illusive barrier she'd created. She left the raincoat in the street and maintaining a slow pace proceeded straight ahead, passing into the pathway the gang had created. The Gophers slowly dispersed and Esme dis-appeared into the darkness.

Astounded at what he'd just witnessed, Johnny couldn't help wondering if it had been nothing more than a game of chance, much like the game Lieutenant Danes made him play before assigning him to the firing squad that would execute Nora's father. From a deck of cards fanned out on his desk, Danes had ordered Johnny to draw one. A red card would excuse him from the firing squad while a black one would secure his position on the front row. Johnny had drawn the jack of clubs, a favorite among Irish card players and a sign of good fortune. It had sealed his destiny.

He searched the streets until midnight, but to no avail. He headed off for his flat, praying to the darkness she'd suffered no harm. He'd never met anyone like her, but his fascination carried a warning: what she appeared to be, even in her own words, was what she wasn't. And yet, he could still sense the fragrance of lilacs.

Chapter 10

Headed home, he was tempted to double-back at every corner. With each passing street the urge grew stronger. He began to sprint hoping to dash through the intersections by giving temptation less time to route him off course. Storefronts swept past as did fragments of the past having no time to establish themselves. He ran with purpose and yet without meaning, and it wasn't a contradiction. It was where his life was now.

Exhausted and sweating, he made it to his tenement. Struggling to find his breath, he panted up the three floors to his flat. Inside the blighted front room, he turned on the dim overhead light. With scraggly wallpaper peeling off the walls and the stench of untended antiquity in the air, the room looked and smelled like the stench of the desolate bog in Kinsale where the Irish had launched *The Pestilence*.

He quickly washed in the cracked basin. The water refused to warm. Shivering, he threw on his woolies and staggered toward the icebox. On the way across the room he became faint and bent over to clutch his knees. Inhaling deeply, he thought he could feel his guts touch his spine. His stomach was hollow. There wasn't a seam of flesh over his belt. His last meal was at Hailey's. Was it yesterday or the day before? He stumbled into the icebox door. To make sure he could still think straight, he muttered a few words of *Puppy in the Rain*, the four-stanza poem his mom had read to him whenever she was dismayed over yet another evening of his father's philandering. Johnny thought of Homer, the poem's drenched basset hound, who, when caught in the rain often stumbled over his long ears, tumbling again and again until, according to his mother, God reached out, helped him to his paws and led him to his kennel.

Poteen was the Savior now, not some preposterous spirit swirling around in the clouds. Johnny grabbed the half-empty quart tucked into the door, along with a chunk of black bread and collapsed on the worn sofa bed. He ate so fast a clump of the cold, dry bread stuck in his throat. He couldn't cough it up or hook it with his fingers and almost panicked thinking he was about to choke to death. He gulped at the poteen until it flowed from his mouth. The whisky began to slip through the bread, gradually unclogging the path to his stomach. He forced a cough and did so until his throat cleared.

He took the turmeric from his jacket and coated the sties. As the stinging lessened, he set the sack and the poteen on the small wooden table beside the bed and crawled under the covers. He tried to convince himself not to worry about Esme. He'd done his best to find her. And after all, she'd survived the shocking fall of the lamppost, with its cutting beams seeming to turn her into the apparition she claimed to be. In awe, the Gophers had parted for her. Maybe in another life she'd been a sorcerer who could not distinguish between her sly tricks and reality, or one of heaven's mystics who claimed she could ride the clouds and to prove it she would jump from the top of tall buildings to float down among those who watched screaming in horror. Maybe she'd escaped from an asylum where she'd spent time entertaining inmates, believing they were an audience in a glorious amphitheater.

As if Nora had been witnessing his thoughts, she abruptly rose from the past, ushering him to the evening festivities at the Obrien's after their brigade had defeated the Tans earlier that day in Bandon. The party was wild. Every time someone mentioned how many Tans the column had killed, glasses were raised for someone else to raise the tally, so they could cheer the increase. The ale was flowing through their bodies as through flumes. Liam started to sing *The Rose of Tralee* and silence fell. To Johnny's amazement Nora stood and joined in the song. He had no idea she could sing and to his amazement, her voice blended well with Liam's. Everyone became tearful but when the song

ended they cheered as though they'd won the finals at Stoke Stadium. Afterwards, when the rain began, he and Nora went out onto the porch and were
listening to the patter on the tin roof. There, she said, "I love you" for the first
time. He'd stared at her in disbelief and said that he loved her as well. She
stared back, smiling, and they kissed.

Johnny corked the bottle and put it on the table. He lay back waiting for
sleep to come, but the memory of those words carried him from the Obrien's
porch to the cliffs of Kinsale where with her gun trembling against his temple
and her scornful eyes awash in sadness, she'd said the same magical words in
a voice filled with sincerity, yet with bereavement, a voice reserved for dying
loved ones. And then she fired the gun into the sky above him. With the blast
ringing in his ears he could barely comprehend that he was still alive.

"I love you!" he shouted into the echo of her horse's hooves.

The memory swept through his body fracturing his senses. Night swirled
around him, wrenching him into and out of the past, arming him with a strong
assurance he would somehow find her before the sun came up.

How and where he would do so came to him as the halo of the moon
floated across the window blinds he'd failed to close. He felt like a traveler returning home after years of wandering. He knew exactly where to search for
her, for he knew well the expanse of trammeled soil and orphaned seed in
Heaven's lower acreage, the region of Naught where without consequences
any lie could pass for truth and any truth for a lie, where he could find anyone
and any reason for their being there, the dead and those simply passing
through. With poteen's help he'd visited the area many times since arriving in
America.

Confident his illusion would blossom into reality, he sank into Heaven's
littered backyard where years were just minutes, cemeteries only temporary
resting quarters and prayers offered too late to warrant an answer lay stagnant
There, in the packed stands of time, wars were watched by millions of souls,
cheering as though at a deadly hurling match between the Rebels and the Tans,

cheering because they knew God would not let the population dwindle. For if He did, He would have less and less to do.

As Johnny searched for Nora, the boundaries of time began to close. His heart pounded and his legs twitched. The mattress springs creaked the moment he turned down the well-traveled road to Naught. Its gilded lampposts were busily spitting flames at the relentless Commandments springing from Earth. One such truth stated that might made right and thus war brought forgiveness to the winning side. Abruptly a lamp's flame lit another Commandment, brightening the faces of those whose lovers had left them and never returned. The script below them read: "Careful what you pray for, lest it be granted." Still another had it that love could never overcome the unwillingness to forgive, and that it was fraudulent to believe several spins around the rosary beads were anything but a ruse.

The last Commandment hung ominously above him as he continued down the road looking for her. The dream now cast a net of sadness over him. Those on the side of the road gave him blank stares. At the end of the road he found himself alone. He looked out over of a field of shamrocks, only to hear her say, as though demanding he not give up, "I love you, Johnny Flynn!"

Momentarily restored, he called her name again and again. Searching far into Heaven's sluggish night, taking alleyways, cobbled roads and golden curbs, he gained not a glimpse of her. In the firmament's muted surroundings, it came to him that perhaps she answered only to her secret name, *Sarosa*. He shouted the name until fate's unmistakable voice rang out with a brilliance more shocking than the last beams of the fallen lamppost, "She's dead Johnny. The woman you call *Sarosa* is dead!"

"Liar!" Johnny yelled, jerking his head from the pillow. He found himself staring between his clenched fists at the icebox. The reflection of the rising sun on its door baffled him. He'd not heard she'd died from anyone on earth, had not even heard it whispered or joked about, nor had he read it in any of the soiled copies of *The Irish Herald* that Hailey routinely filched from a nearby paper stand. Still the refrain declared it was so.

He sat on the side of the bed struggling to keep away from the bottle, and as the sun brightened the room, he did something he hadn't done since childhood. He knelt beside the bed and began to pray.

"Our Father who art in heaven ..." He tried to go on but the weirdness of talking aloud to an empty room got the better of him. He thought about how his mother prayed beside him when he was a boy. "Now I lay me down to sleep..." She would begin and he would repeat with his hands pressed together. It felt silly even then, but when they said, "Amen" together she would always kiss him. He could smell the whisky on her breath but felt thankful that even though the Brits had denied her any money or medicine for her cancer, his dad could afford the spirits she needed to help dampen the pain. Before opening his eyes, he would always pause to say, "Thank you God," and then whisper to himself, "...for making the whisky cheap."

He wondered if it would help to address his plea for Nora's life to Jesus instead of the Almighty or simply towards the ceiling and let the words find their way to whatever source responsible for receiving them. To avoid the embarrassment of hearing his full voice again, he whispered, "Please, God or Jesus, if she's gone, can you find it in Your heart to bring her back."

He stumbled to the window. The Hudson was a dark non-reflective sluice, a mirror without a backing. He stared until his anguish spilled out. But in the pause, the tables turned yet again. How could he possibly believe she was dead? After all, it had come from a goddamn dream, and all the while he'd been drenched in poteen.

Wavering in the turbulence of the room's silence, he told himself he had to get to his job at the pier and take care doing so. His eyes were burning. He reached for the turmeric. Wetting his finger, he found just enough to dust the sties. As his eyes began to quiet, his worry over Nora resurfaced and he shivered. It bordered on insanity to let a dream swap a lie for truth. But even so, even if there was the slightest chance it might be true, he had to know and know as soon as possible.

Chapter 11

He scrambled through the dresser drawers for a pair of washed coveralls and a pleated denim work shirt. He threw them on, slipped on his dock leggings and boots and locked the door before starting down the stairs. He'd go to the pier, pick up his allotment and deliver it as rapidly as possible to Hailey's where he'd find out what, if anything, the old man might have heard about Nora. Then, God willing, if the answer was nothing indeed, he'd collect his payment and try to find Esme for more sage and turmeric. He searched in the night's morning fog for the name of the second-hand store she'd mentioned, but it had escaped his memory. Surely, Hailey would know.

The fastest but most daunting route from his apartment to the pier lay through the new subway passage being constructed from the Kitchen eastward to Long Island. Johnny had only taken the course once because of its inherent danger. The tracks were being laid mainly through the City's most ancient and vile sewers where it was said even an occasional alligator would make its presence known. Allegedly, the route had become home to ghosts as well as brain-troubled veterans, called moles, who, afraid of being shot dead by the advancing Germans or the Black and Tans, remained in the mud-laden tunnels, which were easily mistaken for foxholes.

The moles fed on beer and whisky poured into the sewers by those boozing on the streets, who at the sound of any nearby siren panicked in fear of being arrested. Leftovers from restaurants were frequently dumped into the manholes providing food to those who peered nervously from the openings and frantically waved their hands when they believed the enemy was no longer in sight. If they were passed over, their screams and curses could often be heard caroming off the walls of the row houses. Rumor had it that the rich, who often brought pets home from abroad only to tire of the upkeep, would occasionally drop the animals into the sewers to get rid of them. The moles refused to kill and eat them. Instead they guarded and fed them, giving them the love the rich didn't have time for.

Johnny's head was spinning as he hurried to the huge cellar doors below Barrigan's Tool Shed on 24th. The entrance had been there since the Civil War when the City laid an escape route for the Yanks in case the Confederates managed to make their way to town. It took every ounce of his strength to crack open the oak door. Grasping onto the slippery iron rungs embedded in the walls, he stepped down into the passageway. It was black as coal except for a distant curbside drain that allowed a narrow swatch of morning to enter. Barely familiar with the path to the pier, he was baffled when he arrived at the fork below Thirty-fourth street only to discover he couldn't remember which way branched west to the river and which went east to midtown.

He was struggling to make a choice when a reflection of torchlight emerged from a bend in the tunnel. As the light turned the corner, it took flame. A thin shadow followed, attached to a rickety old man carrying a torch in one hand and a wooden basket in the other. A dirty Irish flag was draped around his shoulders. When he saw Johnny, he stopped and raised the torch to stare at him. The flame lit his gnome-like face. As he spasmed, shaking the basket, the shadows of slopes and outcroppings rose and fell on his glowing bald head.

"Hey, there mate," Johnny called out, "could you tell me which way to pier ninety-four?"

The man gave Johnny a quizzical look and came closer. Johnny braced and the man gazed at him, exploring his face as if trying to determine whether he should be trusted.

"So, you're Irish, are you? Come closer. You might recognize these," the man said in a thick brogue.

Johnny edged just inside the smell of burning kerosene to the stench of mildew and decay. He was familiar with the smell — the hull of *The Pestilence* had been filled with it. The man nodded toward his basket, tilting the torch so Johnny could see inside. The skeletons of a large and small hand, a twisted foot, several human ribs, and as best as Johnny could tell, a clavicle sat atop a thick layer of bones. It was a harsh reminder of the world he'd been a slave to on the ship.

"A few leftovers from the Famine and thereafter as well," the man said. "Those able to make the crossing ended up in these very tunnels because they were not allowed to live anywhere else. Here, they found friends and a kindly place to die. Those who came over later heard the tale of the tunnels and were drawn to them for the same reasons. Many of the poor, especially Negroes come here to be laid to rest, for they aren't allowed in the cemeteries. They happen to be the strongest beings of all, for so many of them survive the vermin and infection and later move inland where train lines were more recently laid."

The word, *infection,* brought Dillon to mind. "Sorry, but I must go. I'm late for my job. Should I go left or right?" Johnny asked, expecting an answer and about to turn toward the fork.

"Me mission in life is to return the bones to those who wish to be united with others or to their families," the fellow persisted.

Johnny stopped. "To their families? You can't possibly know which families they really belong to."

"What's real doesn't matter, if the families accept them as such."

"But why would they?"

"The dead become our memories and anything awakening our love declares its depth yet again. That's what the bones do, even if only as symbols. They pass for the past, much like a photo of kin never known. It's love for those who have known love and often for those who have never loved but only wish they had. Families seldom refuse or question them. Love courses through our bones from the beginning of time right up to the present day and into tomor-row. It doesn't die. It is renewed."

"Is it?" Johnny said, picturing the skeletons of the mother and her twins huddled in the hold, the bones of her arms wrapped around them as though she could protect them from the afterlife. "Hatred and ignorance, that's what the bones speak to, nothing more, one war after another, one kingdom too many, a prince not lauded, a gang disjointed. Where's love in all that?"

"In the sky above us. Understand, we learn to hate our enemies long after the battle is waged, be it between countries or brothers or sisters who come to despise one another. And yet, in time our hatred is overwhelmed by human-ity's love for humanity. That's why on any given evening I bring out me old pipes and play on the street corners."

"Are you meaning bagpipes?"

"Aye."

"Did you play in the War?"

"I intended to, but early on, within a week of the Rising, in the fields of Belfast I set me pipes behind a small barn while I put on me uniform, and before I knew what happened they were blown to bits by a machine gun. I had to settle for a rifle instead. But soon now, with handouts given me for the bones, I'll be able to buy an old Highland chanter, and God willing, when I play it'll contain the memory of a battle won."

The man's throat ran dry. His mouth moved but nothing came out. He looked at Johnny apologetically. "I beg your forgiveness," he rasped, "but sel-dom does one stand before me who is not only alive but willing to listen. Go left, young man, and find your destiny."

Johnny slowly traced the crossbones with his fingers. "May I ask a foolish question?"

"There are none, so please, ask away."

"Would you happen to know if Nora Connolly's alive?"

The man's forehead wrinkled. "What's that?"

"Nora Connolly, James Connolly's daughter?"

"Of course, I know who she is, lad. I just wanted to make sure I heard you right. Yet, surely, had this happened, every Irish man and woman in every part of the world would have heard."

Johnny started to thank him and take leave when the man leaned over, examining the bones as though they contained hidden messages. He looked up at Johnny. "James Connolly was as close to a saint as we've ever had on the Isle, except perhaps for Cuchulain. James avenged his beliefs and love for Ireland by dying for them and in doing so he passed along his legacy not only to his daughter but to the two of us as well. And despite the recent Treaty with Britain, healing will come to replace the desire to equal the bloodshed."

"Let's hope it does," Johnny said, glancing at the dual passageways. "It's been a pleasure but I must be moving on."

"Bless you for indulging my prattle." He stuck out a filthy hand and Johnny took it. "I'm father Doolin," he said, "And you'd be, if you don't mind me asking?"

"Johnny, just Johnny will do. You said *father*? Are you... were you, a priest?"

"Not that kind of father, lad. A much more sacred kind. A Da whose two sons were shot to death in the GPO on the morning of the Rising. Now, make your way."

Stunned, Johnny hesitated as Doolin with a quick wave of his hand bent over to pick something from the sewerage. Johnny wanted to ask about his sons, for he'd been across the street in front of the General Post Office that day. He remembered the sound of gunfire inside and the sight of bullets splattering the large Corinthian pillars. Inside, Connolly's leg was being blown to bits.

It all connected, every tiny bit of the war, from the destiny-changing moment of his duties, both fighting for the Brits and the Rebels, straight into the sewers of Hell's Kitchen where it formed a quagmire of confusion and contradiction into which he would have sunk, were it not for his mission to make certain Nora was alive.

He went left under the arch, leaving Doolin sorting the bones. He exited the sewer and hurried toward the pier past the entrance on Death Avenue where Bile had attacked him. He clinched his fists and told himself today wasn't just yesterday; today was a hundred or more yesterdays, if not a thousand, and he had to free himself from their grip.

Crossing the street into the small park just below the pier, he thought of Doolin and took the crossbones out of his pocket. The memories of the twins were flowing in the bones, warming his touch. He'd never known the twins and yet he'd seen their ghostly images, their tiny faces, their smiles when being fed. They'd risen from the dead and spawned a wave of love and caring inside him. Until now he'd never thought about avenging their deaths and yet, without realizing it, maybe he already had. Maybe by taking them from the hull and crossing their little bones, he'd reminded fate that its mission to create lasting sorrow had failed.

As he slipped the cross into his pocket, he thought of Nora and tried to pull together what Doolin had said about love and its role in detouring retribution. But if she were no longer alive, none of it mattered. And then his heart tripped faster as he grasped onto the lie, for if she were gone, it would matter more than ever.

Chapter 12

The ship from the West Indies was anchored at a distance, but the Swamp Angels, who were usually on the water's edge below the pier loading kegs, were nowhere in sight. As Johnny approached the pier, Seth, one of the Angels who had rescued him from the Hudson, emerged from the far side and waved for him to hurry. The section of the dock closest to the water had been curtained with a billowy tan canvas. When he reached Seth, he put his tattooed hand protectively on the back of Johnny's skull to guide him under the dock. There in the shadow of the drape, the Angels, smaller in number than usual, were madly preparing the carts for delivery.

"What's going on?" Johnny asked. "The cops?"

Seth's green angel, tattooed on the side of his neck, tightened. "No, the Gophers," he replied. "Locust overheard them last night at Diva's. They want our takes from the Caribbean. We don't know when they're going to strike. It could be any day but certainly before long, so we're rushing to strip the ship and fill the carts as fast as we can. We've worked it out with the Del Mundo to let us stack our boats at dawn instead of mid-day to throw them off. That should give us plenty of time to strap the carts early and be on our way."

"But there's whisky aplenty. Why do the Gophers need ours?"

"With Christ's Day approaching, the word *aplenty* gets replaced by *never enough*. The Italians want in, the feckin' mafia, Johnny, and they're paying the Gophers to do their dirty work. It's this young capo, a crazy named Lucky Luciano, and his henchmen. If you think the Tans were bad, you ain't seen nothing yet. These bastards got a torture list. You give them your victim's name and pick a torture based on the price, and then they see to it. All they care about is money and they're willing to wage a whisky war for the taking, and it's not only the Gophers. The black folks want in. They're up from the South and poorer than any Irishman on the streets. The Tar Babies they're called, led by negroes from the Belmont Church over by the Park. So, it ain't about sharing the load. It's about a hellish whisky war! A couple of our mates are leaving because of it. Can we count on you to stay?"

Johnny had had his fill of war, war of any kind, yet the oddly exciting battlefield rush that only a veteran could know raced across his chest. "You and Locust saved my life, Seth. You can count on me."

Seth smiled. "Something I've been meaning to ask you about that day, Johnny."

"What's that?"

"There were two stones left in your rucksack. What were they doing there?"

Johnny braced. "They were from a mine in Galway. They weren't just stones. They were ore, worth a lot."

"And you coming off that boat in the middle of nowhere? Why was that?"

"The Brits," Johnny lied. "They promised me free fare to America if I'd help clean up the famine ship. But they lied. As it turns out they were going to stop any Irishman from making the crossing. I didn't realize it until the end."

"The bastards threw you off in the middle of nowhere?"

"They waited until I could get a glimpse of the Statue. That was my reward they told me."

"Those son-of-bitches! But we've known that's what they are forever, haven't we? Why Collins settled for the Treaty, I'll never know. I guess you don't know a turncoat until the very end." Seth caught himself. "Well, Johnny you're alive and amongst the Irish. A few minutes more and God willing, you're on your way to clamp onto a few schillings for us all. I'll make sure the lads know you're here. Back in a minute."

Johnny slipped out from under the pier. Relieved the conversation was over but still nervous, he watched the Hudson traveling slowly southward under the weight of winter, while at the end of the pier, packers pumped rum from the huge barrels into twenty-gallon kegs, then plugged and latched them. The noiseless rowboats now making deliveries from the ships resembled a group of worms creeping across the water. The small-engine boats normally used to speed the deliveries lay empty and covered on the sand. The minutes crept by as the rowboats crawled ashore.

Seth stepped out and pointed towards the Angels at work. "Yours is the double cart in the rear. You'll find a pistol wedged just above the axle. We're giving one to each runner. I'd carry it about my hip and cover it if I were you. Have it at the ready. By the way, does the main pub you service, I believe Hailey's by name, have music, mate? I've never been there."

"Jazz greats on records and a singer for the holiday season."

"A he or she?"

"She."

"Does she have a fourscore body?"

It stopped Johnny for a moment. There were times in the past when he would have weighed in with a fetching description, but for some reason he felt it was neither his to answer nor Seth's to ask about. "Her voice is like none other," he answered.

Seth smiled. "I'll bring a couple of the boys down one night. But you be careful, mate. We didn't save your arse to have it skinned by the feckin' Gophers, or what is it the niggers call themselves, The Tar Babies."

"The blacks don't call themselves 'niggers,' Seth." Johnny retorted. "I'd watch my mouth, if I were you."

Seth stared at him. "Beg your pardon, Johnny, but I'll call them what I like. *Negroes,* if that'll do for now, are savages and don't belong in a big city. Every white person in the Kitchen feels the same way. They need to be on an island far away from the rest of us."

"Why's that, Seth?" Johnny demanded. "So we can avoid getting infected by them? A white judge down South said they carry disease on the outside of their skin and ruled that a young black boy had to have his legs cut off because the doctors said they found the infection on him. You must've read about it in medical school."

Seth shook his head. "Johnny, what the judge ordered was for the best. Coons don't belong here and if we do what's right, they'll soon be back in the jungle where they belong."

"Don't call them 'coons' either!"

"Go get your cart and get the hell out of here."

It was all Johnny could do to keep from smacking him across the face, but he managed to stay put as Seth walked away. He took the pistol from the axle, tucked it into his belt just over his hip and hid it under his jacket. He was familiar with the gun, a 7.63 Mauser, a Boer War relic used by the Volunteers early in the Rising. He slipped a handful of bullets into his jacket pocket. As he tugged the cart from the sand, the gun felt awkward, but by the time he got to the curb, his body seemed to remember its old friend and gave it no thought.

Even though Seth had given him a special cart with a rear balance and an extra middle wheel to better endure the cobblestones, the kegs weighed heavily on the wheels as Johnny struggled down Death Avenue. It would be too difficult to take the sewers as they were laid with the largest stones and perhaps whatever was left of Bile. Besides, if he made it straight down the Avenue he'd end up more quickly in the midst of the speakeasies and within a couple of blocks of Hailey's.

As he set out, he felt unexpectedly, if not strangely purposeful, as if there were now a semblance of order to things. He attempted to sort through it all:

Nora's welfare, or more to the point, her life or death, and Esme, the eerie, yet strangely alluring piece of bent sculpture, and if that weren't enough, the potential pirate war between the Angel's and the Gophers. At the intersection with Fifty-fourth Street, he remembered what Doolin had said to him in the tunnel, that he had to be prepared to accept Nora's death. But he couldn't. He just couldn't. Her existence meant a thousand times more than his own.

Haze-filtered light from a nearby lamppost created wavelike impressions on the wet street reminding him of the torch-lit swells of rain covering the lime pit at Arbour Hill, the night he led Nora to her father's grave. The Brits had thrown the bodies of the signatories of the Proclamation into the pit and covered them with lime, hoping to banish them from history. When Nora knelt and raised her pistol into the air, sobbing, she looked up into the rain and for a moment he thought she was about to shoot herself, but before he could scream for her to put the gun down, she lowered it. Johnny felt for the Mauser without knowing why. Had she waited until now to take her own life? Is that what the voice in his dream had failed to tell him?

Alongside him, a tram, decorated with a swarm of Christmas lights across its bow, trundled slowly down the tracks like a kind and cautionary mammal. Without warning, its shrill whistle began to blow frantically. Johnny glanced down the avenue to see the new fast train approaching the tram head-on. He jerked the cart to a stop and shouted for them to halt but couldn't hear his own voice as breaks screeched and poured smoke into the air.

The horseback riders that Johnny took to be the Herdsmen - those hired by the City to clear the tracks - broke into view from alongside the fast train, firing madly into the air. But as the vehicles shuddered to a deafening stop, the gunfire continued. A bullet struck one of Johnny's kegs. Rum poured onto the cobbles.

Johnny ducked behind the cart. The veteran's life-preserving reaction to gunfire struck him immediately. He knew the direction of the shots, knew that at least seven guns were involved and knew alarmingly that the horseback riders weren't the Herdsmen he'd assumed them to be, the rustlers and posse

members from the wilds of Montana and Wisconsin hired by the city to clear
the streets and protect the poor.

The evidence stood right before his eyes. These riders were posers, wearing dusters, rumored to be the western mainstay of the violent Irish gang
known as the Gophers whose hero was Billy the Kid. Gophers were leading the
tram under the lie of clearing the streets while doing nothing more than hunt-
ing for whisky and members of the rival gangs who possessed it.

No one else but a Gopher would have been so stupid or so terrible a shot
as to shoot a hole in a cask they were attempting to steal, Johnny thought,
though he'd been told it was the preferred way to hijack a rival gang's booze,
sacrificing a keg to take over the rest. Passersby were scattering and scrambling
wildly to get into the stores. Drifters struggled to their feet and stumbled to the
curb where they sat with their heads tucked into their arms.

Another burst of gunfire broke out, ten shots this time. Rum began to spill
from another keg. Johnny jumped to his feet and started to shove the cart toward the trolley, hoping to use it for protection. But before he'd taken a step, a
large magnum pistol thundered nearby, the roar a cannon within a canyon. The
vibrations ran along the cart's frame, up his arms and through his chest. He
would have recognized the sound of a Colt .45 anywhere.

The metallic smell of gunpowder brought his eyes back to the street. Instantly, bullet holes riveted the front of the tram shattering the windows. The
driver, as if hit by a thousand volts, twisted violently. His head and his shoulders jerked back against the seat. For a moment he seemed suspended between
standing and sitting. Suddenly, his head spasmed toward his shoulder, smashing into the side window. Cracks in the glass spread around his skull like spi-
der webs. The glass hung in place briefly and then crumbled over his head and
shoulders and onto the street.

Dusters emerged from behind parked cars and doorways like roaches
from cracks. Johnny couldn't imagine why they were blasting the trolley and
shattering storefront windows — and then it dawned on him. The Gophers
were in a gunfight with another gang. As in battle, neither side took aim, no

one cared if there was a target. The only concern was to hold down the return fire by firing crazily, randomly in full pursuit of fear and havoc.

Riders were beginning to flee the trolley. An elderly black woman jumped from the door steps. Her legs folded under her as she hit the pavement and she frantically covered her head with her arms. A dwarflike fellow grabbed at his shoulder, spun and crashed bleeding into the trolley's open door before falling onto the pavement. A young reddish-blonde girl no more than twelve or thirteen leaped from the steps and started running toward Johnny. He threw his arms open to catch her, but she fell before she reached him, tumbled in the bundle of her dress and landed on her back, arms and legs akimbo.

Johnny crawled to her as fast as he could. She looked like a rag doll blown into the street by a savage wind. Her light blue dress fluttered up over her waist and the leg tangled under her bottom.

"This is *our* City!" someone yelled.

He pulled the dress down over her knees. He couldn't see any sign she'd been hit and thought maybe she'd smacked her head on the stones and gone into shock. He touched her freckled cheek but she didn't flinch. Her eyelids were still. He knelt and put an ear to her chest. Her heart was beating fast and shallow. The fingers of her outstretched hand were twitching. He leaned over to ask if she could hear him and spotted a stream of blood leaking from above her ear. Pushing her hair away, he saw a narrow crevice along the side of her skull. A bullet had apparently caromed off the bone but hadn't entered her brain. At first glance it seemed no more than a bloody scrape behind a tattered ear. But he knew head wounds were often deceptive. That he'd been taught by Shannon, the nurse in the Irish medical corps, the Cumann na mBan, who'd saved his life. "Let the head wound be," she'd ordered. "Do not stop or blunt the blood in any way, for doing so could clog the brain. The injury must drain on its own, no matter the outcome."

How then to keep the girl alive? He'd treated all sorts of injuries on the battlefield but never a head wound. Keep her warm, yes, but how? Elevate her feet? But with a head wound, weren't the feet supposed to stay below the heart?

Move her? It would be the worst possible thing he could do. Give her water — there was none — perhaps rum? Rum to a child? Would it matter as long as it helped keep her hydrated?

"Do something, for Christ's sake! Her life depends on it!"

Johnny ripped off his jacket, covered her and jumped beside a wounded keg to cup his hands under the slowing leak. He leaned over the girl and let it drip onto her closed lips. They neither moved nor opened, yet the whisky slowly started to sink between them. Her fingers stopped moving.

"You're going to be fine, just fine, little girl," he whispered. The familiar, leaden quietness he'd felt in such intractable moments on the battlefield overcame the noise around him. He leaned closer to her, hoping to feel a heartbeat or hear a sob but there was neither. Kneeling closer he nestled her chin between his neck and shoulder, hoping for a whispered breath. The seeping blood warmed his face. He asked if she could hear him and when she didn't answer, he lifted his head. His tears dripped onto her face and she, too, appeared to be crying. The wrenching emptiness of the battlefield gripped tighter. The moment was over, but it wasn't. The true toll had not yet been taken. But in time it would be, when the memory would replay again and again, trapping him in the grief-stricken moment.

So locked in his despair, Johnny only gradually became aware that the gunfire had ceased.

A shadow covered his shoulder. He grabbed the gun and sprang to his feet. It took only a second to realize he was facing a tall Duster with hands high in surrender. Seth was behind the Gopher with a gun in the man's back. Seth shoved the Duster closer.

"This is the vermin who shot her. He belongs to you, Johnny. Hurry and finish him off before the cops get here. We're taking the others to the pier as hostages to be used for trade bait. I thought about drowning the motherfucker in a keg but that would be too much to his liking."

Johnny heard his brigade leader, Neill Buckley, ordering his column to take no prisoners after they'd caught the British soldiers who'd put Martha Rimes' elderly husband, Ezra, to a pistol dance outside Crossbarry. Carrying out Buckley's command, Johnny and his men had taken the Tans into the hills of the Knockmealdown mountains and hanged them in the trees. Only later did the dangling silhouettes haunt him, tempting him to ask the same God who'd started the war if He might reverse course and grant him and his mates' forgiveness.

With his free hand Johnny grabbed the Duster by the flesh of his throat and jerked him to his face. "Look at her! Look at that little girl, you bastard!" he yelled, tightening his grip and stretching the handful of loose skin until the Gopher was forced to look at her. Her face had turned purple.

"Damn you! Goddamn you!" Johnny shouted. He wanted to let go and sweep the girl from the street, hug her so tightly it would force her heart to start beating again. But for a second, an invisible moment which failed to staunch time, life and death sought refuge within one another. He twisted the barrel of the pistol into the man's neck, forcing his shell-shocked eyes skyward. They flittered with his fear of the afterlife.

"Blow his feckin' brains out, Johnny!"

The voice hadn't come from Seth. Johnny glanced away from the Duster. On the street between the trolley and train a dozen Angels were standing guard over six kneeling Gophers. Another called out to Johnny, "Kill the son-of-a-bitch!"

Johnny's hand was shaking so hard his hostage grimaced. The reality of death widened the bastard's eyes. Johnny felt like he was staring directly into Bile's eyes — Bile, the scourge who had thrown his friend, Seamus, to the sharks. Now, one of Bile's soon-to-be pals in Hell had killed a little girl.

"Be done with him, Johnny!"

Johnny cocked the gun. An explosion burst through the Duster's skull. His blood splattered over Johnny's face and hands. Johnny staggered backward, then righted himself, forcing open his blood-soaked eyes. The Gopher lay dead on the ground. Seth had killed him.

"Goddamnit, Johnny, what's got into you?" Seth shouted as the sound of sirens lanced the air. "The cops are almost here. We don't have time to wait around." He pointed his pistol at the Gopher's head. "The *coup de grace* must be done with the same weapon."

Johnny heard the echo of his own voice whispering into Bile's ear. He grabbed Seth's hand. "No!" he exclaimed. "You're setting him free!"

Seth's eyes blazed. "Setting him free? What's got into you, Johnny? If you're not man enough, I am! Let go of me!" he yelled, but Johnny tightened his grip.

"Listen to me!," Johnny shouted. "The *coup de grace* is what the priests demand, so they can anoint his soul. Otherwise it has no permission to go to heaven. You want true revenge, without any doubt, without any regret? Leave him be or throw him into the Hudson, but for God's sake don't help the son-of-a-bitch find forgiveness."

"That's all crap, Johnny! The *coup de grace* makes sure the bastard's dead."

"Why take a chance? We know he's dead. You shot him in the goddamn head!"

As the sirens grew louder, Seth glanced at the girl, then seized the Gopher's hair and jerked his head from the stones. "You're right, Johnny, he's gone. The motherfucker's gone but I'm still tempted. That little girl..."

"Leave him be. You not only killed the bastard but sent him to Hell as well. You couldn't have done better."

Seth waved at his compatriots standing watch over their prey. "Kill the bastards and let's get out of here!"

"No, Seth, trade them! As you said, they're worth a ton of rum."

He looked angrily at Johnny. "Only to have them return with one goal in mind, to hunt us down, you, me and our mates." He shouted to his men. "Get it over with!"

Macabre kicked his prisoner in the ribs and shot him. Cahal brought the handle of his pistol down on his captive's head and then again as blood poured from the Duster's eyes. Locust had no gun. He stood like a child himself, staring in disbelief. Jacob grabbed him by the hand and the Angels fled, all but Johnny who knelt and swept away the Gopher's blood as it sought to pool into the girl's.

The black woman who'd fallen from the trolley stumbled over to kneel beside the girl. She put her hands together in prayer, sobbing through her angry, bloodshot eyes. She glanced at Johnny. "Why *didn't* you shoot him like your friend told you to? The child would have blessed you for all eternity."

With the sirens piercing his ears, Johnny could barely hear the woman but he easily read her lips. The question left him groping for an answer as he searched for more than the anointment justification. "I couldn't. I've been party to too much killing. Forgive me, I just couldn't." He reached out to touch the girl's cheeks and withdrew his hand. The impression of his fingers lightened her skin for a moment but quickly faded to blue.

He stroked her cheeks, traced his fingers to her wound where the blood had begun to clog. He sniffled like a child. The sirens faded into his sorrow. And then, her stained lips quivered. Stunned, he reached out to place his shaking hand over her heart and leaned close to her mouth. Her heartbeat was occasional but her sparse breath warmed his face.

He watched dumbfounded as her skin lightened to pale. His heart pounded. "Are you... are you..." When her lips moved he shut his mouth and waited.

"I... I... went to heaven," she whispered.

"You went to heaven?"

"Uh-huh."

"Was it nice there?"

"I like it better here," she said, regaining her voice. "Heaven was cold and you could see through everybody."

Johnny wanted to lift her into his arms, but worried he could still do more harm than good, he stroked her cheeks again. "We need to get you to a doctor."

The woman removed her scarf and wrapped it around the girl's head, covering her battered ear. "I'll try to find a cop to take her to the hospital."

"Thank you, ma'am. Thank you," he said.

He remained on his knees anxiously smiling at the little girl as the woman stumbled through the massacre on the avenue. She tugged on a cop's arm and he leaned toward her, glanced in Johnny's direction and rushed toward him. He crouched beside the girl, put his ear against her chest and asked if she could move her arms.

"Yes."

"I'm Officer Chandler. Can you repeat my name?"

For a moment she appeared confused. "Do you have a gun?" she asked.

"I do."

"You can't take it to heaven."

Chandler smiled. "That's okay. We won't need one up there. Here, let's see if you can sit up." He slipped his hands under her. She groaned as he raised her. "What's your name, child?"

"Jenny."

She smiled looking at Johnny. "What's your name?"

"Johnny."

She glanced at Chandler. "Johnny gave me wine, the same wine Jesus drinks."

Chandler looked at Johnny suspiciously, then bent down to the girl. I'm going to take you to a hospital just to make sure you're alright. We'll call your parents from there."

"I only have a mommy. My daddy got lost in the War, but he's coming back someday." She looked at Johnny. "Can you stay with me?"

"He cannot," Chandler said, glancing at the kegs.

"Would you like me to go with her?" the woman asked.

"That would be great. Let me let tell my buddies." He got to his feet, looked at Johnny and pointed to the kegs. "Are they yours?"

"Yes," Johnny admitted.

"Take them and be gone before one of my guys comes for them, as well as for you. You stayed with this child. That merits a favor. Now, go."

"Sergeant, you need help?" an officer shouted.

"Your last chance," Chandler said to Johnny. "Or they'll take you and your leftovers."

Johnny kissed Jenny on the forehead, seized the cart and shoved away. Her face was imprinted on his vision. The thought of leaving her lanced him like a poisoned arrow. He'd left without getting an address or asking the woman for a phone number or how he could get in touch with the officer. He'd run away on a battlefield impulse to protect himself and his whisky.

The wonder of what he'd witnessed hit him squarely. Jenny's return to life had nothing to do with what he'd done, for he'd done nothing but trickle rum on her lips and stroked her cheeks. There was more, more than anything he'd ever experienced on the battlefield. He could not identify it, but it was there, somewhere, waiting to be identified.

His chest ached as he ran. His stomach rolled and his legs weakened. He dared not stop. She'd survived! By God she had! And the Gopher who shot her? Johnny made sure the bastard had gone to Hell; he was probably already there. Granted, Seth had pulled the trigger but *he*, Johnny, had guaranteed the

Duster's punishment forever. And then it came him. Perhaps the girl had avenged her own death. By somehow turning fate on his heels, she'd over-thrown death, his most chosen and rewarding punishment.

Johnny found himself on Twenty-eighth Street. It was raining and his eyes were burning again. The glow of Christmas lights strung along the telephone poles were a blur. Their glow shimmered off the stones. All around him hov-ered the dank smell of wet asphalt and the sound of voices in the shadows. At the corner of Thirty-fifth, he stopped to catch his breath. He remembered the blood on his face and jacket, wet his hands on the stones and wiped his face as best he could.

Resentment blended with gratitude. A hate of hate, a fear of fear, a desire to strangle all of mankind's so-called justifications for which the worst wrong-doings were committed, came to him. But more importantly, what did one have to go through to muster the courage to refuse to give up — as the child had somehow done?

He crossed the street and continued down the avenue. Jenny's resolute, victorious image appeared everywhere: on the storefront windows, on the slick stones and in the darkening clouds. In one moment her tomorrows vanished forever and in another she'd miraculously wrapped her heart around them and brought them back. She'd outperformed the legerdemain of Houdini and equaled the story of Christ Himself.

The cart bounced over the stones. Darkness moved into the corners of his eyes shuttering his sight. He continued across the street, hoping he was headed to Hailey's. Overhead, the sky was dark, but the storefronts glowed, layered by the rain into rings of holiday light.

The image of Nora's face appeared. Emblazoned in her eyes were the in-escapable forces of love and hate, combined with a fierce, begrudging resigna-tion as if she were waiting for him in that nightmarish cemetery of his dreams. Jenny had returned and so, too, had the love of his life.

"She's alive!" he shouted.

As if fate were tight on his heels and brimming with jealousy for having Jenny wrenched from its grasp, the voice shouted again. "She's dead, you fool!"

Johnny ran even harder hoping to outdistance what he feared was now his madness, fate's favorite joker when he dealt the cards of irony, the fifty-two human perplexities very few could resolve.

Chapter 13

After Sunday church, the pubs opened. Awnings were descending. Workers were placing signs on the curbs listing *two-for-one* dinner specials, which had become code for a free shot in each tumbler ordered, but no more than three. The waiters and tenders preparing the thinly veiled speakeasies for the evening glanced at Johnny and waved cautiously, not wanting to draw the attention of any cop short on his monthly take. Irony struck again as the cart bounced wildly, causing even more to spill from the wounded kegs.

A man wearing a waiter's apron stepped from the shadows. With a hand cupped around his puzzled face he moved into Johnny's path. "Pull over, lad, and while you wash the rum from your face we'll suck them kegs dry for a guinea!"

Johnny made an effort to smile as he turned down Twenty-fifth. Halfway along the block he stopped and dipped his hands in the gutter flow to wash his face more thoroughly. Barely yards away, the sidewalk opened into the upward sloping parcel of land that hosted Hailey's. Gasping, Johnny struggled up the hill. The thick rear door was surrounded by blue and lavender Phlox that defied the season. Hailey tended the leaves as if they were children, talking gently to them as he cupped the petals with his fingers and flicked away the snow. To protect them from the cold, he kept small boxes of candles on the shelf beside the plants. Late in the day he lit the candles and waved the heat over the Phlox to dry away the night's dampness.

Johnny knocked on the door. A minute or so passed without an answer. He banged on the wood. "Hailey, are you there? It's Johnny. Eoin, can you hear me? It's freezing!"

"I'd recognize that panicky voice anywhere," Hailey called out. "Could only belong to an Irishman recently ashore or an escapee from Blackwell's Island."

"An escapee from Ireland, you mean," Johnny replied.

The door's small, iron-laced window opened. Two huge eyes appeared. "So 'tis the pirate himself. Have you our stash?" Hailey's mouth fell below the aperture making it seem as if his voice was being channeled from the halo of Christmas lights crowning his bushy grey hair.

"Here 'tis," Johnny replied.

The door opened and Hailey glanced at the carts. "Whoa, what are you bringing me lad, holy whisky already prepped for Atonement? He smiled and leaned over to run a finger around the bullet holes. "Forty-five magnum, so it wasn't the coppers?"

"No, the Gophers. They opened fire up by the pier. This little girl named Jenny…" Johnny couldn't resist. When he told Hailey the story, especially when Jenny asked to stay with her, he choked up and paused to wipe his eyes.

"The bastards," Hailey said, putting a hand on Johnny's shoulder. "Thank God, she's alive. To shoot a child. What the hell's wrong with them?"

"They're trying their damnedest to oust us."

"Ousting, the oldest game in the Kitchen, if not the world. A form of knighthood in these modern times, I guess you could say, except for those who become its victims." He nodded toward Johnny's Mauser. "Let's hope that won't be you." He started unstrapping the kegs. "We'll get them below and based on what's left in them, I'll figure out what I owe you. By the way how're your eyes? They still look a bit red."

"Better, but Esme said I need to keep treating them."

"So, you found her?"

"At The Woebegone as it's called… but there's something else I want to…"

"She's amazing that one," Hailey interrupted. "But for the crook in her waist, she's the most enticing young woman I've ever laid eyes on." Breaking into a smile, he threw his head back. "Jesus, listen to me. I'm old enough to be her great grandfather, for Christ's sake." He reached for a keg. "Here, let me lend a hand."

Johnny felt his only option was to grab onto the cask and get the delivery behind him. Perhaps then would be a better time to ask Hailey about Nora. Groaning at the difficulty of carrying the riddled casks without spilling more, they fought their way down the steps into the stonewalled pouring room.

As he helped fit the kegs between the handmade stocks, Johnny tried to find a moment to ask about her but the smell of leftover rum and the room's tightness distracted him. He wondered if the rebellion against Prohibition somehow managed to entrap time, jailing one and all in the speakeasies where time couldn't flee or allow anyone to flee from it.

"We're done at last. Let's go to the counter, lad," Hailey said.

Upstairs at the bar Hailey was breathing hard. Halting between coughs to catch his breath, he put his hand on Johnny's shoulder for support. Gradually, he righted himself. "You seem befuddled lad. What is it?" The words were broken by short gasps.

"Hailey, are you alright?"

"Sorry, I was just thinking about the little girl. You described her so vividly, I felt I could actually reach out and touch her."

"It's time for me to apologize, for I have something else… something I have to ask you."

"Don't worry, lad. I know where you're coming from. As soon as I load the cash register I'll pay you as though the kegs were full and a bit more. God knows, with all you went through to get here, you deserve it."

"Thank you, but it's not about the money. It's about..." he paused, wondering if Father Doolin had answered the question as well as anyone. That is, he'd had no answer. "Hailey, I know you're a reader of the *Irish Times*."

Hailey nodded, attempting to clear his throat as he slid his hand along the counter and slowly circled the bar, heading toward the register. "Whenever I can filch a copy. I'll surely not pay a cent to read about how the Treaty-ites are *allowing us* to live in our own country."

"Hailey, I know it's not so, but I just have to ask. Would you happen to know if Nora Connolly's still alive?"

Hailey's brows crevassed his forehead. He brought a hand to his mouth to catch a cough about to erupt. "What's that you're asking?" he gasped, reaching for a towel.

"Nora Connolly, do you know if she's alive? You know who she is, don't you?"

"Of course, I know who she is, lad," Hailey said, narrowing his eyes as his voice strengthened. "That's like asking a Catholic if he ever heard of the Virgin Mary. All Ireland knows James Connolly's entire family, even his youngest, Mona, who was caught in the fire. It's as though we all grew up together. What do you mean, is Nora alive?"

The mention of the youngest sister gave Johnny pause. He saw Jenny's frightened face as she ran toward him with open arms.

"Johnny, where are you, mate? Are your eyes giving you grief?"

Trying to find his reflection in the mirror, Johnny struggled to answer. "I just heard somewhere, that Nora had died."

"Heard it where? Did you get a call from back home? There's been nothing in the *Times*. I've heard nothing to the effect." Hailey stared at him. "I'm asking you, Johnny, where did you come about it?"

Johnny had walked right into the most obvious question anyone would have asked, and because the source of the rumor was a nightmare imported by poteen, he was unprepared. To lie wouldn't help and the truth would only make things worse. "I'm not exactly sure. I might've dreamed it or maybe it came from somebody here Saturday night, someone in their cups who was just making it up."

"Johnny, you were too drunk to remember anything. Even if it had been whispered in your drunken ear, it would have bypassed you like a hurricane around a raven's caw. And besides, had something so God-awful taken place, it would be on everyone's tongue this very minute. Forgive me for saying it, but maybe you're a bit off in your head. We all are off for a while after we first come here. The crossing confuses our hearts and minds. Soon we start to get lonely and yearn for home, the way things used to be, the way we remember them or think we remember them. It can take us away from the ground on which we stand today and rob any hope for tomorrow. It's not uncommon, Johnny."

"The way we remember them or think we remember them," stayed in the air

"Forgive my rambling, lad, but as for Nora maybe you aren't aware. They say that after the Treaty with the Brits she joined Sinn Fein and is now a public spokesperson for Irish rights. Don't worry, I'm sure she's as alive as the two of us, only thinking straighter than either. But if you don't mind me asking, your enquiry begs the question — why the concern? She's like so many famous folks we come to love and admire. They're family in our hearts but no more than distant relatives in reality. Maybe in your present state of mind that's what's bedeviling you?"

Johnny rubbed his eyes. Trying to hide his wobbly feeling of relief, he took a deep sigh, knowing he had to answer. "I met her father once, when I was a boy," he lied. "He was a cobbler in those days and taught me the trade. I met Nora at his shop. She was young and... she was kind. He called her Sarosa. It stands for freedom and I guess it's the cause she's serving now, though I'm not sure James would have supported the Treaty."

"I imagine it's going to work out even though he and Michael Collins didn't want it. I'm certain she's found something there, some link to her father's beliefs. Most likely she's taken up where her Da and Collins left off. She's gar- nered the freedom they left us and is doing her best to make the most of it.

T'will be fine and so too all the members of the Fein. What's this about, lad? Are you thinking about returning to the home land?"

As much sense as it made, Johnny found himself irritated. Nora, the fighter, the outlaw, the unshakable portrait of a Rebel, if not a female version of Cuchulain himself, had become a politician. "No, no, I never think about returning. Things here are to my liking."

Hailey nodded at the pistol. "Just fine, eh?" He reached under the cash register and opened what appeared to be a tool box stuffed with bills and coins and handed Johnny ten dollars. "Given what happened on the street today, it appears you have a price on your head. So, your fee just went up, lad," he said, chuckling. "Just jesting. You'll be fully rested soon. It's no doubt due to the craziness running through you, and those eyes ain't helping matters. They're dark yellow again."

"They're acting up for sure. I'm off to try and find Esme now," he said, ruffled by the reminder that he just might have a price on his head.

"If you want to wait for Eoin, I'll ask him to go along with you in case your eyes...."

"Thanks much for the offer and the pay, but I'll be off."

"Just leave the cart by the shanty. I'll have him watch it. Meanwhile, welcome to the new world. May you stay for a while."

Chapter 14

Johnny's eyes wouldn't let him enjoy the balm Hailey had provided. He couldn't make out the street numbers and could barely discern the names of the stores he passed. He took license with the quote from Mathew that that his mother had often cited while lightheartedly distorting what Jesus said about the eternal need to forgive. "Squeeze the cursed eyes seven times and the pain should stop, and if not seven, then seventy times seven."

How had his mother always found a way to forgive those who'd wronged her? Even when the Irish refused to pay for absinthe or whisky to help ease the pain of her breast cancer, she'd forgiven them. She'd forgiven Johnny's father for his every affair, every drunken night he'd spent before the fireplace praising the body of the most recent woman he'd bedded, every tongue thrashing he'd given her on the porch when she sat with him daily to weather the insolence in his hangovers.

Once when he and his father were sitting out on the steps of Ineeb, his dad's favorite pub, the old man tried to explain why he drank so much: "Because being forgiven by your mother for every goddamn time I sin lays far more guilt on me than God intended. To wash it away, I drink."

Did that indirectly explain why Johnny drank so much now? Because he felt James had forgiven him time and time again for serving on the firing squad? It made no more sense than his father's explanation.

Johnny halted and looked up to test his eyes. Floating snowflakes dotted the dark clouds with a spectral whiteness. Chilled by the snow's nibbling moisture, he squinted down the street where the name "Rags-to-Riches" glowed from a small, theater-like marquee. He quickened his pace. As he drew closer, he spotted a hand-made manikin below the lights. Its neck was made from the handle of a broomstick and the head, from a smooth, round piece of taped parchment decorated with bright red lips and Irish green eyes. The sign of infinity was stitched over the breast of its tattered red dress decorated with paper roses and sporting a torn fur collar. The lengthy dress dropped below the fringe of the coat to the spindly wired feet strapped into gold, high heels, one of them missing a heel. A cardboard sign hanging from the manikin's gloved hand read: "Ask inside — you'll be surprised!"

Johnny looked through the window barely able to make out the scarves and handbags on the shelves. Leaning closer, he could see that several of the scarves were worn and tattered while others had stitched together tears. The prices were pinned to each. Inside, standing mirrors framed the opposing walls of the room. Lamps hanging above the mirrors created a stream of endless orange and amber reflections between the walls.

Opening the door, he thought he could hear Esme's soft voice whispering as if reciting an odd poem, asking imagined shoppers to keep their voices down and raise a hand if they needed help. When he stepped inside, the voice faded.

"Anybody home?" The floor creaked behind him.

"May I help you?"

He pivoted to find Esme by the window smiling. Where in hell had she come from? As she moved past him toward the counter, her reflection remained for a moment in each passing mirror, partially blocking the flow of lights. She stepped playfully back and forth in front of the mirrors, dragging the reflection with her. She watched him watching her. "It's like being in two places at once, in the past and present at the same time," she said as she slipped behind the counter.

"I'm sorry to trouble you," he said, astonished at what he'd just witnessed. "My eyes are starting to burn again. I can still see, but it's a bit worse."

"You're sure the body of this less than curvaceous lass standing before you isn't playing tricks on them."

He chuckled quietly. "I wouldn't swear to it."

"Let's have a look," she said, leaning closer. Alarm crept into her face. "They have gotten worse, Johnny, much worse. Lift your lids, carefully." She searched from his nose to the corners of his eyes and back again. "It has to do not so much with what you can see, but what *I* can. Have you been treating them?"

"I used up what you gave me, both the sage and turmeric."

"The infection's defeating them. Your eyes are buttery with tiny flakes of red, which means the infection's drawing blood from the lids and sockets. We have to do more or it'll only be a matter of time before you won't be able to see a thing. You can choose to go to a doctor, if you'd rather, but he'll tell you the same thing, hand you a cane and suggest you avoid stepping off a cliff."

"Is there anything else I can do?"

She stared over his shoulder toward the front window as if in an inner debate, then scanned his face. "Can you see into my eyes?"

"I can see where they are but little else."

"Neither the moon nor the sun?"

"What are you talking about?"

She pulled a silk handkerchief from a drawer and handed it to him. "Wipe them again. I'll bring you something much, much stronger. Give me a minute."

On the trail of her voice she disappeared into the back room. Johnny heard several drawers open and close, each louder than the one before.

"Where's the damn vase?" she shouted as another drawer slammed shut. "Thank God!" Moments later he heard a sharp, grating sound, like sandpaper on wood. After a minute it stopped. Silence filled the void.

She emerged from the room and slipped behind the counter. "Can you tell what I'm holding?"

He rubbed his eyes and squinted at her fingers. "Maybe a piece of a ladies stocking… filled with powder of some kind."

She untied the lace binding. "From Cuchulain's stone at Clochafarmore, to the toe of a lady's stocking with her blessing," she said, placing it on the counter. "A few days after the Tans beat me, I developed gangrene where the butt of the rifle split my hip. Ina, my dear friend, who was nursing me, had no place to go for drugs because the town had been abandoned, except for the church, that is. Ina could barely sit with me without crying. One day she showed up bright-faced to tell me she went to see her priest and he'd given her a prescription to help me. The prescription was a set of instructions from God, he told her."

Esme smiled and opened the stocking. "Ina helped me out back and went to relieve herself in the lilacs. Mixing her pee with the greenery in the woods, she made this potion for my wound and after using it for a week, my hip healed. So, I'm thinking, if it can cure gangrene, it should certainly take care of your sties. The priest's prescription, Dash, as it's called, is waiting to help you." She licked her finger and dipped it into the stocking. "Bend over."

Johnny leaned toward her. The powder was green, the color of a fern and smelled oddly like peppermint. "There's pee in this?"

"As in us all," she giggled. "Trust me and come closer. Open your eyes and try not to blink, or think."

"Shouldn't you put on some gloves?"

"Not with this on my fingers. Not even if I wash the Dash off and then touch the sores. It sinks right away into the skin and keeps the surface impenetrable for hours, plenty of time to find a basin." With three dips into the powder, she coated the lower part of his lids and wet her fingers again.

"Pinch your lids and turn them outward, towards me." Her finger gently brushed his lids. It tickled and he flinched. She removed her finger, spat on it, dipped it into the sac again and ran the tip across his lower lids. "Squeeze them tight, open them in a long blink and do it several times."

Johnny's eyes stung so badly he had trouble opening them. He started to wipe at them but she swiped his hand away. "No, you must let them drain on their own, and don't be alarmed at the greenish tint. It's not infection. It's the shamrocks and peppermint leaves and… let's just say, the main ingredient."

His nose started running. He sniffed, throttling a sneeze. As he fought the urge to wipe his eyes, his forehead began to ache.

"Steady, steady. T'will be over soon," she whispered.

Like a lamp slowly extinguishing, the stinging sensation began to weaken. Esme handed him another handkerchief. As he dried his eyes, her partially hidden face emerged from the drape of her wavy hair. In slowly disappearing layers, the haze faded from her cheeks. It reminded him of Nora resurrecting the young rebel who lay dead in the street of Kilmichael, his face caked with dried bog. The Tans had rolled him in the mud until he'd drowned. They threatened to kill anyone, citizen or relative, who made any effort to bury him. She'd brought a semblance of life back to the lad by covering his face with hot towels to soften the casing. Caringly, she'd wiped it away. As the young man's face began to return, his little brother stepped out from behind their mother's skirt to announce that an angel had come to tend his brother. He pointed to a raven perched high on the pitched roof of a blacksmith's shop. "It's the raven on Cuchulain's shoulder, the same one!" he said happily and lowered his fingers to point at Nora. "It brought her in his claws all the way from heaven."

As if delivered by the same angelic raven, Nora now appeared behind the counter. Johnny couldn't speak, yet fear played no part in his bewilderment. Surely, what he'd been suspecting for a while, and came to him more frequently now, was true: he was going insane. And yet because of Hailey's explanation of madness being a common result of the crossing, he felt something frighteningly enjoyable about the apparition, something mystifying, as if he were journeying back and forth in time with no help from the whisky. He saw into her eyes and she into his and for a moment they were together again on the O'Brien's porch listening to the rain.

Like a tapestry slowly coming to life in changing swells of color, the two women stepped sideways into one another. Esme's tanned skin gave color to

Nora's face and Nora's dark hair deepened the waves about Esme's cheeks. Their mouths melded into a cave of temptation.

"Is something wrong, Johnny?"

His heart fell at the sound of Esme's voice. He wondered if he was about to collapse. The dual image moved slowly from behind the counter, coasting toward the mirrors, bringing the past forward while somehow erasing its connection to tragedy. Time began to move around him. Suspended in the amber reflections, it danced in Esme's eyes. As if the magic had sheathed him, the smile on Nora's face backed into her own reflection and disappeared. The sharp, green color of Esme's eyes remained before him.

"I can see," he said, astonished and yet embarrassed he'd taken so long to answer. "I'm sorry. I got lost for a moment."

"Dash can have that effect, causing people to believe they're in another world when trying to reroute the mind's doubt that the wounds would heal," Esme said. "I felt it often when I was recovering, and if the powder weren't so scarce, I'd still be using it, but poteen's available at a much cheaper price."

When she laughed, Johnny was tempted to grab her by the shoulders, lift her over the counter and hug the bejesus out of her, but he held back as she laced the sac and handed it to him.

"I can't thank you enough," he said, digging for his wallet. "Here, let me pay you for it."

"You already have, and someday you'll realize how expensive it was. On the other hand, if your eyes continue to improve, maybe I'll bill you twice over and keep a portion from Lars," she said smiling.

"Lars, your boss? I'd almost forgotten his name."

"He's not 'my boss.' We work together as equals. He's gathering on the East Side."

"With friends?"

"No, no, not that kind of gathering. He's gathering hand-me-downs hands from the trash bins of the wealthy, the things they've worn but twice and still grown tired of. The holidays are when America's rich women clean their closets out to make room for their gifts from their Santa Husbands. Sometimes I gather but mainly Lars because he's faster. He can outrun any cop in New York when he's high on absinthe. He just flies over them. My job is try on all the clothes and footwear and tell him the size of each, at least from the waist up. I love doing it because I can feel the souls of those who've worn them. It lets me know who among our donors has passed away and who's still alive, who's bereaved or tortured or has overcome their past and set out anew, which is seldom. As with ravens, for it is said they, too, can feel the souls of the bygone, as did the raven on Cuchulain's shoulder."

"Did you come up with the idea for the store or did Lars?"

"Lars. He's from Denmark, near Kronburg Castle, or Elsinore as 'twas named by Shakespeare, the setting he used in Hamlet. Lars claims that the Castle's where he began to have ideas about selling used clothes to those who couldn't afford to buy them new, as he took pity on the poor, wretched witches who inhabited the Castle."

"Why did he come to America?

"The World War. He'd gone to visit Elsinore when Belgium was invaded by the Germans. His family was killed while he was there. He wanted revenge and thought America would be the side to be on. So, he came here but they wouldn't let him join the armed forces because he couldn't control his hallucinations. They've driven him deeper into the absinth, but for a wonderful reason, he claims. As he puts it, his illusions combined with the whisky help him 'find love where it's nowhere to be found.'"

"And where would that be?" Johnny asked, as the lights seemed to swim through his words in coils of mimed sunset.

"Here," she said.

"Here? Here, in a second-hand store they find love? Johnny said, more with astonishment than sarcasm.

"Rags-to-Riches is more than a store. It's a refuge for lost souls, a place where they can gather and share their feeling of being alone, where they can escape their past and feel love for another and thus for themselves when, until then, they have none. "

" How do you know that? How would you even suspect it?"

Though his tone was now unmistakably skeptical, her lips became a forbidden smile. "It reveals itself in the strangest ways. For instance, the dress on the manikin outside. Within seconds of trying it on, I could feel the soul of the woman who'd owned it. I knew right away she'd overcome something strangely unusual and death-defying.

"I wanted desperately to meet her, so I used the dress as a guise — I'd return it to her and apologize for taking it. Lars told me where she lived. At her front door, when I tried to hand her the dress, she smiled and said she hoped it fit, and of all things, I believe she saw through me and asked me to tell her the real reason I'd come. When I told her our intentions in creating such a store, she said that she, too, understood the flow of gratitude and kindness from one to another and asked if I would like to hear her story. She waved me into her house with a leather-bound hand. We introduced ourselves and sat down by the fireplace."

Johnny listened as Esme told the story.

"She was attacked by a bear when hiking in the Knockmealdowns. It gnawed her hand and jerked her to the ground. She knew she was about to die. Then, grenades began to explode near the British barracks. The bear let go and fled into the woods. She was crawling toward the noise when a rebel spotted her and went to get the medics who bandaged her wounds and saw her home.

"The woman, named Faye, was grateful to God for the Rebels, but said that every time she took the wrapping off to wash her wound, she seethed in anger. So, weeks later she set out with a shotgun to the very spot where she'd been assaulted. On the way she came upon a bear cub whose fur had been lit aflame by the ashes of a campfire. The little creature lay smoldering on the coals. Faye lifted her dress, pushed aside her underdrawers, straddled the fire pit and with every ounce of pee inside her, she pissed out the flames. As it turned out, the cub belonged to the very creature who had attacked her."

"How in the world could she have known that?"

Esme nodded as if he'd asked the perfect question. "The momma bear came rushing out of nowhere into the clearing. In a panic, Faye fell and twisted her ankle. Just when she thought her life was over, the bear lay down on the ground beside her baby and licked and cuddled it, all the while taking time to lick Faye's ankle as well. The bear knew what Faye had done and that she was no longer an enemy. Faye eventually got to her feet, unloaded the shotgun, dropped it into the ashes and using a broken branch as a cane, limped home. Her need for revenge had been overturned by kindness, her anger by gratitude, if not the love in the mommy bear's eyes."

It had to be a fantasy, Johnny thought, a story Esme had extracted from her fairy-tale world, and yet it left him wavering in the gap between disbelief and awe.

Chapter 15

"You're sailing toward me from three thousand miles away," Esme said, coming from behind the counter and clasping his hand that held the Dash.

"I owe you more than I can pay just now," he said.

She released his hand, tugged on her locks of hair, nervously tightened them under her chin and disappeared behind the counter. Johnny must have blinked because in an instant she rose in front of him with a shambled suitcase and a sullen face. "All I've just shared with you is but a prelude," she said, opening the suitcase. It was packed with what appeared to be women's clothes. "These were Sally's."

"Sally's? Dillon's mother?"

"Yes. I'm selling them for Joshua. They need the money. To make a bit more, he's joined the Tar Babies."

"The Tar Babies? I'm told they're meaner than the Gophers and the mafia put together," Johnny said in disbelief. "Joshua seems like too kind a fellow."
"Joshua seems like too kind a fellow."

"He is kind and wouldn't lift a finger to hurt you or me, about the gang, but I do know he *is* kind and wouldn't lift a hand to hurt you or me, but he needs money and according to him being in a gang that steals and sells whisky is the best way to get it, especially now, during the holidays."

"I'm sure he could find a regular job."

"He has one, if you call racking the tables at Blimey's pool hall over on Lexington, a regular job. They pay him a dime an hour, while the white rackers get twenty-five cents, but Blimey, himself, lets Dillon come with him and helps him with his homework, so Joshua puts up with the wage." She handed Johnny the flask. "Here, you might need this."

Glancing at the manikin and back to Johnny, her unfocused pupils settled on his. Her breath came in long, self-calming gasps. Her lips moved silently, changing from side-to-side as if she were in a debate with herself or alone climbing the Knockmealdowns in search of the little cub. He thought of little Jenny and wondered if his summoning her was what Esme was doing, summoning kindness from far away. He wanted to touch her but held back.

"Johnny, there are certain things I must share while there's still time."

"What do you mean, *while there's still time?* You're young, talented and full of energy." He stopped there, remembering Seamus. Before he'd smashed against the stern of *The Pestilence* and thrown overboard by Bile, he, too, had been young and full of energy. He could fill three baskets of bones to Johnny's one and return from the stern to the hold within minutes, having fed the sharks.

When Johnny returned from the memory, Esme was gazing at the window. He thought maybe a customer had appeared, or perhaps a stranger who might be following him, so he looked as well but saw only the manikin.

The streams of light eerily lined Esme's eyes. She seemed lost, a nomad from another world. She took a deep breath and let the words slip out on its release. "Joshua's trying to save enough money to buy a gun. The Tar Babies don't have money to supply guns to everyone, so each person has to save up enough on his own. The more armed they are, the more they can steal. But that's not the whole story." She hesitated, pressed her hands against the counter and stared at them. The hesitation became a minute. "I need help to finish the story. Would you prefer absinthe or poteen?"

Chapter 16

She raised the bottle of poteen to her mouth and gulped. Her fetching cheek bones rose in her flushed face as she coughed. Fighting for breath she handed Johnny the bottle. To prepare for whatever she was about to reveal, he took barely a sip and returned it. Slowly, she leaned onto her elbows. "I promised I'd never tell."

"Neither will I, Esme. It's all right."

"Joshua needs extra money... to pay off the conductors. You see, if black people are let on a train at all, it's normally just in one of the freight cars or in the caboose, and even so, they need more than the normal price of a ticket to stay onboard."

"What train? What are you talking about?"

"He's determined to return to Melville, to kill Aiken, the judge."

"You can't mean it. No possible way."

"And soon. That's what I meant by *running out of time.*"

Alarm overrode Johnny's sense of relief that Esme wasn't the one in trouble. "What the hell's Joshua thinking? He'll never get out of there alive. I've heard they kill blacks in the South for sport. With all that he's suffered, I can't believe he'd even consider going down there. What about Dillon? Surely, he's not taking him?"

"Joshua's looking into a black children's home over in Brooklyn for when he's away."

"For when he's away? Away?" Johnny said, incredulously. "Esme, he isn't taking a holiday, for Christ's Sake."

Esme sighed. "I've tried my best to reason with him, but he sincerely believes that killing Aiken is the highest calling in his life, the greatest gift he could ever give Dillon and Sally."

"Killing Aiken's not a gift! It's theft of the highest order, grand larceny of a child's life. I can't believe it. He told you all this?"

She nodded and sipped at the bottle. "One night when Dillon went backstage to a kids' party the mothers were giving, Joshua asked me to have a drink with him behind the curtain. He threw down three or four bourbons before saying much of anything. Then he started talking about Sally and how when they came to New York, he brought a suitcase stuffed full of her clothes. He said the sight and smell of them brought her soul into their little apartment where he and Dillon would cry together feeling her presence. He asked if I would sell the clothes to help raise the money to avenge her death. I could see the furor in his heart as he sobbed." She stared at Johnny. "I'm sure you've seen it yourself, in battle, the hatred chained to one when the need for revenge cannot be overcome with reason or assuaged in any way, but by might."

He nodded. "I have seen it, but with war it's different," he said. "In war revenge and killing are one and the same. Revenge is the order of the day and there's never a reason to question how you achieve it. It has no boundaries."

She patted her chest and cleared her throat. "The next morning I woke up wondering exactly that. I was so worried that I couldn't go to work and went to Blimey's to find him. I wanted to know if what he'd told me was the truth or some drunken fantasy. I repeated what he'd said word-for-word, never once taking my eyes off him. He sat for the longest time staring at the floor. The sound of hustlers jousting and billiard balls striking nearly drove me crazy as I waited for his to answer. Finally, I raised my voice above the clatter and told him how disappointed I was that he wouldn't tell me the truth. When I started to leave, he grabbed me by the arm and asked if I would help take care of Dillon while he was gone. I told him that if he ever left, even if he stopped showing up at The Woebegone, I'd call the cops immediately."

"What did he say?"

"It took a while for him to find that huge smile of his. 'I've been bullshitting you all along,' he said, then tried to lie his way out of it. His words are stuck in my head. 'I went way overboard with what I told you, Esme. Believe me, I didn't mean it. It just came from my nightmares about what the fucking Judge done. I should'a killed him when I had the chance, right in that courtroom in front of the white trash who sat pretending to be an honor-bound jury when all they was, was Klan members happy as hell with Aiken's ruling to chop off Dillon's legs. I got up and screamed at him, and they took me off to jail until it was over. But I'm not going nowhere, Esme. Nowhere, I can promise you that.'

"Who's bullshitting who, Joshua, I asked him and then repeated my promise to tell the cops the minute I found out he'd left town."

"You think it gave him second thoughts?"

"Oh, he knew that he could easily outfox me by skipping a few nights at The Woebegone and try to make me think he'd had to work or something else to lower the bar. If I called the cops and they found out I'd misled them by saying Joshua had left the City, they probably wouldn't bother to track him down, if I called a second time."

Johnny's could feel his heart pulsing "He'd do all this while locking Dillon in a nightmare for the rest of his life — in a children's home?"

"He thinks he can do his killing and make it back. But he's *killing* somebody, and even if it's a piece of scum he's killing, it's still a killing. I'm doing my best to prevent it," she said. "Like the promise of God to Isaac. 'Give one something more than he has and he will depart from the nonce,' and at the risk of speaking for God, perhaps there's a way to provide Dillon more than he has and have it include Joshua."

"I'm not following."

"I want to give Dillon a larger world." Her voice began to move with passion. "If I can give him a love of something, a love that Joshua himself could feel part of, a greater something that would convince him there's so much more to life than revenge. If I can do that, then maybe he'd bury the need to kill forever."

"What could you possibly do?"

"It's not what I *could* do, but what I've done." Her breath fluttered. "You're going to think I'm crazy — well, I'm sure it's already dawned on you — but here, let me show you something."

Esme ran into the back room and came rushing back with three pairs of coconut shells, each pair bound together with thin straps that resembled boot laces. Each hollow coconut had its top covered with tightly drawn pieces of thin leather.

"Take a guess," she said, grinning proudly.

"Bongo drums made out of coconuts."

"You win the prize!" she said, extending a pair across the counter. "Tap them with a finger."

Johnny thumped a drum with his finger. The hollow sound slipped through the bottom of the coconut to echo briefly in the silence. He placed the fingers of both hands on the smooth surfaces and slowly ran them back and forth, tapping them gently. After a moment he tapped faster until the taps blended into a patter. He stopped and smiled.

"Not bad, Johnny. Now stroke them to the sound of my voice as I sing a song yet to be written but plays often in my mind, a song that speaks to what I've been saying about Dillon and Joshua, and now you as well. The name of the song will be, "The Day I Decided to Stay.""

In the harbor of Kinsale, I heard a foghorn calling,
Johnny, they are sending you away
For you chose to leave the rebels cause, so you might find love abroad
A famine ship to take you is waiting in the Bay.

Each word pierced his heart. As if she'd seen into his past, she'd offered the famine ship as a metaphor for the drums.

She sang as though reciting a poem, slowly but with ardor, squinting, yet unable to prevent her eyes from glazing over. She repeated the song several times before he realized she was waiting for him to join in. After the fourth refrain, he found the harmony and started to hum and say the words. When he realized he was singing solo, he stopped, opened his eyes and saw the delight on her face.

"You found the chord. You blended in perfectly."

"You wrote that?" he said in awe.

"With a little help from beyond.

"The drums are for Dillon."

"Hopefully, to help him move into a new place and coax Joshua to go with him. Like the toys in the bogs and caves where the parents would take their children when the Tans were coming. Not only the children but also their parents survived because of them. Their love of the toys kept them alive and even today their hopes and dreams are still fueled by them. So, yes, the drums are for Dillon."

"But how do you know...?"

"You haven't heard Dillon play the tables, have you?"

"Play the tables?"

"On occasion, he and his dad come early on Wednesdays, long before the doors open. One night a couple of weeks ago I was backstage getting dressed when I heard this pattering like rain on a tin roof. I went out to find Dillon sitting at a table nodding and swaying as he tapped and swished his hands

across the surfaces. As soon as Joshua spotted me, he grabbed Dillon and
stopped him. Dillon told me he'd started playing the tables early one rainy
night at The Woebegone, before anyone else showed up. Swishing his hands
on the floor and clicking his fingers, hearing music no one else heard, he said.
That's when I knew it was more than a young boy playing a game. I couldn't
afford to buy him a drum, so the day after Joshua told me what he was planning
to do, I ran over to the Jamaican market for the coconuts, went to an instrument
shop by the Bowery to learn how to bind and cover them."

A siren outside the store shrieked and then faded as if in apology for
screaming in error. "Incredible," he said. "You are incredible."

She blushed and moved so close he could feel the warmth of her breath.
"Here, Johnny, close your eyes and pretend you're praying."

"I just might be," he said, closing his eyes.

"Now, open them."

Disappointed their lips hadn't met, Johnny opened his eyes to find her
peering into his.

"They're clearing. The butter-coat is thinning," she said, moving back to
her side of the counter. "Thanks to them for watching over us."

Once again he had no idea exactly what she meant, and yet her use of the
word *us* gave him a feeling of wonder and tenderness. A pang of guilt shot
through him. "I have to go," he said, turning for the door.

Chapter 17

As he reached for the door, she called to him, "Johnny, I know we Irish love Billy the Kid, but isn't carrying a gun on your hip taking things a little too far? I hope I don't have to start worrying about Joshua *and* you."

Johnny's hand went to the pistol in an awkward attempt to hide his embarrassment. "They gave it to me at the pier... just before..."

Aware of his tenuous voice, he knew what was about to happen but could do nothing to avoid it. He was on Death Avenue between the trolley and the train. Gunfire and screeching brakes were bursting around him. He saw Jenny's purple face and drew the pistol from his belt and wheeled toward the window. Was the figure outside a Duster or someone sent in Bile's footsteps to kill him He took aim.

"No, Johnny! Put it away!" Esme shouted. "Put the gun away!"

Her voice altered his vision. A strange skeletal figure in a red coat stood outside the window. Gradually, it shifted from a suspect back into a manikin. Johnny glanced at the pistol shaking in his hand. He began to tremble. Convinced more than ever he was losing his mind, he lowered the gun and turned to Esme. "I'm so sorry," he said. "I was on the streets this morning. Gunfire broke out. I don't know what just happened. The memory was just too fresh. It rolled over me. I got spooked."

"Here," Esme said, "let's set the gun down and rid ourselves of the poteen. We need neither, lest we end up drunk and dead on the floor." She spoke in a light, reassuring tone as though trying to calm an upset child.

As she put the poteen in a drawer, he set the pistol on the counter and released his grip as if dropping a snake. Esme's eyes relaxed and searched for his. The lamplights were streaking through his reflection and he couldn't help but feel as if fate himself hung in the air, vast and weighty, indistinct yet accusatory, demanding yet again to hear why he hadn't fired.

"I couldn't bring myself to," he answered.

"Couldn't bring yourself to what?" Esme asked. "To shoot a manikin? Why in God's name would you, unless you've truly gone mad?

"I didn't stand up for her."

Esme slid the pistol to the far end of the counter. "What are you talking about? She's made of wire."

"No, she was made of flesh and blood," he said. His lips worked nervously. "This morning on Death Avenue, a little girl... no more than twelve or so..." He looked through the streams of light toward the manikin to finish the story. "She died in my arms. There was nothing I could do. Then I covered her lips with rum and... stroked her face and she... she returned. Somehow, she came back to life."

Esme took his hand. "My God! Why are you so angry? You did more than anyone could have."

"Her eyes seemed to turn inward and closed," Johnny said. "Her fingers were ice cold. She swallowed and began to tingle as if tiny insects were attacking her skin. She started to hum, as though she were considering something being said over her and swallowed again. 'Thank you,' she said, and she opened her eyes. The cops rushed me out of there before I could get her last name or address. I can only hope she's alright."

"She'll return, Johnny."

His fingers coupled with hers. "I should have done more. They caught the shooter and brought him to me for street justice, but I couldn't bring myself to pull the trigger. Seth, another of our runners, shot him dead and asked me to administer the *coup de grace*, to make sure." Johnny paused to free his hand and wipe his eyes again. "But I refused to. I tried to justify it by telling myself something a priest in Kilmain... I mean in Dublin... once told me. Unless it is certain a body is dead, it cannot be anointed and without anointment the soul is denied heaven. I don't know why it hit me there in the street. It's so stupid. A person dead is a person dead. The Duster was unquestionably dead, but I should have shot the bastard anyway. The memory of pulling the trigger would have been far more gratifying than acting like a coward based on something a feckin' priest said. Priests don't serve on the battlefield. What the hell do they know?"

"What indeed? That you feel you should have shot him, I surely understand. Believe me I do. From the bottom of my heart to my father's last breath, I do. But the child's alive. That's what you must take away. Leave the rest on the street."

When she touched his hand again, the sensation crept into his wrist and up his arm. Her face narrowed as her eyes took a cue from his. Creased at the corners, they began to flicker. She straightened, emerging from her own trance.

The words of this beautiful misaligned woman could resonate like a prayer in an empty church, Johnny thought. He'd not had such a conversation with anyone, ever, except possibly with himself on the battlefield where fate kept rising up to worsen the tragedy. "Will you be at The Woebegone tomorrow night?" he asked.

"I will, and God willing, Joshua and Dillon will too."

Chapter 18

When he awoke the next morning, he opened his eyes slowly to prevent the lids from pulling the crust from the sties. To his surprise they peeled open smoothly, allowing him to see through the partially open shutters. The snowbound sunlight was showing crystalline and sugary. The slats in the blinds were well-defined lines between the opening and closing cords. It took a moment to realize he could actually see.

He climbed out of bed, grabbed the stocking and ran into the bathroom where he bent over the sink and looked into the mirror. His troubled face stared back at him, and though it was scary, it didn't possess the same eerie features that emerged Saturday night after having more glasses of poteen than he could remember. His eyes, irregular and drawn, were still red but not fiery, the buttery glaze had lessened to faint yellow, the retinas were still, the eyelashes steady. He wiped them gently with a wash cloth, easing it over the lids without a shred of discomfort. He took turns prying each eyelid open as far as possible to make sure he wasn't being fooled. The powder called Dash had restored them.

He thought of Esme and tried to piece together her ideas about replacing tragedy and bad intent with what *can*, as she put it when explaining her reasoning behind the drums she'd made for Dillon and how going out of one's way to help provide hope to others brings out the best in us. It came to him that this was exactly what he'd tried to do for Nora's father. James had wanted a better life built on hope. His wish to die wasn't how most people would define the essence of hope, but it had been just that for one of the most passionate authors of the Proclamation. James had encouraged Johnny to serve on the firing squad without regret, for his death would encourage Ireland to unite behind the cause of freedom. Johnny had done the right thing by the old man and whether Nora admitted it or not, he'd done the right thing for Ireland. Had he refused to serve on the firing squad, he would have been jailed and executed along with the those who'd joined together to draft the Proclamation. But had he chosen death he would have forsaken James, and that would have been the greater of the paradox. Yet, for having served James and the cause of freedom, he'd been condemned by Nora and the rebels alike.

The pier stretched so far out into the Hudson that the end was lost in the settling fog. Johnny thought of the soldiers' oft-repeated dream of crossing a bridge that led homeward only to have it narrow until they were prevented from returning. They'd called the commonly seen illusion, the Bridge to Nowhere.

Seth greeted him under the pier, his arms folded across his chest. The handle of his Mauser stuck out from its holster. He dropped his arms to pat the gun. "Where's yours, Johnny, in your hip pocket?"

"Jesus," Johnny said, knowing full well he'd left the gun with Esme. "It's still in the apartment. How in hell could I have done that?"

"So, you've not had a chance to use it?" He leaned toward Johnny. "Let me take that back. We know you had the chance but refused to. Isn't that right?"

"What's *right* is the reason I refused."

"Forgive me, Johnny, I forgot. You refused to kill the Gopher and when given a second chance by administering the so-called *coup,* you chose to take your revenge by keeping him from heaven. Have you been lying to me or do I have it right?"

"At last, you do."

Seth shook his head. "With such pure Catholic blood, I'm surprised you aren't from Belfast. You've been to war and must know there are times when might makes right or there'd be no winning side. Time's coming when you'd better accept the idea or die pretending it's not true. Gangs are sprouting up everywhere. Now we have the Tar Babies, the black panthers who call us white trash and want to poach our liquor and kill us in the process. In fact, I'm told they prefer killing to money. They put forth the nonsense that we Irish are somehow bleached messengers from Satan set here to rid the world of color, which in their mind includes Italians and Jews, and anyone who sports a tan in the wintertime."

Johnny couldn't even force a smile. He turned away from Seth and gripped one of the kegs thinking of Joshua's determination to return to Malville. Given the horror of what had happened, to his family, Johnny could surely understand how little else would occupy Joshua's mind. But Joshua was on the verge of committing a far deeper cruelty by failing to understand that he'd be wrecking Dillon's life.

Seth strapped the keg onto the cart and knelt to pick up a piece of splintered pier and toss it into the sand's thin cover of snow. "I'm not joshing you, mate. We're the ones who possess no color whatsoever and happen to be the most giving folks on Earth. Therefore, we need to have the world shinny white, like the snow around us. If we were all black we'd get lost in the night, now wouldn't we?"

"I can't listen to anymore, Seth," Johnny said. "We're all people here and not one of us should be defined by color, whether white, black or in between. I gotta get going." He wheeled and grabbed another keg.

Seth pursued him. "So, then what defines us, eh? Cowardice? Like you in the street the other day? You had the bastard in your grip. I seen the muzzle of your gun poking into his throat. There won't no argument to be made about right or wrong. He almost killed that little girl, for Christ's sake! Whose permission do you need greater than the Almighty's? He had your back. You would've been doing Him a favor by letting the scum show up at the Pearly Gates, only to be denied entrance and sent off to Hell."

Johnny tried to come up with an excuse that would satisfy Seth. His trigger finger shook and his eyes flickered. "I've killed way too many in my life."

Seth smiled unevenly. "Bad joke, mate. Come on what's your reason?"

"You ever been to war?" Johnny asked.

"No, I stayed away from it back home. I was too young."

"Count yourself lucky. I fought three years for the rebels. I've held the death of both friends and enemies in my arms, I've killed with guns, rifles and hand bombs. I've seen our Volunteers die, young boys most likely your age when you lived back home, aware of only what you'd heard by the fireplace. I've served on a firing squad and led good people to their death. And I can tell you, I still see their faces, every one of them. They stare back at me like photographs on a mantle. It's their revenge. I'll see them until the grave and afterwards I'll meet up with them either on the streets of heaven or down below."

"Wait a minute. You served on a firing squad?"

Johnny tensed. Why in God's name had he said that? "No, no. Not on a firing squad. A couple of Tans who'd killed one of our informers, we hanged him from an arch in the town church," he lied.

Seth finished latching the kegs. "I don't know what to make of you, Johnny. You don't seem to be joshing. If you aren't, I'd say you're losing your grip on the real world. Maybe all that guilt's eating away at your brain. Maybe that's what killing does to the weak, chews up your manhood and turns you into a coward. You probably don't get a hard-on anymore." Seth looked at the kegs. "I can give you an extra one, if you like."

"Four is all Hailey can handle," Johnny said.

"I'm not talking about kegs, Johnny. I'm talking about a gun. It could save your life when you're in danger and all your excuses burn down to the need to stay alive. It's in us all. Nothing changes it. Staying alive is whispered in our ears the minute we squeeze out into this world, and if we fail, we fail the wish of God, which is the ultimate treachery."

Johnny thought of the moment at the sewer entrance when all his thoughts had been instantly reduced to survival. He'd thrown Bile down the manhole. Had there been any difference in shooting him and refusing the *coup de grace*? "Maybe God's playing both sides, like betting on a duel between outlaws? The winner's right because he won and the loser's wrong because he lost?" he said.

"God wants us to stand up, not run away. That's what you're missing, Johnny. Now stay put and I'll go get you the type of Mauser they say Countess Markiewicz carried before the Brits caught her and locked her up. That, in and of itself, ought to boost your manhood."

Johnny was shocked to hear her name. He would never forget the day General Maxfield overturned Countess Markiewicz's death sentence. A fiery leader of the Rebellion, she had been a prisoner in Kilmainham. Johnny had been standing guard outside her cell when a captain approached with the news she'd been spared. When she asked the captain why, he said it was because she was a woman. She screamed at him, called Maxfield a fool who couldn't tell the difference between a woman and a man and demanded her execution be carried out. Maxfield wouldn't hear of it. She was removed from death row, sent to a neighboring jail and later released. Johnny wondered if she still regretted being alive.

"I don't ever plan to carry a gun again," he said.

Seth rolled his eyes, looked out at the water and shook his head. "If ever there's a day when you don't come for the whisky, I'll find somebody to take your place because more likely than not you will have joined another gang. We won't take time to find out why you turned on us because there's no use in wasting time trading lies. You'll be marked for dead. It's a rule we've followed since the beginning, and nobody's gonna change it now, especially you."

Johnny put his hand up to say, Enough.

Seth's face hardened. "By the way, when are you going to tell us your last name, mate? Or is there a reason you're hiding it? Maybe they threw you off that ship because you killed somebody on board and felt so guilty about it, you couldn't bring yourself to shoot the Gopher? Is that what happened?"

Johnny felt his face flush. "Flynn, Goddamnit! My name is Johnny Flynn, and no, I didn't kill anybody on that ship! I actually fought to save somebody, a mate who was injured in an accident on board and then fed to the sharks. I tried to save him. *That's* why they threw me off the ship."

"You tried to save a dead man and they threw you off the ship? Makes no sense whatsoever," Seth said. "But maybe it does explain the man who came by the other day asking if anyone knew you or by chance had ever seen you? He wore a coat and tie and a Fedora hat. And I should mention that he had a gun strapped under his arm."

Johnny tensed. "Did he say why he was looking for me?"

"No, but by the look in his eyes I knew he wasn't playing games. He did say he would find you if he had to turn over every cobble and visit every pub in the Kitchen. He described you to a tee. He said he'd collected a number of descriptions from those who'd known you in Ireland. It was urgent that he find you, he said. Considering the gun and the fine way he was dressed, I took him to be a hitman sent by somebody with money. It must have something to do with why they made you walk the plank." Seth stepped into Johnny's face. "What did you do back home, kill somebody? Did you run away from something or somebody for your sin?"

"I just told you everything I ever did in Ireland," Johnny retorted.

"Bullshit! He asked if I'd ever heard of anyone on the piers by the name of Johnny Flynn. At the time I could honestly say, no, but now that I know who you really are..." Seth grinned. "He said he'd been searching for you for a fortnight. He looks for you on the streets during the day, stops at the stores, and visits anyone behind an open door. The pubs at night, as he said, lurking like a sober-sides from one to the next. Seems he's worked his way down to Thirtieth street. Only a few more blocks to Hailey's."

Judging from Seth's description, the man had money, Johnny thought. Who had he known with money enough to search him out? No one, except maybe Nora, who didn't have money but certainly could have raised it. Maybe she couldn't explain herself to her comrades for not pulling the trigger that terrifying day on the Bluffs, then went to the brigade to ask for money to pay someone else? But would she hire someone to kill him? Would she reach out to avenge James' death yet again?

"Do you suspect anyone?" Seth asked.

Johnny turned from Seth without a word and hurried off, pushing the kegs ahead of him. Everywhere he looked, he felt that eyes were fasting on him, from the shadows and the windows of the tenements to men in cars or on horseback. He took to the sewers for protection. He could hear a train approaching overhead. The rumbling of the wheels grew louder, so loud he had to stop and cover his ears. The stones shook as though they had the chills and his body shuddered. A hitman. By now everyone had heard he'd survived. They'd likely heard of Bile's fate and would stand in line to make sure the deed was done.

Could Nora possibly be behind it? He'd heard the sorrow in her voice and seen the regret in her eyes when she whispered her last words before leaving him on the Bluff? *"I love you,"* she'd said. Those words, those unforgettable words that made the crossing with him. Had she hired a gunman? No way in hell, he swore to himself. But someone had.

Maybe he should bypass Hailey's and just keep running, jump the freight trains as Joshua and Dillon had done and ride the tracks. To where? Had the stalker been the one who'd missed him and shot holes in the kegs and then fled when the cops came? Surely, he would have spotted such a person. Such a creep would have stood out, even in all the havoc.

He stopped to catch his breath. He wrapped his arms across his chest and held fast reminding himself of the woman holding little Jenny. From some lost region in his brain, a feeling of goodness flowed through as he thought of her.

He regretted not taking just a second to ask her full name. It was too late now, but he knew, or at least trusted, Esme's suspicion that Jenny was fine.

With keen eyes he shoved the cart ahead. Even as the tunnel darkened, the sadness of losing Nora that rose relentlessly as the sun went down, gave way to the memory of the song Esme had written for him.

In the harbor of Kinsale, I heard a foghorn calling,
Johnny, they have sent you away,
For you chose to leave the rebels cause, so you might find love abroad
A famine ship to take you is waiting in the Bay.

Chapter 19

Johnny showed up with the whisky at Hailey's garden door, its blue color bright even in the feathering snow. He knocked and waited for Hailey to answer but there was no reply. He tried to open the door but the knob wouldn't budge. He knocked again but heard only the thud of his knuckles against the thick wood. Shivering and glancing over his shoulder, he waited. There was nowhere to go and he had to stand guard over the whisky. He had no choice but to quickstep in place to stay warm. He wondered if he should tell Hailey about the stalker, but backed away from the idea. It would lead to too many questions and possibly cause more trouble than the stalker himself. It was Johnny Flynn's problem. He'd brought it on and he had to cope with it.

A vision of Esme replaced the ordeal of waiting in the cold. He saw her reflection as she stood among the mirrors in the store with the rays from the overhead lamps shining through the room like starlight, making it seem all the more likely that the faeries had exchanged her body into that of a clairvoyant. She rested her chin on a beam of light, while gold emblazoned the waves of her long hair. An amber tint crossed her waist just above her raised hip and another just below the rise. Covered tightly by her tattered, red party dress, the edges of her taut midsection dovetailed between her legs. He couldn't help but follow the muscles as they stretched down towards her womanhood. He felt a twitch and his coveralls began to tighten. His freezing face cracked into a smile. He couldn't remember the last time he'd had an erection.

Guilt flooded over him as he remembered Nora's love of sex. Once had never been enough for her. With her appetite she'd had to reach consummation twice each time, even when they'd been standing against an oak tree behind O'Brien's barn. She'd given him about ten minutes between episodes and then leaned him against the tree, threw her arms around his neck and hoisted herself above his hips and slowly settled upon him smiling as her eyes closed.

"Jesus, mate! I didn't know you were here!"

Johnny braced. "Sorry, but I knocked several times."

"Was in the cellar curing the poteen." Hailey's cheeks began to shake. "My God, this must be what it's like to wake up in Norway. Here, let's get the whisky inside before it turns to ice." He reached out to grab the handle of the cart. "Where've you been, lad? I was worried. We're coming up on the weekend with Christmas closing in right behind. There's work to be done, thank goodness."

Johnny took a deep breath. "Sorry, there's been a lot going on." He helped open the door and stepped aside for Hailey's huge body to wedge past him.

Hailey peered into Johnny's eyes. "My God, lad, no longer a fire in them. They're clear, totally clear. Esme was right, eh?"

"She changed from the sage into something she called Dash. It burned like crazy when she put it on but that's what it took. Something to torch the infection. During the night they cleared. When I woke up it took a while to convince myself I could really see again."

"You did good, lad, and so did she. Like I told you, she's different than anyone I can remember. Her voice, her face and her soul. There's beauty in them all, vast beauty I'd say, were I a poet and thirty years younger." Hailey hiked the cart up over the step. "She's faring well?"

"She is. She just made a gift for a young Negro boy who lost his legs. The boy's a musical talent, so she came up with the idea to make him some bongodrums. She made them out of coconuts and fine leather. They're amazing."

"Is the lad she made them for one of the children she helps at The Woebegone?"

"That's where I met him. Jesus, stupid me, I stumbled over him on the curb. I couldn't see where I was going and tripped over him. His dad was there to help out."

"You never know where kindness is going to come from."

Johnny smiled weakly. "Joshua, his dad, helped me up and found me a seat in the theater. He made sure Esme knew I was there."

"Well, if the youngster likes the idea of playing the drums rather than running rum, someone's bringing him up right. Let's get to the basement where it's warmer. I won't charge you for the heat."

Together they carried the kegs down to the mixing room, then went back up to the bar where Hailey offered Johnny a shot of poteen and some cold chicken he'd skewered the night before. He downed them both in a hurry and was about to excuse himself when Hailey looked up from the mug he was drying. "How did the boy lose his legs, Johnny? Do you know?"

Johnny slipped to the center of the seat. Remembering that Esme had trusted him to keep it all to himself, he hesitated, but then asked Hailey never to repeat what he was about to hear. He told the story of the judge's order, Joshua's desire for revenge and what Esme had done to try and prevent it. Hailey set the mug by the cash register, turned away to stare at the baseball bats. Johnny wondered if Dillon's situation was just too much for Hailey or if he might be searching for some of his usual sarcasm, but he felt the old man was seeing far beyond the wall.

"Joshua and Dillon, father and son, a tale as horrible as anything I've ever heard," Hailey said at last. "The veterans have shared plenty of terrible stories here at the bar but nothing even comes close. The fucking judge ought to be hanged." Hailey stared at the counter. "Johnny, I understand the need for revenge. Believe me, I do, and I'll tell you this, it can be damn near impossible to escape it. Bless Esme for trying, but Joshua is trapped in his hatred... and the drums... I just don't know."

"No one does at this point, except maybe Esme."

Hailey stared toward the basement steps. "I knew a man once who lost his son," he said, pushing two chubby fingers into the folds of his neck. Suddenly, he slapped the counter and shouted, "Come here you little sonofabitch. I'm gonna beat the hell out of you!"

Johnny cringed and readied to jump off the stool. The threat seemed so unlike Hailey. "Are you okay, mate?"

Hailey slowly nodded and opened the cash register to remove a set of long keys that reminded Johnny of those he'd used to lock and unlock the cells at Kilmainham.

"Come with me, lad. I've something to show you."

"Wait a second. If you don't mind, who were you threatening just now?"

"Don't worry, Johnny. It wasn't meant for you it. 'Twas meant for me. Come now. I'll go first down the stairs, so if I turn to smack you, you'll have the advantage."

Johnny recognized the familiar smile as pure Hailey, making fun of himself. He knew there was nothing to worry about but wondered what prompted the outburst.

Hailey grabbed a flashlight from behind the counter and led the way down. At the foot of the stairs, he handed the light to Johnny and moved across the low ceiling, cell-like chamber, bypassing the mixing room, toward a barely visible door set in a shadowy nook of the far wall. "Shine it over here," he said, unlocking the padlock and cracking open the door. The aged stench of mildew surged out. Covering his nose with his elbow, Hailey glanced at Johnny. "Keep your distance, mate. It's not a body in here, but the smell will eat at your innards. Hand me the light."

Hailey opened the door to its fullest and worked his way inside. A wave of disgusting odor rolled out as he jerked a dozen putrid sandbags from a stack, dropped them on the floor and pulled out four burlap suitcases sitting atop a shattered steamer trunk. From the space where they'd been hiding, he carefully removed what appeared to be the remains of a bicycle.

Twisted like a corkscrew, Johnny thought it could have been mistaken for Cuchulain's gigantic arteries had it not been for two large, wood-spoked wheels resembling those of a small hay wagon. The flat rubber tires, attached to rusty sections of a bent steel frame, were three times the width of a normal bike's tires. The handlebars were no longer handlebars, but crimped rods that resembled a bat's wings. Hailey struggled to bring the relic to his chest.

Awkwardly wrapping his arms around it, he kissed the steel rod that once had run from the seat to the handlebars but was now simply a pipe attached to the air. "I made the bike when I was but a lad. I suspect I know every nut and bolt," Hailey said, sadly. "It's got no seat now. It was a pony's saddle with the stirrups cut short so I could reach the pedals when I was a youngster. It got stolen during the crossing. If only memories could change the past...."

Johnny ran his fingers along the crooked frame. "You made this?"

"My penny-pinching dad wouldn't spend the money to buy me a real bike. He said I had to figure out how to cut corners and build one on my own. I drew sketches on the kitchen floor, with my mom's help, and over time we stole pieces of broken bikes and wagons wherever they showed up. We put it together out by the chicken coop. From time to time my Da would come watch us and laugh and tell us how stupid we were. He said my Mom's side of the family were idiots and in my case the apple hadn't fallen far from her tree."

Johnny's mind cycled home to his father, the drunk philanderer. He died in Johnny's arms one night outside Ineeb's, having chugged two quarts of whiskey on a dare. Johnny had carried him home in a cart only to be greeted by his mother who was standing on the porch of their log cabin. She came down the steps, cupped his father's face in her hands and said, "Home at last, my love. Home at last."

Silence surrounded the memory until Hailey's voice broke through. "Like Dillon's father, I too, understand revenge," he said. "I've hidden from it since I was a lad, always trying to walk far behind my memories to try and escape it, but to no avail. The hatred of my Da has stayed pent-up inside me like a witch with a pitchfork. Once my Ma broke a leg when she stepped into a gopher hole and was confined to a wheelchair for a while. He'd run her up and down the hills until she cinched up from fear of crashing into something. Then he'd stop and laugh at her. One day in a mad fit he wheeled her over to a nearby bog, shoved her and the chair into it and took off, leaving her there, most likely hoping she'd drown. But she grabbed onto the limbs of a low hanging willow, made a thick rope out of them, and pulled her way out. She wheeled herself home soaked and dressed in mud. I wouldn't have known her but for the wheelchair." Hailey shook his head. "That vermin, a fucking sneak-thief who trusted no one including himself. He drank to keep the stars from whirling in his head and when they'd stop, he'd fly into a rage, seizing anything he could get his hands on and smashing it to smithereens."

"Did she always say she forgave him?"

"Forgave him? Hell, no!" Hailey eased the frame to the floor. "One day he got drunk, and Ma locked him in the chicken coop and ran off to town to get our milk and honey. After a while I went to check on him. I'd cut this hole in the wall of the shed where I could stick my hand inside and feed the chickens when it rained or snowed. I peeked through it to see him standing at the door like a huge gorilla. He was shaking two squawking chickens by the neck. All of a sudden, he spun around and caught me looking at him. His eyes were full of fear and anger, like I was some wandering curse sent to kill him. They had a fierceness I've never forgotten."

Hailey thrust his finger at the closet. "'Come here you little son-of-a-bitch! I'm gonna beat the hell out of you!' That's what he yelled at me. Then he dropped the chickens and kicked the door off the hinges."

"Jesus!"

"I jumped on my bike to go warn Ma, but he caught up with me before I could get through the gate, flung me off the bike, carried it over to the tool shed, jerked out his sledge hammer, smashed the hell out of it and then clamped it in his vice and twisted it with this huge pipe wrench. I ran like a scared rabbit and when I couldn't hear him shouting at me, I turned around. He was at the bottom of the hill standing over the bike like somebody who'd just beat a ten-foot rattler to death, huffing and puffing and sweating. It came to me he was about to have a heart attack. I just stood there waiting, afraid to go to him, but when he collapsed it got the better of me and I ran back to him. His heart had stopped. It pissed me off because I'd always dreamed of the day when I'd be big and strong enough to beat the hell out of him. I threw water on him and even kicked him in the side a few times to wake him, but he was gone."

It struck Johnny that Hailey, like Esme, had told his deeply tragic story without hesitation. Why had they picked him to listen? Was it because they suspected that he, having been to war, had seen, heard and weathered many stories more heart-breaking than theirs?

"He died on me without giving me a chance to show him how much I hated him. The son-of-a-bitch died on me!" Hailey wiped his eyes. "I'm going to remake my bike somehow. It'll be a replica you can't tell from the original and wherever my father is these days, in heaven or hell, he'll watch me fix it and he'll seethe."

Suddenly the obvious took possession of Johnny. He thought himself such a fool for thinking of it only now, and spent the moment cautioning himself about what he wanted to ask, worried about intruding in Hailey's revelation after he'd struggled all these years to resolve the dilemma on his own terms. Yet with the terrifying world Dillion was about to inherit, Johnny couldn't hold it in any longer. "Hailey, I don't know if this would work, or if it's too far from the reason you're about to build the bike to ask but…"

"The reason's clear Johnny, and I won't stray from it. What's on your mind?"

"This isn't fair and if you tell me to shut my mouth, I'll understand, but would you consider making the bike for Dillon as well? I realize it's not what you had in mind…"

Hailey put a finger to his lips and then reached out to stroke a wheel. He breathed in deeply and let out a long breath as he pinched his eyes and stood staring at the remnants of the bike. "It *is* more than what I had in mind… and thankfully so. My idea was all about me. I was too busy trapped in my hatred. I should have thought of it. It should have been my first thought. Two blessings for the price of one. Thank you, Johnny."

"It's you we have to thank, Hailey."

"This will now be revenge at its fullest," he said emphatically. He leaned toward the bike's distorted shaft. "Old fellow, you had the hell beat out of you. But now, if you'll forgive the play on words, we're going to set things more than straight. I'm going to make you over into something new, something you'll recognize but cannot imagine." Hailey went silent. In the powerful blend of quiet and darkness, he stood examining his hands as his breathing quickened.

Johnny tensed, wondering if he was about to collapse from a heart attack. "Hailey, you alright?"

"I can see Joshua pushing Dillon to school, if the boy's running late, or guiding him to The Woebegone in the dark or even all the way to the Yankee Stadium while the boy plays his drums. It may help take Joshua's mind off killing and realize, as I have just now, that retribution can be had apart from violence. What do you think, lad? You've known it all along, haven't you? Do I have it right?"

In his mind Johnny could only think of what Esme had said about replacing the chains of catastrophe when she told him about the drums, and perhaps the reason Nora had turned the gun away from him at the last second. "More than right!" he exclaimed. "You've come up with a new commandment!"

"I can take no credit, for 'twas yours all along. Would you be willing to help with this here?"

"By all means."

"Then, what do you say we get started."

"Let's!" Johnny's eyes scanned the bike, trying to picture the shape it might take. "I guess these tires could serve the stern and those from a cart the fore."

"We're not making a ship, mate, but put this in your head as well," Hailey said, chuckling. "To have the boy's arms do the work instead of his legs, imagine hand throttles, pumps, if you will, instead of pedals, to allow him to steer. Like this." Hailey began to push and pull his arms as if he were rowing a boat. "It'll take some getting used to but he'll work up to it. And to help him I'll weld a rail to the rear so Joshua can shove him along."

"We have to move fast. Joshua could leave any day."

"And that we will! The sooner we get to it, the better for Dillon, and the sooner my father turns in his grave."

"Just tell me what to do."

"You can help gather the parts and turn a few bolts. I've got a bunch of tools I used to build the bar and stage when the pub opened. As for the rest, once I take everything apart and straighten it out, I'll see what else we need. We'll have to find a seat. How long are Dillon's little legs?"

"I'd guess a foot or so, just short of his knees."

"A saddle wouldn't work then. We'll need a comfortable seat, firm but with some give and take so his arms and legs can move like crazy when he's in a race and at the same time, keep him steady. It'll come to me. Meanwhile, I believe we've got just enough time to celebrate," he said, heading into the mixing room and returning quickly with two tumblers of poteen. He handed one to Johnny and raised his glass. "Two redemptions for the price of one. Without you, there'd be only one. 'Twas from you the idea came."

As Johnny clinked glasses, a vision of Joshua running behind and shoving the bike came to him, accompanied by an almost unbearable sense of purpose.

"Johnny, something just came to me," Hailey said. "Would you try to find us a wheelchair, maybe an old throwaway at a sordid place like the Knickerbocker Hospital up on a Hundred and Thirty-first. Think you could go in the morning and check it out?"

"Sure. The Knickerbocker, you say?"

"Yes, but don't linger there. I've heard it's plenty dangerous. They tend only to poor and disheveled white people. Rumor has it some of the doctors aren't really doctors but students, at best. They say the head surgeon's a drug addict who laughs and dances when he operates and feeds his patients morphine and cocaine to avoid the cost of giving them ether. So, could be that the likelihood's high you can steal a wheelchair and nobody'll know. If you get out alive, I'll see you tomorrow afternoon. Meanwhile the poteen's on the house but no more than will let you find your way home."

Johnny didn't feel bad about stealing a wheelchair. He'd been asked to find a gift. Despite a full glass of poteen in front of him, he only took a sip. He made it home easily, saw no one following him, went to bed excited for the morning, and for once in a long while, sank into an untainted sleep.

Chapter 20

He slept through the night without being flooded by the strange, lurid dreams of loss and love that often altered his whereabouts. But when he awoke, there was no hangover or blurred vision to cause things around him to appear shapeless and forlorn. For the second straight day, he could actually distinguish the squinting blinds from the light cutting through them. Rapidly, his fresh, vivid mind mapped out a day unlike any since the crossing, a day he looked forward to, a day when he would actually *do* something rather than hover in his woes. Purpose had made the crossing somewhere in the night. Let the man in the Fedora be damned. He could stalk all he wanted, but Johnny would outrun him.

He had to get his hands on a wheelchair, visit the pier early for his stash and head straight to Hailey's, even though he'd like nothing more than to stop by Rags-To-Riches to let Esme know about the gift for Dillon. But he knew he'd have to wait until late in the day to see her, or if he and Hailey worked well into the night again, he'd have to wait until Saturday at The Woebegone when hopefully they could surprise everyone.

Before leaving Hailey's, he'd jotted down the address of the hospital on a slip of paper and put it on his nightstand when he got home. In a place made to help the misbegotten, he would ask if he could borrow an old wheelchair – even a broken one might do — to help him escort a poor boy with missing legs back and forth to school. It was basically a lie, but given Hailey's description of the Knickerbocker, chances were that lies went undeciphered.

He slipped on his denims, a tweed sweater and an old war jacket of grey-green serge, then gulped down two raw eggs, gnawed a chunk off the crusty black bread and rushed out of the apartment to catch the tram, for the new fast train had been suspended since the attack.

The snow fell gently on the tram's windows. The buildings lining Eighth Avenue slowly ground past as the trolley lumbered out of the Kitchen. Johnny kept wishing it would move faster between the more distant stops in the north, but it remained mulish in its sluggishness. He tried to imagine what the bike would look like when complete. He laughed to himself as he imagined Dillon surging past the tram, pumping the oars like lightning rods.

At his stop across the street from the Knickerbocker, he stepped onto the curb and looked up at the huge, orange-brick building which, because time had eaten away at the bricks, resembled an aging tenement. Three horse-drawn ambulances were parked in front of the bullet-shaped entrance. The drivers and nurse-men were cleaning the wagons and feeding hay to the horses. Johnny hurried across the street to the hospital's gigantic wooden doors.

The large reception room resembled a church at twilight. A split stairway encircled the receptionist's desk while a massive, arched window, stained so darkly with deep blues and reds it barely let in enough light to touch the shoulders of a woman sitting before him. The orange halo brought back Pearse's comments when Johnny apologized for having to blindfold him before his execution. The rebel smiled and said in a prisoner's struggling, mildewed voice, "No matter the blindfold, lad, for I needn't open my eyes to follow the aura of the angel's lamp into the darkness, for I want to face head-on, fate's intention to have me weep and beg to stay alive."

Johnny headed over to the desk with the memory unable to temper the murmurs and groans of the sick and feeble waiting for help as they lay sprawled on the floor and in the worn leather chairs. A group of women sat bundled on a sofa. They moaned in a choral of pain. A one-armed man lay on a table which was so hidden by shadows he appeared to be adrift. It reminded Johnny of a battlefield.

He had to be careful to avoid tripping over someone. He felt his way by gently nudging the shadows with the toes of his boots. Suddenly, he heard a distant cry followed by a stream of screams as if a group of the helpless were being flogged. He stopped, and as his eyes adjusted to the darkness, the screams slowly abated.

The receptionist, a thin woman with one outsized earring and an uneven jaw looked up at him. "May I help you?" Her annoying, office smile immediately gave way to stern, irritated lips.

"Yes, if you would," Johnny said. "I'm in urgent need of a wheelchair. A used or even broken one, would be most helpful."

"You seem to be fit enough. I saw you walk in and your voice is strong, so your lungs would seem intact."

Johnny didn't know if she was trying to make a joke or if she was being serious. He chose the latter and didn't smile. "It's not for me. It's for someone I take care of, a young boy who lost his legs in an accident a while ago. He's getting too heavy for me to carry him back and forth to school and while it's only a block away from our apartment, I could use some help."

"I'll need to take some notes." She reached for a pen and paper. "Is he your son or a relative, by any means?"

"No, ma'am. Dillon's a young black boy."

She looked up. Her eyes firmed. "A black boy?"

"He was in a terrible accident when he lived down South. His shanty gave way and now he can't walk."

"I'm sorry but you'll have to look elsewhere," she answered wearily, as if to say he should have known better than make such a request. She set the pen down and straightened her shoulders. "This is the Knickerbocker Hospital. We don't treat Negroes here. We specialize in the poor and downcast whites, especially veterans who've lost a limb and can't stand on their own or feed themselves. Best you try Harlem Hospital, though I'd be careful of infections. It's just a few blocks uptown on Lenox Avenue."

Johnny felt like he was in the presence of Judge Aiken's nurse. He placed his hands on the counter and leaned toward her. "Let me make sure I heard *you* right. I believe you said this hospital doesn't treat Negroes? Is that what you said?"

"This hospital specializes in diseases and disfigurements of Caucasians only. We haven't had time to learn about Negro sufferings. We're flooded with veterans and there simply weren't enough black soldiers on the battlefields. We've just been too busy to branch out. Try your luck at Harlem Hospital."

"Lady, I don't know how many Negro soldiers there were in the War, but I can tell you, the streets of Hell's Kitchen are littered with them!" The irritation in Johnny's rising voice blended strangely with the crackles and cries of those around him. "And by the way, the War's got nothing to do with the boy or his family. Dillon's legs were cut off by orders from a white judge, a hateful son-of-a-bitch who believed infections from black people carry such danger they could worm their way out of their coffins to infect all the rest. I imagine you people believe that's the case as well."

The woman drew back and reached for the telephone. "I must ask you to leave."

"Gladly." He pivoted and started for the entrance when a gaunt black man in a grimy yellow gown grasped his shoulder and cut his eyes at the woman behind the desk.

"Miss Townes, I'll handle this," the man said.

As he removed his hand, the man's gold fingernails flickered in the desk light. "Young man, I'm Dr. Bishop. Let's step aside and take a minute to catch our breath."

"Get him out of here, James, before I call security and they sedate him."

The man raised a glittering finger and pointed at her. "It's *Doctor* to you, Miss Townes, not James."

"Maybe in *your* eyes, but not in the hospital's," she replied.

The doctor's face tightened squeezing a deep scar on his cheek into an ee-rie bend that resembled a scythe. "Come with me," he said to Johnny, taking him by the elbow and guiding him carefully through the sickbay toward the entrance. Johnny buttoned his jacket to the chin preparing for the cold wind, but Dr. Bishop routed him away from the doors into a narrow, carpeted hall-way lit by lamplight creeping from under the sills. They stopped outside a set of double doors marked, *Morgue*.

Doctor Bishop took a keychain out of his scrubs and tried to fit one of the keys into the lock. When his attempt to open the door failed, he looked at Johnny.

"Forgive me," the doctor said, "but for a moment I forgot you were a stranger here. It's more a storage room now than a morgue but it still serves the dead. I didn't mean to frighten you. I'm here to help, if I can. What's your name, son?"

"Flynn, Johnny Flynn," Johnny said without hesitation.

"Well, Johnny — may I call you by your first name?"

"Of course."

"I ask only because here they have strict rules for the staff. When we ad-dress a patient or relative, it has to be formal, and if you're a Negro employee you must heed all the rules of the Confederacy. I was in a room across the hall spoon-feeding an elderly woman when I overheard your conversation with Mrs. Townes. Feeding patients isn't something doctors are normally called upon to do but as Mrs. Townes said, in this hospital a black doctor is no more than a misconception because we're not thought to possess the brainpower to be a doctor, even if we've made it through medical school and passed all the same tests many of the white doctors have failed. But would you be so kind to tell me more about the child's condition. I think you referred to him as Dillon?"

"Yes, Dillon," Johnny said and related Esme's version of the story. At first, the doctor didn't wince or show any sign of being affected, but when Johnny came to the judge's order, Bishop's eyes narrowed in fury. When he finished, the silence between them refused to go away.

"I know, it's too horrible to comprehend, but I'm told it's the way…"

Bishop put up his hands. "I understand, for I, too, am from a small town in the South where such things take place. When I was ten years old, back when the Century turned, two fun-seeking members of the Ku Klux Klan found me lost and looking for my parents on a street corner in a town called of all things, Ruffage, Tennessee. I'd been shopping with them in a grocery store and we got separated. So, being a dumb little *nigger* boy, if you will, I went outside. It was storming and I was scared they'd drowned or got hit by lightning. So, I asked the men if they would help me find my parents. One of them grabbed me, called me 'a queer', and threw me into a gutter raging with water. He kept a grip on my wrist and ran alongside me, dragging me in the flow toward a man-hole. I still can feel the panic when I slammed into an old rusty fox trap too large to pass through the opening. One of the pinchers clamped onto my cheek. That's how I got this." He pointed to the scar.

"My God," Johnny said, aghast.

"Yours *and* mine," the doctor said. "Next thing I knew, an old man who turned out to be a veteran of the Civil War scooped me up and pried me free. He tore off a piece of his shirt and then helped me find my mother and father who were still in the store looking for me." Bishop took a quick breath. "The irony that a Confederate soldier, of all people, saved me from the Ku Klux Klan has stayed with me forever. Because of it, I made a commitment to serve in the War. Blacks had to serve in separate units, so I joined the Harlem Hell-fighters who, by the way, spent more time in combat than any other American unit. I got shot in the Battle of the Argonne. They sent me home and years later I finished medical school at the ripe old age of thirty-one."

"And to think what that woman at the desk said."

"Here's another irony — serving the Country helped get me a job here. They most likely wouldn't have hired me otherwise, but they seem to have forgotten about it."

The doctor smiled and made another attempt to open the doors. This time it worked. They stepped into the now deserted morgue, which reminded

Johnny of a huge barn, with hundreds of shelves filled with everything from operating tables to lockers for the dead.

"Those at rest stay here until we locate their family or someone who claims to be related and if not, after a month they're taken away and planted in Potter's Field off the coast of the Bronx. In all this, you might have missed the reason I brought you here. Look over there, behind the door."

Stacked in a line as if waiting to march into battle, stood a row of what appeared to be new wheelchairs. The doctor went over, pulled one from the line and rolled it to Johnny. "Here, take this with my blessing and be in touch with me if young Dillon needs care. I can see him over at Harlem Hospital where I work a second job to make-up for lost time, which at this hospital would be the time I spent fighting for our Country."

"Doctor Bishop, I don't know how to thank you. May I ask you one question before I go?"

"Please."

"The Klansmen who dragged you to the sewer and called you... those names. Do you ever want to go back and make them pay?"

"I already have. I went to war and became a doctor and married a man my age. All of the pursuits toned down my hatred and after a while supplanted it entirely. The Klansmen, as we so kindly refer to them, never need to know. I know who I am and I'm proud of it." He paused to grin. "Wait no longer to leave, young man. There's an exit to your right. It'll let you out on Eighth, , about a block from the nearest trolley stop. Here I'll get the door. Godspeed."

"To you as well."

Before the doctor reached the door, a worker with a white hatchet face bound by a red, grizzled moustache came rushing into the room. Eying the wheelchair, he stopped. "Hey, Jimmy, you going for a ride?"

"His name is Doctor Bishop," Johnny said.

The man glanced at Johnny. "My name is Julian, Mister Julian by the way. Now let me apologize to the doctor," he said, bowing sarcastically with palms in prayer. "You say you made it through med school and passed the exams. No one here believes you, would-be *Doctor* Bishop."

"I passed the boards some time ago," Bishop said calmly. "Maybe before you flunked out of grammar school."

"What about those gold fingers, *Doctor*. That's why they don't let you operate on anyone."

Johnny grabbed the man by the shirt and stepped in front of him. "The doctor fought in the Argonne and has scars to prove it — apologize!"

"Sorry there, *doc*, didn't mean to hurt your feelings by telling the truth," Julian said, smiling and plucking at his mustache. He glanced at Johnny. "Now, you Irish piece of trash, let go. I have to get back to work."

Johnny tightened his grip on the man's scrub. "Forgiveness is earned, asshole, not doled out like a bunch of *Hail Mary's*. Apologize like you mean it!"

"That's enough, Johnny," Bishop said.

Johnny bowed abruptly, spun the man around into a chokehold and bent him backwards over his hip until he started to choke.

"No, Johnny!" the doctor said, urgently. "Forcing him to apologize is forcing him to lie!"

Johnny hesitated and, as the words sunk in, released him. Julian slowly coiled onto his knees, wheezing and coughing as his hands trembled. Bishop helped him to his feet and led him to the door.

Burrowing through his anger, Johnny realized fate had tricked him, taken advantage of the confrontation to remind him that his new happiness was about to disappear like winnings at the track. When the door closed behind the worker, Bishop appeared surprisingly calm, as though nothing out of the ordinary had taken place.

"Please accept *my* apology, Doctor Bishop. It got the better of me. I just couldn't hold it in."

"You certainly do not owe me an apology, Johnny Flynn. On your way now. Take the chair with you and be sure to tell Dillon I'm here if he needs me. Let me correct that. I'll be at Harlem Hospital, if he needs me."

Pushing the wheelchair Johnny hurried out through a back exit. He went straight to the stop and just before the trolley arrived, he thought of Jenny and decided to take her streetcar, over on Death Avenue. When it arrived, he climbed aboard clumsily carrying the wheelchair up the steps. Searching for Johnny's invisible injury, the driver looked at him in sympathy and offered to help him to the rear where there was room for the chair. Johnny thanked him and guided it back himself, wavering along the way as his anger faded and his spirit loosened, reopening the gates through which he'd entered last night, into the world of Dillon's, to come.

Chapter 21

The trolley moved no faster than a rapid walk. Passengers could get on without it stopping. Cardboard-like silhouettes filled the seats in front of Johnny. He wondered where Jenny had been sitting when the Dusters shot out the windows of her trolley. How in God's name had she escaped? He sat looking out the windows, hoping she was well and blaming himself for not getting her full name.

Clouds were gathering near and far with the promise of more snow. The sky had begun to clamp down on the buildings, seeming to force them apart into white-laced alleyways that crossed the trolley's windows with an eerie, lurching motion. Johnny held onto the wheelchair, picturing Esme's face alongside Jenny's. Their togetherness removed the pain and purple tone from Jenny's face. She smiled, as if to suggest that she and Esme were sharing a joke he would never understand.

If an elderly gentleman in a felt red, skull cap hadn't pulled the cord, Johnny would have missed the pier. He got off quickly, set the wheelchair on the sidewalk and scanned the area. Seeing no one, he pushed the chair along with a huge smile on his face, moving with the sense of anticipation he'd awakened to. Stopping on a snowy slope to overlook the pier, he worked to convince himself that his uplifting spirit would refuse to give way to the customary melancholy that came in the late afternoon

His rum-running mates were already out on their deliveries, having left early to avoid the Gopher's vengeance. Only tiny Locust Mari was under the pier. He said very little, and when he spoke his chin and lips trembled as the words were sliced by his stuttering. His arms flickered without provocation. His mates said he'd missed his calling as an insect, and they had named him *Locust* as a reminder.

Locust stared at the wheelchair and his lips quivered. "You all right, J...John...ony?" he asked. His chewing tobacco had scorched the enamel of his teeth and yellowed his lips.

"I'm fine, mate. Don't you worry. This chair's for a friend of mine."

Locust shook a finger at the only cart left under the pier. "Them ke...ggs be yours. I been watching over them. Seth t'told me to che...ck if you was carrying your gun."

"Damnit, I forgot and left it behind this morning," Johnny said, retelling the lie he'd told Seth.

"I won't t'tell no one. I put on an extra keg... on... on the cart for you. Maybe it'll bring you... lots of money.'

"Thank you, Paddy. I'll mark a dollar for your kindness," Johnny said, fastening the wheelchair to the extra keg which sat like a cannon atop the load.

Locust raised a trembling hand. "Be care...ful. Seth's an...gry at you."

"About the gun?"

"For talk...ing sharp to him the other day. He said we shud'uv let you drown."

Johnny was tempted to say Seth had it coming but bit his tongue. "We're fine, Locust. Don't you worry. But for now I'd better get a move on."

"Be careful, Johnny." Locust looked around, put a hand to his mouth and leaned toward Johnny. "Early... this morning when we — we were done loading a man... a man come to the pier and said he was look...ing for you." Locust stopped to clear his throat and gather his voice. "He told us what he thought... you looked like and said he could only find you with other people's help, because he didn't have a ... a photograph... of your face."

"Did Seth say he knew me?"

"I didn't hear... all they talked about, but Seth said... he didn't give you away." As Locust quickened his pace, his voice improved. "But, but he did say he hoped the guy ... got you on his own."

"Got me?"

"He was wearing a gun strapped to his chest. He had on a business suit under a wool coat but I thought I could see the handle sticking out under it.

"Did he look like a boatman, a sailor?"

"No, Johnny. He wore a Fedora hat pinched... at the brim and his shoes were ... slick and shiny. Seth thinks he's a hitman. Seth said that's way they dress, to hide what they really are."

"I got to get going."

"Don't worry, Johnny. Nobody can find you. We're the only ones who really know you."

It was true, Johnny thought as he shoved away. No one in Hell's Kitchen but Seth even knew his last name, and just a few knew what he looked like — unless the stalker was a boatman from *The Pestilence* dressed in disguise.

To make up some of the time, instead of taking the sewer route, Johnny chanced the Avenue with its thinly frosted cobbles. With Christmas so near the cops seemed to be backing off a bit, for it benefitted them to make sure the liquor flowed into the hands of the rich who were quite willing to make a pay-off to avoid being arrested when singled out for having booze.

Surprisingly, the garden door was open. Just the same, Johnny knocked. Moments later Eoin appeared. "Hailey's downstairs, Johnny. He's been there all night building this lorry or maybe a dray. I couldn't figure it out, and he's too intent on finishing it to spend time talking. He's been asking your whereabouts every ten minutes and cursing from time-to-time, calling his Da a bogsucker and far worse. Help him out because we're going to need him upstairs

later. Folks are coming in already. I'll take care of the kegs. You go on down. I
got to man the bar." He looked down at the wheelchair. "What's that there?"

Johnny heard a crash.

"Goddamnit!" Hailey shouted. The sudden silence churned like butter-
milk.

Raising the wheelchair over his head, Johnny carried it down the stairs
into the metallic air. The candlelit lamps scattered across the basement floor
created the image of a pond of slippery copper. Hailey was kneeling on the
floor, staring at a poster-sized sheet of white paper and didn't acknowledge his
presence. Johnny was about to saying something when Hailey looked up and
grinned. His eyes were doused with fatigue and his face twitching with exhaustion.

"I see you got it, lad. Good job! Set it aside for a minute to take a look at
what we've done and see what we're about to do. Yonder lie all the parts."

Johnny opened the chair and rolled it through an assortment of screwdriv-
ers, pliers and socket wrenches scattered among the remains of the old bike
and what seemed like an additional one, for there were far too many parts to
be just Hailey's cycle. The main frame of his bike was mostly straight and resembled a long snake. The re-inflated, wooden-spoked tires rested against the
wall. Their tread still appeared to have miles remaining. A traditional bicycle
tire rested nearby. The handlebars of both bikes had also been straightened and
cut into six rods that lay aside gleaming in the lamplight as though thrilled to
be free. A thick pile of chains sat by the closet where the bike had been stored.
Next to the chains, layered in size, were both large and small sprockets.

"How in hell did you do all this?" Johnny asked.

"It would have been impossible anywhere else because when I went to
untangle it, the Devil's fires softened the frame and kept me warm in the process."

Johnny chuckled. "Did you get any sleep last night?"

"A couple of hours. Didn't want me Da sneaking up on us. Look here at the sketch, lad. What do you think. I drew it on an old copy of the *Irish Times* — see there, a picture of the Royal Castle on the front page. It felt like Mom was looking over my shoulder and whispering in my ear, 'Revenge at last!'"

Johnny knelt to get a closer look at the smudged drawing. The statue of the angel on top of the Castle had her face to the sea and her arse to Dublin, in one of the city's proudest jokes. Behind the Castle's doors, his memory climbed the staircase to Connelly's guarded room where Nora was sobbing at his bedside. They'd just gotten word that General Maxfield had okayed his execution.

"I know it's hard to make out with all the splotches," Hailey said, "but I had to follow Ma's instructions to the letter, and she's prone to changing her mind quite often. What do you think?" When Johnny didn't answer, he went on. "You seem to have it under careful scrutiny, lad. Have you found some flaws?"

Johnny shook off the memory. Even though Hailey's sketch was smeared with eraser marks, he was able to make out the image of a strange looking vehicle that bore only a faint resemblance to yesterday's twisted version. It was a bicycle and yet it wasn't, more an inverted swan, its neck resting on a sand dune before rising to stare at its belly. Whatever it was meant to be, it had three wheels, the two huge ones from Hailey's bike in the rear and a smaller one in front. There were chains aplenty. A wide space for a seat with a footrest only inches below, formed the opening between the rear wheels.

"Never seen anything like it," Johnny said. "Do you call it a bike?"

"Now, mate, you've hit upon a fine point. Would you mind if we called it The Indy? They're opening the Speedway this year, first time since the War. I've followed the race since it began, years ago. Would you mind?"

"The Indy, it is. But I can't tell from the sketch where the power's going to come from to win the race."

Hailey pointed to two, black goblets, one on each side of the handlebars. "These are mounting cups with sprockets. The chains around them run to the front wheel." He reached to his side for two baseball bats. "See here. The thick ends get bolted into the cups. Dillon will grip them about here," he said pointing just above the midsection of one of the bats. We'll whittle them down so they're not sticking up like rabbit's ears."

Johnny's eyes caught the signatures. "They're Lefty O'Doul's, the bats you mounted over the bar?"

Hailey nodded. "Your eyes are sharp, Johnny, but have no second thoughts, for Lefty's a hard drinking, kind man who's being traded around so much he probably doesn't remember the night he came here. He overcame all his odds, like Dillon. Well, no one is better qualified than Dillon to claim that honor."

"I get it. Dillon pushes and pulls on the bats and in both directions the chains drive the wheels."

"While using his chest to help his arms. Last evening when I was lining the whisky bottles on the shelves, I reached out for this tumbler, to dry it, and as I picked it up I saw the bats reflecting in the glass and it came to me."

"Where did you get the other bike?"

"From Eoin, bless him. When I told him what we're about, his eyes went inside his head and he ran out behind the shanty and fetched his own. I offered to pay him, but he wouldn't hear of it. His dad's a biker — well, not really — but let's just say he can find Eoin another one in a heartbeat. He's Italian and they're born on bikes."

"I saw Eoin when I came in. He didn't tell me."

"And maybe I shouldn't have, for there's more to the story, but we'll let it stay there for now." Hailey halted and his voice seemed to bite into his cheeks as he stared at the wheelchair. "My Da… if only he was sitting here wrapped in those chains. If only, I'd share every thought in my head about how we plan to put the Indy together, right down to the last detail. Every feckin' word would be a bullet in his heart." Hailey's face relaxed. "Forgive me, mate, and bless you for listening. The anger's still well within me but a bit gets squeezed out with every turn of the screwdriver."

"How can I help?"

"Would you mind taking the wheelchair apart while I solder the shafts to the axles? We'll try to figure how far back Dillon should sit and mount the seat. Thanks to me Da's fat ass, Dillon's going to have a lot of wide and roomy comfort."

Lacking rust and wear, the wheelchair's nuts and bolts turned easily. The ends of the leather seat were stitched around its rails but once Johnny removed the wheels, the seat slipped off with no cuts to the threading. It stretched easily across the allotted space. Johnny slipped the holders onto the rods and stepped back.

"Perfect, lad. Perfect! Now would you give me a hand with the rest?"

They went to work like surgeons, teasing two long chains from the bundle, then paring, snipping and twisting them to make sure they fastened tightly around the front sprockets. Then they went to the rear and slipped the long axle through its rod, bolted it to the wagon wheels and stood back, gazing first at the Indy and then at each other.

"Time to make it glow," Hailey said. He went to the closet and came back with a can of polish.

Johnny straddled the front wheel, dipping a washrag into the polish and snapping the cloth back and forth until the handlebars sparkled. As he wiped the seat, the leather began to shine like polished shoes and reflect his vague shadow.

Hailey wiped his hands on his pants. "Here, give me a little room," he said, and proceeded to saw the bats in half, insert the thick ends into the cups and fasten the bolts. The handles of the bats stood fast, waiting to be griped.

Johnny gazed at the Indy in awe. It was beyond anything he'd ever expected, resting somewhere between a bicycle and a racecar. "Incredible. I don't know what to say."

Hailey clasped him by the shoulders. "My father's hatred becomes more than a source of revenge, but a gift. 'Twas you who brought it to me. I'm sure that peace, peace I've never had or ever thought possible, will follow. Let us go to the bar and raise a cup to the Almighty.

"And to Esme, who gave Him the idea," Johnny said, wondering how he could possibly wait for the hours to pass before showing her the Indy.

Chapter 22

The next morning on the way to the pier Johnny counted his blessings —
most of all, his sincere belief that Nora was alive and all the rest; his pain free
eyes, the abandoned gun, and The Indy.

His spirits soared as he delivered kegs to four taverns he'd never stocked
before. Each was busy cleaning and making ready for Saturday night. The excitement blended well with the cold air and the sight of his breath, as he hurried
from one speakeasy to the next. Amidst the clatter of tables being shoved about,
glasses clinking and brooms swishing the floors, he felt the incomparable spirit
of Saint Paddy's Day, the blarney and the liquor, the times at the Ineeb when
his father, deep in the throes of drunkenness, broke out in song praising the
Saint.

Once when the old man finished a slurred version of Molly Malone, he
climbed up onto the bar to set his own rhythm in the ritual of "Treble, Batter,
and Rally", known to all as the most ear-splitting Irish jig. With the bar as his
stage, he jammed his legs in the air and clicked his heels from one end to the
other. Exhausted and struggling to find his breath, he fell into the outstretched
arms of his astonished friends who carried him to a chair next to Johnny where
he confessed what Johnny had known forever, his whoring and giving his vacant excuse again and again. "Lad, I seek my pleasure over and over because
of your mother's forgiveness. She's forgiven me for every sin, which makes me
feel so feckin' guilty. I came to hate her for it. I've tried to make her throw me
out of the house just to put an end to it. I even went so far as to bring a young
fleece home one night and introduce her. Your Ma had her sit by the fire and

read the Bible to her. Your mom's dying breath held these words, 'the Lord forgives you and so do I. Forgive yourself and I'll see you in heaven.' But I couldn't forgive myself because she never stopped forgiving me!"

"Why didn't you leave her, if you hated her so?" Johnny asked, knowing the old man was too drunk to take a swing at him.

"Because I loved her beyond words."

Did love have such power, Johnny wondered? If so, why hadn't it overcome Nora's hatred for him, or had she never really been that much in love with him?

On Forty-fifth Street, Johnny stopped outside a coffee shop and stuck his head inside, calling for a hot cup of black coffee to be brought out because he didn't dare leave the kegs on the street. A waiter with white freckles indistinguishable from snowflakes brought it to him. Shivering, Johnny thanked him with a quarter tip and asked if he could sit on the curb for a minute to enjoy the drink.

"The curb is for the distressed. Stay on your feet or they'll think you're one of them and come to take your trove," the waiter said.

Johnny sat down anyway. Before he could finish his coffee, a bedraggled young couple, who with their sullen expressions seemed decades older than they appeared, slowly approached him. The lass asked for a nickel or a dime. Johnny fished in his pocket and gave them each a dime. They brought their hands together.

"Bless you," the woman said.

"Twice over," her mate added with a joyous sigh, as if twenty cents would let them make it through the day.

Johnny finished the coffee and got to his feet. The cold air pressed through his denims. He was late for the last delivery before Hailey's. Most likely there'd be no tip but he didn't care. He cared only about getting to Hailey's before

Esme arrived. He had no idea when she usually showed up because he'd been too drunk to think about such a thing the previous Saturday.

Even though the daylight was still shoulder high, the Christmas lights dominated the streets, re-instilling a sense of celebration in the air. Though the decorations glowed more handsomely on the avenues, they appeared more rewarding on the side streets: a green bulb here and a red one there, isolated but not alone, versus the never-ending streams of lights on the avenues that seemed to carry time away. But when he reached Hailey's, the illusion lost its allure, pummeled by jazz from the cavernous gramophone.

Johnny had no sooner stepped inside when he noticed the shadowy markings of Lefty's bats left on the wall. He felt a twinge of regret. Given how Hailey had described O'Doul, the ballplayer would have approved.

Hailey waved from the stage and pointed vigorously to the stairwell. Johnny rushed down into the basement. Hailey had strung Christmas lights across the ceiling and along the walls. The closet door was wide open and inside, propped up against the stack of ancient suitcases, a golden framed, sidewalk painting of a smiling Jesus glowed. The lights lit the frame, casting an orange halo onto the floor around The Indy. The leather seat carried a soft, auburn effervescence that reminded him of the candlelight on the narrow mahogany mantle where his mother had posted the tintypes of early Dublin — she would edge her way past them, running her fingers over the glass, never saying anything but speaking in silence about her regrets for leaving.

Johnny knelt to touch the wheels. The spokes sparkled like polished tines. Hailey had created a chariot. Johnny was tempted to climb in and give it a ride across the Forum, but the first ride belonged to Esme.

As music filled the stairwell, the sound of shoes began to clatter on the basement ceiling. Johnny went upstairs and took a seat at the bar. The room was filling up as the seemingly random sounds of a flute and bassoon nagged at one another, only to come together and swoon harmoniously when the sound of a drum grew stronger in the background.

Hailey was grinning from ear-to-ear as he set a tumbler of poteen on the counter. "Tonight you have a job before you, lad."

"To finish the glass?"

"That and more," Hailey chuckled. "To show Esme the Indy. I pray she'll like it."

"Like it? You must be joshing. She'll love it. When do you expect her to show up?"

"Usually around seven, just a few minutes before she starts. Maybe it would be best for you to take her downstairs after she's done on stage. So, try and go easy on the poteen until then."

"Hailey, you made the Indy. You're the one who should show it to her. Other than finagling a wheelchair I had very little to do with it."

"No, she's your friend while I'm but the old goat who hired her. She most likely had the vision first and passed it along generously, to make it seem that God had sent it through you. I simply gave the vision shape, that's all." He glanced across the room. "It's getting crowded." He started away and halted. "Remember, go easy on that there. Hate to have you get run over by a race car."

The mood in the room was already building toward jubilation. Johnny watched in the mirror as couples shoved against one another to fill the floor. The women appeared even more festive than usual as they removed their heavy winter coats to reveal jewelry, fashionable tops and short flapper skirts decorated with Christmas glitter. The ladies preferred a glass or two of champagne to begin with, followed by juiced martinis and Rob Roys while the men went straight to shots of rum and bourbon.

Shouts of enduring rebellion kept getting louder but never peaked, suggesting higher levels to come. Dancing abounded. Couples who earlier had widened their moves across the room were being forced to draw closer as more patrons joined them. With the exuberance soaring, Hailey kept visiting the stage to turn the phonograph louder.

Johnny stared at his drink. Hesitating, he brought the glass to his mouth and sipped. His lips softened as the liquor slid over them. He closed his eyes to watch the rum seep through Jenny's lips, and gasped as the poteen streamed through him. He'd never gotten used to the searing sensation as it dipped past his heart into his stomach. It happened the first time he drank the whisky, when Seamus McCulahy, the volunteer spy who introduced him to the drink while sitting at a rebel bar named Buckles — a pub in Tipperary where Johnny had fled in hopes of being recruited into the rebel forces. From the rafters the owner had hung the buckles of the Black and Tans killed by the Volunteers in the neighboring villages. And when the Brits came by for a drink, he told them the buckles belonged to the rebels.

After an inquisitive conversation, bordering on an interrogation, McCulahy shared a copy of the Proclamation, which Johnny had never read. He struggled to recall the paragraph which had so affected him when he read it that day, for the first time. It evaded him for a while, but as his focus began to overcome the commotion in the room, the words returned: "The republic guarantees religious and civil liberty, equal rights and equal opportunities to all... its citizens... "

A hand touched Johnny's shoulder. "Would you by chance be Johnny Flynn?"

Johnny looked into the mirror and froze at the reflection of a tall, grey-haired man in a Macintosh and a red Fedora. The fellow placed a flat, leather attaché case on the bar as he wedged himself into the seat next to Johnny. A strap ran across his chest. His eyes locked on Johnny, who sat unnerved, unable to speak or move. The sound of a trumpet, a flute, voices, shouts, heels clicking the wood coalesced around him like a set of chains. As the lights dimmed, the fellow's image faded. If his plan was to shoot Johnny, it would happen now.

Johnny's fear erupted. He turned, seized the wooly collar of the MacIntosh and jerked the man within inches of his face. He tightened his grip, distorting the stranger's face so drastically he barely resembled his reflection. Johnny thought he felt the handle of a pistol jutting from the man's chest. "Give me your gun," he said, attempting to keep his voice down.

The man's eyes widened. "I don't have a gun."

"Under your coat. I can feel the handle."

"That's a tourniquet, not a gun. I broke my collarbone in a fall. I can assure you there's no gun. I'm a solicitor, not a gunman. Go ahead. Feel my shoulder. See if you find a gun."

"Raise your arms."

The man lifted one arm above his head. "I can't raise my other. The brace won't allow it."

"Don't move an inch."

Johnny released a hand from the coat and traced the strap across the man's chest to his shoulder. He found no gun, only a small cage-like device covering what felt like a wooden brace. He was familiar with the shape, for he'd often seen the battlefield wounded bound in such a way. Connolly's shattered leg had been trussed by a similar contraption, only much larger.

Johnny let go of the coat and grabbed the attaché. "What's inside this?"

"My credentials, Mr. Flynn, and the reason I've been trying to find you. I'm a solicitor from the High Court in Dublin. My name is Johnny as well, Johnny Ryan. I'm here to serve you."

Johnny tensed. "Serve me, for what, damn you!"

"Easy now. For your role in the execution of James Connolly but it's not what you might think."

Johnny grasped the man by the collar. "He wanted to die, for God's sake!"

"Not only for God's sake but for yours and mine as well, Mr. Flynn. James Connolly and the Lord Almighty, as well as the High Court, have united to set you free."

"Set me free? What are you talking about? Free from what?"

"From yourself and all of Ireland. May I please open the case?"

Somewhat relieved but still dubious, Johnny slowly released his grip and slid the attaché to him.

Ryan pulled a file of papers from the leather case, opened the file and placed a typed sheet in front of Johnny. The paper appeared to be officially stamped by the High Court of Dublin.

"Please read the order, Mr. Flynn."

"To Johnny Flynn, an Irish born, former British soldier, and a member of the firing squad that executed James Connolly." Johnny's hands began to shake."

"Shall I read it to you?" Ryan asked.

Johnny brought the paper closer and read to himself: "All Irish born members of the British firing squads that assembled to execute the Signatories of the proclamation are hereby redeemed by the High Court of Dublin, for it has been realized that in the inexcusable pressures of the day, these citizens had no choice but to comply with the most atrocious demands of the Kingdom's army. Thus, any application of the word, traitor — or any such term with a similar meaning — to each of you receiving this declaration shall be dismissed as false by the elected members of this Court. These papers, signed by eight members of the Court — the number of signatories of the Proclamation of Freedom — maybe used by the recipients as proof of false claim and reestablish their standing as welcomed citizens in Ireland and abroad."

Aghast, Johnny stared at Ryan. "I cannot believe it."

"As is said, believe it or not, it is your declaration of innocence. There are two copies. The one before you is for you to keep. This one is for you to sign." Ryan took another paper from the file and placed it on the counter. "I'll return the signed copy to the Court and it will be kept on file in the vault." He handed Johnny a pen and pointed to the line above his name. "Sign here, whereupon I'll take my leave."

Johnny signed and handed Ryan his pen. Had he had more to drink than he realized or was he lost in another weird dream?

Ryan was getting off his stool, briefcase in hand. "Best of luck to you, Johnny Flynn."

"*This* is the best of luck, right here in my hand," Johnny said. "If you knew what this meant to me."

"I can only imagine. I've seen it on the faces of the others I've had the pleasure of serving. A few were still afraid to leave their homes, for fear that some of our citizens would offer no forgiveness and demand repayment. But not all. In one case a man's wife had no idea what her husband done. I'll never forget the look on her face. It was a mix of shock, anger and relief, all in one. 'You never told me' she said to him, perhaps upset he'd withheld it from her, and perhaps simply surprised at what he'd done. The gentleman couldn't respond, until he did. 'I love you', he said. She just stared at him, trying to make sense of it all. I knew at that moment I should have left, but I couldn't bring myself to, and I'm glad I didn't because she looked at him and whispered, 'I love you, too.'"

Johnny's eyes fastened on the order as the story's full impact soaked in.

"Do the families of the executed know about this?"

"Each was visited before the order was drawn. Everyone's understanding and consent were of utmost importance. Without it, the Court would not have proceeded."

"Did you go to the Connolly's?"

"I met with Mrs. Connolly and her eldest daughter. Mrs. Connolly fully understood our purpose, for by now, she'd come to believe that her husband had wanted to die for the Cause. She signed the paper with forgiveness in her heart."

"And her daughter?"

"Only the next of kin were authorized to give permission."

"But did she say anything?"

"Not a word but just after her mother signed, Miss Connolly jerked the paper out of her hand, stared at it until tears began to run down her cheeks and with a trembling hand, handed it back to me. I left in silence. Speaking of which, I must go now, Johnny."

Johnny watched Ryan leave, then stared at the order with a sense of exhilaration he'd not felt since coming to America. Ireland had forgiven him and possibly Nora as well, though he would never know for certain. He'd always felt he'd done right by James in serving on the firing squad, but now, having read the order, he *knew* that he had. His reflection in the mirror smiled back at him as he kissed the order and slipped it into his jacket pocket.

The chatter and clatter swirling around him disappeared into the sound of Connolly's voice once again calling out to Johnny as he knelt before him with his rifle. "Shoot straight, Johnny Flynn!" Johnny's hands steadied. The rifle settled on the small paper target pinned over Connolly's chest. He pulled the trigger and returned from the Stonebreaker's Yard, an unrequited Rebel.

As a joy surged through his being, Johnny tapped his fingers on the bar and tried to give thanks, but no words were available, so he took a page from Esme's book and using a poem his mother had taught him about the merits of forgiveness, he put the lines to song.

> *I touched your fingers as a child*
> *And felt your warmth as you smiled.*
> *That I had left you alone far too long*
> *Was my sin you just forgave.*

Johnny was well into his second glass when Hailey lifted the stylus and took the microphone in hand.

Everyone kept moving to the remnants of enthusiasm, but as Hailey repeatedly begged for quiet the activity in the room ebbed. "Thank you! Thank you all for coming," he said. 'Tis a glorious holiday season writ in purpose, the freedom to drink what we will, and wish to the dungeon those who would take it away!"

Raucous cheers sent vibrations up the stool into Johnny's rear. Hailey raised the mike to his lips. "And here to help us celebrate the idea that Jesus loved His wine and 'twas not the lesser for it, is an Irish lass with the most beautiful voice ever from the Emerald Isle. Aptly, her name means beloved: please welcome Esme!"

She rose onto the back of the stage in her mystical way, veiled in the customary emerald mist that seeped from beneath the flooring. Johnny realized that the red dress she wore wasn't the same as before. She'd borrowed the manikin's. While she hadn't patched the rips in the velvet, the dress seemed better for it because her skin appeared to turn the openings into artfully shaped designs. He straightened to try and steal a look at her entire body but a horizon of shoulders blocked his view.

The crowd began to clap and call her name. Hailey handed her the mike and leaned over to kiss her cheek, but his face disappeared into the glow of her hair and he stumbled toward her. Esme grasped his arm to help him from the stage. She returned, bowed to the audience and as she straightened, caught sight of Johnny. Her smile expanded to include her eyes and cast no doubt that she was happy to see him.

When she started to sing, he relaxed, watching her every move while sipping on his whisky.

"It's a Long, Long Way to Tipperary" brought tears floating on whispers from many in the hushed crowd, as did "The Wearing of the Green." People hugged when she sang "Irish Eyes."

Johnny grew nostalgic. He wanted another drink but Hailey was over by the stage and Eoin was lost in the scurry. He told himself it was okay, he could handle the sober side, that is, until she sang the ancient song, "The Girl I Left Behind Me," the story of an immigrant longing for a lass he'd left behind in

Ireland. The moment came again, the unforgettable moment. His mind left Hailey's for County Cork where he and Nora were standing outside the O'Brien's under the porch roof. It was pouring rain. The patter on the tin reigned softly, a light drumbeat in a forest. Slowly she turned to him and for the first time let him kiss her.

Eoin came to fill his glass, and Johnny gave a regretful nod to the lad. He brought the glass to his mouth, only instead of taking a swallow he placed it on the counter. His mind sped back to the kiss and even though the song ended, the memory remained.

Amid the ovation Esme turned her back to the room, bent over until she was hidden by the horizon of shoulders and curly bobbed hair. Abruptly, she rose and spun around to face the crowd. Beaming at their startled expressions, she jammed her flask into the air and brought the mike to her lips.

"Do unto others, as you would have them do unto you! Bottom's up!" she shouted tilting the flask towards the rafters. Without turning away from the crowd, she grabbed her skirt, raised the hem to her thighs and tucked the flask into the stocking atop her sensually curved leg.

Approval rang out. Glasses lifted, shoes stomped the floor and shouts of "Freedom!" filled the room. Gradually, the roar became a murmur slowly squelched by anticipatory sounds of "Shhhhhh" throughout the room.

She began the Christmas carols with the oldest of them, "The Wexford Irish," a melody dating back to the twelve-hundreds and then the "Holiday of the Birds," and "Once in Royal David's City." The silence harbored the audience's emotions. She spun around and as if playing a magic trick, jerked the flask aloft, and sipped from it as a woman cried out for her to repeat, "The Girl I Left Behind Me."

Flask in hand she stepped forward and glanced at Johnny. Her lips opened slightly as if to whisper, not to worry, that the message of the song would be fine. Then she began.

The hope of final victory
Within my bosom burning
Is mingling with sweet thoughts of thee
And of my fond returning
But should I n'er return again
Still with thy love I'll bind me
Dishonors breath shall never stain
The name I leave behind me."

Johnny shivered, expecting Nora's image to return, but Esme's eyes held her at bay. She kept glancing in his direction, and he, too, looking through the mist, watched her until Nora's voice pierced the trance, crying, "I love you."

Before he realized it, Esme had drifted into "Silent Night". The trills in her voice carried the gentle waves of the carol, and when she finished, the room's stillness resembled that of a church after the last hymn bade the parishioners farewell. Silence prevailed longer than Johnny could have imagined. At last, he heard a sad but generous clap, followed by others until the spell was broken.

Hailey mounted the stage. He kissed Esme on both cheeks and lingered to whisper in her ear. Still clapping, he reached for the mike to remind the crowd that she would be back the following Saturday. Glasses were raised in gratitude. A gent offered his tumbler and Hailey drained it.

"The refill's on me," he said into the mike. "Meanwhile ladies and gentlemen, the best, or should I say, the surest way to repeal Prohibition is to disregard it altogether!" Laughter and cheers followed him to the phonograph where he set a wide vinyl spinning.

With everyone remaining out on the floor, the barstools were empty. Esme came down from behind the stage and circled the crowd to reach Johnny.

"Hailey said you had something to show me. Down below, I believe," she said snickering as she slipped onto the seat next to him.

"I do," Johnny said, chuckling while overwhelmed by the midnight blue of her eyes. Strangely, he remembered them as shamrock green.

Hailey showed up to pour them a drink. "Lass, you were incredible," he said. "Where in heaven's name did you learn to sing like that? You must've been born with it."

She glanced at Johnny with a glint in her eyes. "I was, indeed," she said. "It's my mother's voice. She called out to me in song whilst I was being born and I answered in accord."

Hailey chuckled. "Thank her for me. She did us all a favor larger than life. Now, we'll try to show our appreciation. Johnny will escort you."

"Can I trust this Irishman to take me down into a basement?"

Hailey laughed. "Not on every occasion, but tonight we'll make an exception."

"Hailey," Eoin called out. "They're yelling orders from the floor. Can you handle the register?"

"I'm there, lad!" Hailey pushed away from the counter and spoke out of the corner of his mouth. "By the way, I've lighted the way for you two. Now, to the stairs."

Chapter 23

Hailey had wrapped a string of Christmas lights around the Indy, turning the stairway into a translucent cave.

"Here, put your hand on my shoulder," Johnny said.

"I'm fine," Esme answered, "unless you need me to steady you."

Johnny made nothing of her refusal as they made their way slowly down the steps. When he reached bottom, he glanced over his shoulder. She'd stopped half-way down to stare in bewilderment at The Indy.

"For Hailey's Da and for Dillon," Johnny said.

"What do you mean, Johnny?"

He turned to her and told her the story about Hailey's lifelong desire to avenge how his father had treated him and his mother, and then he confessed that he'd told Hailey about the drums and why she'd made them, realizing all the while he'd promised her that their story would stay with him.

Esme said nothing in response to what he'd said or to the abrupt silence. Her breathing did not increase, nor did her eyes light up in admonishment. She stared at him with an eager, almost haunting look of anticipation.

"Johnny, please, go on." Her voice carried a tone of both approval and encouragement.

He gathered himself. "After a while, standing there, listening to Hailey, it came to me at last, thanks to you. I realized the drums and the bike could serve the same purpose. I asked Hailey if he would possibly include Dillon in his plans. He went straight to work making it happen. My only role was to find a comfortable seat for the lad. Again, I apologize for breaking the trust you placed in me."

Esme approached The Indy with her eyes filled with tears. "You didn't break any trust, not at all. You deepened it by extending it into the land of what *can* be." She reached out and smoothed her hand over the leather seat. "It's so soft and glistens like... like I don't know what. Like someone's dreams, I suppose. How does it work?"

"I'll show you."

She moved aside to let Johnny unravel the lights and place them in a pile. When she climbed on and seated herself, he grasped the bats and pulled them back slowly. The Indy edged toward the closet. He turned his shoulders to guide it around the lights.

Her gleeful eyes followed him. "I'd love to have a picture of Dillon, here in the seat grinning from ear to ear, and send it to the fucking judge with a note, saying, 'Thank you, you cruel bastard,' and sign it: 'Dillon's Revenge.'"

"You won't have to go that far," Johnny said. "Let's hope Joshua will lay down his claim to retribution once Dillon's in the driver's seat. Just like what happened to Hailey the whole time he was building it. Now he can have the rest he's entitled to." Johnny glanced at the stairs, thinking twice about what he was about to say. For a second he had a clouded vision of Hailey as a boy watching petrified as his father smashed the bike. "Come closer," he said.

She moved cautiously toward him. He wanted to whisper but knew his voice would drown in the noise from upstairs. Unflinchingly, she lifted her dress to take the flask from her stocking and hand it to him. "Here, I *trust* you'll save some for me."

"Indeed, I will." Johnny said, aware his eyes did not leave her legs until she let the dress fall. He sipped at the flask but took-in less than usual.

"Trust *flows* between us," she said, reaching out for it and grinning.

"Johnny? Esme? You down there?" Hailey called through the ruckus.

"Yes!" Esme replied, exuberantly. "Come join us!"

Hailey descended slowly, grasping the rail with both hands. When he'd made it down, she threw her arms around him. "From the bottom of my heart," she said. "Thank you!".

He smiled. "Thank *you* and your rum-running friend here, for you conceived the underlying idea and Johnny was the child's messenger. I was merely the midwife."

Esme slipped her arms from his shoulders. "It matters not, for the baby has come to life."

Johnny could tell by the mellowness in her voice that Hailey's play on words had touched her.

"Can we take it for a ride?" she asked.

"More than that, lass," Hailey said. "If you trust the streets at this hour, and if you have a place to keep it, you can take it with you and give it to the Dillon whenever you think it best. The bar's thinning now. In a few minutes it'll be empty and we'll take it outside."

"We can keep it at my store," she said. "There's plenty of room in the back. Johnny, would you help me learn to drive and steer it."

"Of course, and as far as the streets go, it's late. Everyone's passed out by now. It should be safe enough — and if not, we can always outrun them with the Indy."

Esme questioned the name with her eyebrows.

"It's for the car race in Indiana, in Indianapolis, the Indy 500 it's called. I'm a huge fan. It stopped running during the War and just this year it's starting up again," Hailey explained. He looked up the stairway and framed his mouth with his hands. "Eoin, come give us a hand."

"Almost empty! Give me a moment. Be right there!"

Hailey unbolted the bats and removed them from the collars. He and Johnny lugged The Indy up the stairs and when they reached the top, Eoin joined them to help wedge it through the doorway.

"Everyone gone?" Hailey asked him.

"A couple at the bar is all."

In haste, they started past the couple. The woman raised her head from the counter. "What's that you're carrying?" she slurred.

"Santa's sleigh." Esme replied. "We were called upon to make it lighter, because the reindeer are getting older.."

The woman gave a contorted smile and raised her tumbler.

Chapter 24

They carried the Indy down through the garden to the street. Hailey reset the bats and tugged at them to make sure they were solidly in place. "It's all yours, lass," he said. "Jump in and take her for a trial run."

Esme climbed in carefully, gripped the bats and sat staring ahead as though she were about to blast into space. Yet she took off slowly, pushing and pulled effortlessly on the bats and bounced easily over the cobbles. "Dillon's going to love this!" she called out, holding onto the bats and tilting sideways to turn around just before reaching the intersection.

"You've got it, lass!" Hailey called out. "Oh," he said, turning to Johnny, "I almost forgot. Yesterday you were asking the whereabouts of James Connolly's daughter?"

Johnny stopped. "Did you hear something more?" he asked, anxiously.

"As it happens, she's coming to America, this Sunday, that is."

He was stunned. "She's coming here, to America?"

"To the very soil you're standing on. Apparently, she was scheduled to speak in Boston but the weather up there shut down the trams and buses, so she had to change her plans. She'll be speaking at St. Brigid's Church to spread the word on Sinn Fein. I guess they want us emigrants to know we're joining forces with the socialist movement now. With America's feelings about communism, she'd better speak behind a brick wall, if you ask me. That said, I have to get back inside."

A draft of cold wind added to the tremors Johnny felt at hearing Hailey's news. His senses erupted with anticipation. Nora was coming to America!

"Dillon's going to love this!" Esme repeated, pulling up behind him. "Johnny, are you ready to shove off?"

Hope rode on the sound of her voice as if, somehow, she, too, in addition to The Indy, had an invisible hand in raising his spirits. "Ready?" he asked.

She grabbed the bats and leaned forward. "Let's go!"

"Now!" Johnny shouted, shoving the bike into the street. Esme's head snapped back and the bats surged out of her hands.

"Oh my God!" she yelled as the bike sailed toward the intersection.

Johnny slowed down for her to grasp the handles.

"Keep going!" she yelled. "Faster!"

He surged forward. Nora was coming to America! He would go to hear her, to seek her out, if only to have her refuse him again. He wondered if the Court Order had changed her mind or had it confirmed her hatred for what he'd done? Regardless, the thought of seeing her thrilled him.

Storefronts passed by rapidly. Lights came on in dark interiors only to flash by. A car door slammed and a siren wailed. Shadows lengthened under awnings while Esme, lost in her own motion, having caught the stride, pumped like a drunken boxer throwing punches at the darkness. They pulled into a short alley and came to a rest. Gasping, Johnny leaned over the handlebars.

"Turn on Fifty-fourth, " she said. "Best we leave it in the storage room for now. It's but a short way from there to The Woebegone, so I'll bring it over Wednesday night when Dillon and Joshua show up. That is, they damn well better!"

Johnny was whipped but unfazed. They started off again, almost running into the back of an old hearse with its rear doors sticking out into the street. Esme cheered as Johnny swirled her around them, but he couldn't help notice a raised platform inside the vehicle with guide rails for a casket. At any other time it might have given him pause, but not now. He ran forcing Esme to pump as fast as she could. He sped forward joyously, unconcerned his heart was about to explode. Alone and together they whirled down the streets to arrive almost unexpectedly at Rags-to-Riches.

Breathing hard, but laughing, they made it around back to the huge barn doors battened with a thick wood beam. The heavy doors reminded him of the thick oak gates to Kilmainham, where just inside those about to be executed waited for their escort to the Yard.

"Wait here," she said.

She lifted the beam and set it down before he could help her. He watched her hurry into the corner of the rear room and light a lamp sitting by a vase on the shelf.

"My God, how did you lift that beam?" he asked when she came out.

Her eyes smiled. "I had help."

"Help?"

"Recall the Dash I gave you? Just a fingernail on my breast makes me stronger."

As he stared at her smile, wondering if Dash had become her secret name for opium. The silence became uncomfortable. "Here, I'll bring in the Indy," he said.

She stepped in front of him. "Before you do, come inside for a second. There's something I've been wanting to tell you, in that it seems to be confession time in the church." Her smile lingered in the corners of mouth but appeared to frame the seriousness of what she was about to say.

He had no idea what to expect but in no way did he want to discourage her. "Please, if there's anything…"

She interrupted with a sense of resolve. "The name Dash comes from two words," she said. "*Da*, as in father, and *ash* in reference to the obvious. The mixture that just gave me strength and saved your eyes was a combination of my Da's ashes mixed with turmeric, shamrocks and lilacs, and admittedly, a bit of absinth, courtesy of Lars. Ina, the nurse I told you about who helped me heal after they broke my hip, well, her uncle owned a small ice plant in Kilmachael and let us store my father's body there. When I was able to walk again we cremated him on a bier in the backyard. We did so early in the morn so the light from the fire wouldn't be very noticeable. When his ashes had cooled, she taught me how to make the Dash and we used it to kill the infection which by then had set into my hip… and elsewhere." Esme nodded toward the counter. "Da's ashes are in the urn you see there by the lamp."

Johnny was speechless.

"I didn't tell you because I thought maybe you'd think I'd lost my mind and wouldn't give it a try. I wanted you to know even if I am running the risk of having you believe I'm crazy, although, as we now both know, everyone is at one time or another." She paused, watching his eyes, and as if getting an okay, she continued. "I've never thought of my recovery as revenge, but maybe that's what it was, mine and my Da's. Much like the little girl, Jenny, and with Hailey as well — maybe absolution can come from the heart instead of the sword." The lamplight dovetailed through her hair to her cheeks, turning her lips gold.

"Anything left in the flask?" Johnny asked, wanting to make sure he wasn't seeing or hearing things.

Her smile widened with relief. "Of course. It refills itself," she said, raising her dress. "You want a swig now or after we bring in the Indy?"

"Now, if you don't mind. I could use a taste."

They passed the flask back and forth while pausing to grimace and laugh between swallows as the poteen burned its familiar path down their throats. When they'd emptied it, she set it on the counter. Together they eased the Indy over the doorstep into the center of the room.

"Let's give it to him Wednesday at The Woebegone. What do you think?" she asked.

"Best *you* do that," Johnny said. "You're the one who really matters in their lives."

She pushed the hair away from her eyes. The green had returned to her retinas and held him a moment longer. "I'm going for a swim in Long Island Sound tomorrow," she said. "Any chance you might like to join me?"

"A swim? In Long Island Sound? You are crazy! You'll freeze to death."

She laughed. "Yes, I'm crazy! How many times do I have to tell you, crazy is what we all should hope for because it sets us free! The cold water is balm to my hip. The colder the better, so this is the best time of year. The pain returns every few days and freezing the bones takes it away. I've done it ever since I came to America. I used to go to the Hudson but the water by the Sound is much calmer. The pier right off Coney Island. They have an extra tram now, takes you straight there after only four stops in Manhattan. I don't expect you to go into the water — not at all. I just thought you might like to take a holiday break."

He wanted to say, no. There was so much on his mind that he didn't want to be distracted. Nora was to coming to America!

"Johnny, would you care to go to the Sound?"

Even before the word made its appearance, he knew the answer. "Sure," he said, having no idea why.

Chapter 25

It was snowing lightly when they met the next afternoon at the newly named Coney Island Station on Thirty-ninth Street. The falling snow made it even harder for Johnny to believe he was accompanying a young woman to the beach during Christmas time in order for her to take a swim in freezing water. Yet when it came to Esme, he knew better than to let his doubts get the better of him.

When the huge locomotive arrived, the platform shook like it had palsy. The wheels stood as tall as Johnny and after clanging to a stop, the monster engine gave off a long gaseous sigh as though relieved at the opportunity to take a brief rest. Esme climbed aboard first and gave the conductor a quarter for each of them.

The ride was slow and noisy, the windows barely shutting out the great clatter of the train's wheels as it toiled eastward. They had trouble hearing one another due to the crunching of the wheels on the rails, so they seldom spoke. Occasionally, Esme pointed to the skyscrapers in Manhattan, the empty boats along the shores of the East River and the elevated trams. In Brooklyn they spotted a fellow wandering the streets in the dark garb of the Orthodox Jews, his curly hair spinning out from under his hat down to his shoulders. The man's bearded face, tilted toward the pavement as he walked along, reminding Johnny of his fatigued, battle-weary mates plodding back to camp after a fight, on the weathered roads of Bandon.

As Esme's mysterious fragrance settled around him, guilt slipped through his chest. He told himself he hadn't betrayed Nora in any sense of the word, and then she reminded him: *"You allowed me to fall in love with you, which I would have never done had I known, and you damn well knew that. You betrayed me and in repayment you are hereby forgotten!"*

He tried to put her words aside. After all, she was coming to America, so why betray the moment when he would see her again? A moment when, even from his seat in the pews, he could search out her eyes and witness her reaction to finding him there. The thought warmed him far more than the double layer of jackets he'd worn in preparation for the beach.

"We're here!" Esme exclaimed, reaching up for her travel bag. "Shall we?"

As the train ground to a halt, they eased out of their seats. Staggering down the aisle, they made their way to the exit and stepped onto the raised platform to look out over the ocean. The water lay motionless, a still, deep blue frame undercoated with ice floes, some several meters long.

"Esme, did you ask me to come along so you'd have someone to pull you out of the water when you turn blue?"

"Azure," she said, chuckling. "I turn azure so no one will mistake me for dead. The fairies saw to it. You'll see."

"Do all apparitions fancy azure?"

She looked at him mockingly. "You think I'm joking?"

"I must confess, you're slowly winning me over."

She smiled. "Seriously, I won't be in the water long, and then, after I'm dry and warm, we can visit a pub if you like.

"If they're still open."

"Out here they're open from dawn to midnight every day of the week. It's like they say about the Wild West, there's no law this side of the Hudson. Come on, let's get to the pier before the sun disappears."

A block away, a gigantic Ferris wheel appeared to rise to the height of a flying airplane. It stood still, but for its snow-covered seats rocking gently in the wind. In an area named Luna Park they passed an enormous roller-coaster called The Wonder Wheel and a wavering set of platforms named Cakewalk. The rides were closed due to the weather but as Esme said, the bars and restaurants were open. A string of hot dog stands boasted patrons, many of whom sat outside eating and drinking on the wooden sidewalk sheltered by tent-like awnings. No one seemed fazed by the snow.

Johnny spotted an empty contraption labeled the Tan-o-Meter. A sign below the name listed the amount of time it took one's skin to acquire any shade of color. A photograph next to it pictured a man dressed in a blue suit with a black tie. He was smiling a charlatan's smile while handing out tickets to a group of women dressed in sleeveless bathing suits stretched over their thighs. Behind the sign, standing alone in the sand like a huge gravestone, sat a scale so large it looked as if it were meant to weigh elephants.

"I got on it once and it failed to register, not even a pound. Crazy, isn't it?" Esme said as they hurried past.

"Maybe apparitions have no weight," he said.

She laughed. "It's always something I've wished for."

"Never seen anything like this place," Johnny said. "Makes you wonder if those people sitting outside are real or from another planet?"

"They'd do well to choose Venus," Esme said, pointing her finger. "Look ahead, the Steeplechase Pier. That's where we're headed."

What appeared to be an iron structure lit by its own shade of silver stretched far out into the ocean. Hems of mist were narrowing the pier making it appear to have no end. Again, Johnny thought of the bridge that he and many of his fellow soldiers had often imagined when, exhausted from battle, they'd wanted nothing more than to be rid of war and be home with their loved ones. The bridge had been their conjured route home, fate's lying promise. Some hated the image, because it led them to believe home no longer existed and they were soon to die. A few called the vision, The Passage Home, and others, The Road to Hell.

The small, splashing waves drifted ashore on the receding tide. For a moment Johnny felt he and Esme were truly alone for the first time. No music, no worries about the streets, no patrons to entertain, the Indy resting comfortably in its temporary home. They left the boardwalk for the sand and moved beneath the pier where narrow slits let in enough sunlight for them to see one another. Esme took off her coat.

"Here, I'll go behind the posts while you change," Johnny said, even though he suspected she'd already put on a bathing suit beneath her clothes for some added warmth.

"You need not do that but *suit* yourself," she said.

Chuckling, they turned their separate ways.

"You can come out of hiding now," she called after a few moments of silence.

When he stepped from behind the post, she'd stripped naked and was on her way to the water's edge. Her body was shaped by long sensuous muscles running from her neck to her calves, each finely connected, like those of a ballerina he'd once seen dancing by the Quay in Dublin. Esme's thin left leg tapered naturally into her damaged foot. Her flawless rear end flexed as if smiling with every step.

As she moved toward the water, the foam crept over her feet. She pressed her hands tight about her hips and waded in. As the water rose to her thighs, the muscles in her back and shoulders tightened but she didn't flinch or shudder. Johnny briefly thought of Nora's body, smooth and textured with hidden yet inviting muscles, but Esme's beauty showed differently, in a way he couldn't describe, other than as *strangely beautiful* or *beautifully strange* for she possessed two infallible bodies sculptured as one.

She moved deeper between two snow-covered floes. When the water began to rise over her shoulders, he thought she would stop, but she slowly disappeared below the surface. He couldn't believe his eyes. As he waited for her to emerge, a few seconds became a minute and a minute forever. He started to worry. Had her foot caught in an unforgiving swash or a forest of algae? Worry became panic. Had she been carried off in the jaws of a shark or perhaps a fisherman's line from some distant boat had hooked her flesh and dragged her deeper?

Or did she intend to drown herself? Is that why she'd come, why she'd brought him, to save and cremate her body as she'd done for her father? Maybe that was what she'd meant when she told him she was running out of time. He began to count the seconds. There were no bubbles, no wavelets, nothing to suggest she would surface.

"Esme!" he shouted, immediately realizing how stupid of him to think she could hear his voice. Nonetheless, stumbling in the sand as he tried to run to her, he kept calling her name. The moment his boots splashed into the water, she began to rise. With the tide just below her chin and a thin veneer of ice covering her face, she stood seemingly frozen in place. So strange, Johnny thought, for salt water required very low temperatures to freeze.

He started to slog toward her when the thin covering around her mouth cracked open. "Go back!" she called out.

The sharp trill of her voice struck him like the strident surge of Begley's pipes — Begley, the piper who'd fearlessly led the brigade into battle so many times that the Brits had become as afraid of him as a rebel with a rifle. When Johnny found him lying shot on the battlefield, Begley rolled over on the airbag, releasing the shrill burst from his pipes. When Johnny knelt beside him, he tried to reach out and touch his face but his pale arm collapsed onto the deflating bag. His last words were meant for those lying beside him on the field. "The sound of the pipes is the lullaby of God." No sooner had he spoken than his breath gushed from his chest and his body stilled. Johnny shook him gently, then fiercely as the sight of the Begley's dying eyes welled up inside him and the pipes continued to hiss.

Afraid Esme might disappear if he turned away from her, he backed onto the shore. Her body didn't seem to move but inched toward him entirely veiled in a thin coat of ice. She waited on the edge of the water for the ice to melt, leaving her skin a purplish blue. Azure, as she'd foretold. The oddest thought came to him: maybe she'd been waiting underwater for the faeries to return her to this world. Glistening in the glow of the horizon, she seemed to be a layered reflection of her two selves, each bound to a common heart by the figure eight shinning on her breast.

She pointed to the figure. "Infinity," she said, "the swerving racetrack each of us travels, not to mention the Indy."

Beneath the passion in her voice, Johnny felt he heard an apology as if she realized words alone were insufficient to explain what she meant.

"I've never known anyone like you," he said.

Her purple lips began to turn pale. He thought of Jenny and broke into a smile.

"I'm sure *anyone* is grateful," Esme said. "Would you please hold the blanket, so I might put on some clothes?"

"But I've just seen every inch of you."

"Please know, Johnny, I cannot be the object of a man's fantasy."

Believing she was playfully returning his joke, he smiled and raised the blanket to give her privacy. It shifted and rustled as she moved and when the movement stopped, he draped it over her shoulders. She slipped it on and turned, leaning toward him. For a moment he thought she was about to give him a playful kiss for having helped, so he closed his eyes and bent forward, then opened them again to see she had turned her head to the side. Unable to help himself, he reached out and touched her cheek, guiding her face to him.

"No, Johnny," she said, smiling and veering away again as though they were rehearsing the same scene for a play. Her eyes were teaming with kindness that became subdued anguish. She looked off into the distance and turned to him. "This is what I was afraid of. The truth is, I am attracted to you, Johnny, but having you beside me is as close as attraction can bring us."

Guilt passed through him. Guilt for sensing he'd crossed some inexplicable line drawn between them since the moment they'd met. It gave way to shame when he realized he'd almost broken his unrequited vow to Nora.

She cut her eyes at him and quickly glanced away, only to have them return into the baffling emptiness. She sighed. "I'll tell you why it cannot be, and I want you to know it is not what I'd want if things were different." She exhaled a thick, almost endless cloud of cold. "With others I've been able to walk away without regret. But with you it's very different." She fell silent again. "Could we go up onto the pier? What I'm about to tell you would be better said in the mist. Then you won't have to see me cry."

Chapter 26

They came out from under the pier to the sight of countless boardwalk Christmas lights penetrating the mist and made their way to end where the mist was so heavy their hands disappeared when they went to brush it away. They sat down together, drawing the blanket around them. Within seconds, they were trembling. Johnny felt some relief when Esme slipped the flask from her rucksack. "Me first this time," she said in a light tone. She took a deep swallow and handed it to him. He took only a sip, but held the flask to his lips to feign drinking more.

Esme shivered and leaned into the mist. "Things are seldom what they seem, are they? The sea is always moving but most of the time it doesn't seem to be, especially from a distance. Yet, even though mountains are motionless, they always appear to be on the move, because of shifting shadows."

"I never thought of it that way."

She looked at him, her fresh, radiant smile at odds with the moment. Her wet hair was still bonded partly to her face, flattening the long wavy curls, but the change only revealed more of her captivating beauty. Her high cheek bones were visible and her storybook eyes seemed wider.

"What is it you wanted to tell me?" he asked.

She wiped at her eyes and let her breath out slowly. "Life steals our bodies but not our souls. I don't know who said that, maybe no one, but it's true. War teaches that, I would imagine? I apologize, for I know you are much more familiar with war than I am, but it brings me to what I have to tell you." She took another swallow of poteen, but this time when he thought she was about to hand it over to him, she helped herself to yet another gulp and let her voice out just above a whisper.

"I told you about the gun-dance the Tans put my father through, but I didn't tell you the whole story. There was no reason to at the time, but now there is." She jerked her head back and appeared to drain the flask. Her eyes flashed at Johnny. The pain of what she was about to say was embedded in them.

"After the Tan cracked my hip, they dragged me to this thick log and laid me over it. One of them held my face and arms in the mud and then... then another bastard...'"

Johnny put his arm around her shoulder, but she shrugged it off, only to stare down at the pier. Her jaw locked and she jabbed her finger into the mist as though the Tan had just sprung up in front of her. "Goddamn you!"

Catching herself, she turned to Johnny. Her words rushed out. "He took a bayonet to my privates, both sides, to make sure I didn't have a weapon buried in me. Then, while I bled, he raped me in both places. Before they left, he knelt down beside me laughing. I'll never forget what he said, his every word, never: 'Lass, you're bleeding down below, but you should be grateful....'" her voice stuttered to a halt but slowly returned. 'You should be grateful, for if you survive, you'll be able to fuck as much as you want without ever have to worry about birthing a baby. That's a damn sight better than having to make sure your lover remembered to wear a husk.' I can still hear their laughter as they slapped him on the back and called him by his military name, Sergeant Perry."

Tears poured from her eyes. "A full life is not mine to have, Johnny. I cannot be a mom, nor can I fully enjoy the pleasures of trying to have a child, or the pleasures that all should otherwise have." She wrapped her arms around him. Gradually, her crying eased into a sob.

Johnny held her and looked over her shoulder into the murkiness, trying to see beyond the horrid image of her being raped and rendered childless. "It'll be better," he said, his voice toneless, knowing it would never be better and knowing full well he had no way of truly comforting her. He wished he'd kept his mouth shut and just hugged her.

The mist became a dense layer of fog. The sun had almost sunk behind the horizon. As Esme straightened, his arms slipped from her shoulders. Their eyes were just a few inches apart, but it was as if they were looking at each other through a thin, drawn curtain, certain who the other person was on the other side while doubtful they had ever seen each other before. Johnny told himself to stay put but he couldn't. He reached out with both hands and touched her cheeks. He expected her to brush his hands away, but instead she let them stay and leaned toward him.

"My eyes, Johnny, look into my eyes," she said in a tone assuring him he'd crossed no boundary line.

Johnny saw how in her left eye the setting sun resembled a dying fire, how in her right a rising moon beamed like a gilded marble. She slowly slid her eyes from corner to corner, toying with his astonishment. The images floated across her retinas, each isolated on its own lamp-lit horizon. For a moment they paused in the far corners. Then the moon slid toward her nose while the sun stood still before slowly reversing directions. Each image gradually settled in the center of its eye where both locked on Johnny, who was speechless.

"The fairest stars in all the heavens," she said softly, raising her eyebrows to ask if he caught on. A clumsy moment of silence followed but before the awkwardness could blossom into embarrassment, she said, "Romeo and Juliet, the greatest love story ever told."

Johnny's awkward grin collapsed, followed by a wavering smile as he wondered who this woman really was? An unsettled child born at the point of death into madness? Or as she had declared, born into a world inaccessible, but to the few?

"One of the saddest stories ever told," he said, wondering if she'd take it to mean Romeo and Juliet or hers.

"Sad for us who know the story, we who sit on the balcony overlooking the stage with our hearts reaching out to Juliet. But for her it was love at its height, love she could not escape, not even in death. To feel such passion for merely a moment, I would trade places with her in an instant."

In the pause that followed, she stared at Johnny. Her voice arrived on her breath. "If I had been given the gift of love… and if it had ended, I would have wanted it to be just as pure, just as heart-breaking as theirs — with the claws of love buried in my heart, had I survived to wake another day, and buried in my soul had I not. Johnny, have you ever known such love?"

Johnny heard his voice emerge from his nerves. "Aye, I have." In part relieved by the confession, he had the urge to say more, even as it seemed awful to tell someone who'd never been able to find love, that love had come to him. He was about to offer his story the way a player of twenty-five lays a bet, with pride, fear and a shaking hand. "It's with me every hour of the day. Nora is her name. Nora Connolly."

He could see the rise in Esme's throat as she swallowed the shock. She did not have to ask, because he knew the question she withheld. "Yes, *that* Nora Connolly," he answered. Even in the fading light he could tell she was aghast.

"How did…?" She let her question drift toward him..

"We fought side-by-side for the Volunteers and fell in love on the battle-field. At the end of the War, I chose to leave Ireland. The idea that I'd given my life to the Cause and seen life taken from so many around me, forced me to leave. I simply could not live under a Treaty that still subjected us to British rule. Nora stayed and joined Sein Finn, at least as I understand it. Hailey read about her in the *Irish Times*. She's a politician now. She's coming to America this Sunday to give a talk at one of the churches. I think it's called St. Brigid's, a Catholic church on the east side."

He'd lied both outright and by omission, that he knew, and though he felt guilty he was glad for having done so. The full story wasn't Esme's to know, nor did he feel compelled to tell her. What did it matter? It mattered only that he'd answered her question with an honest admission, of sorts. Yes, he'd been in love before and for what it was worth, he still was, though he wondered why that mattered. He would see Nora again, and she knew he'd been forgiven, if not by her, then by her mother and possibly most of Ireland. That's what mattered, despite knowing the sea between them would never again be crossed. He knew it made no sense, but he was thrilled she was coming.

"Will you go to hear her speak?" Esme asked.

"Yes."

"You love her even now, don't' you? I hear it in your voice."

He nodded.

"And that's the beauty of love, it grows far beyond its barricades," she said, capping the flask and putting it into her coat pocket. "We don't want to miss the train," she said. Her voice carried no identifiable tone as it drifted into the fog.

They spoke little on the way home. Esme stared out the window, her back toward Johnny in the aisle seat. She seldom moved. The overhead lights in the Pullman were so dim the glow barely made it to her shoulders.

The rhythmic clanging of the wheels, the repetitive clamor perfect in its harmony, coaxed Johnny to close his eyes. Absently, he leaned his head on the back of her shoulder. She did not move away or turn toward him or pat and caress his hair, which lay against her neck as he drifted into the outer reaches of his mind, that expanse into heaven's shamrock fields and golden streets where only two nights ago fate had taken him on a punishing excursion to search for Nora.

Though now in his dream the dead were gathered outside Angels where the apostles were laughing and joking and knocking back shots. They raised their glasses when they spotted him. The same voice that nights before in his poteen laden dream had told him Nora was dead, rang out in suspicious joy. "Nora's made it home, Johnny!"

Johnny felt his silent response rush into the dream. "You lying shit!"

"Up here lies are acceptable, if the intent is pure," the voice replied. "You need not come looking anymore. She's coming to America!"

Johnny snapped out of the dream and lurched forward.

Esme gasped. "What's the matter, Johnny?"

"She's coming to America, to the Church of the People!"

"Saint Brigid's, you said?"

"Yes, thank God, yes!"

They looked at one another. The wheels of the train pounded out a confirmation that it was so.

When they were getting off the train and about to part, Esme stopped him. "Would you ask Hailey to come with you to The Woebegone on Wednesday? He must be there when we give the bike to Dillon."

Chapter 27

For the next three days Johnny ran as much whisky as possible. The anticipation of seeing Nora drove his energy as the Court Order gave him hope that maybe she now viewed her father's fate differently, from his heart. Johnny asked Hailey to meet with them Wednesday night at The Woebegone, but he replied as Johnny had suspected, saying things at the Pub were getting crazier every night and he had to be there. He reminded Johnny he wanted no credit for his role in building the Indy but would love to meet Joshua and Dillon, if perhaps they could come by the pub afterwards.

The speakeasies were bursting with patrons, due mainly to the holiday spirit that belied the violence and crime occurring far from the bars' lights and conviviality. The Italian Mafia and the Tar Babies were competing with the Gophers and Swamp Angels to take over the rum and sex market while finding humor and reason to raise a glass to every crime, regardless of its brutality. Two women of the night were hanged from the spire of St. Raphael's, while at a crazed bar on Forty-first named, Freedom, the Hebrews gang threw an awards ceremony for the ten most revered hookers in the Kitchen. A Christmas tree was decorated on Fifty-fourth with bones coughed from the portals of the sewers. On Death Avenue, Dusters pounded a rebellious vagrant to death with cobblestones recently dug up to make room for the train tracks.

Yet, the true spirit of Christmas found its way through all the acceptable horror, and while the burlesque of the Kitchen's streets was vast and inescapable, Johnny knew well the nature of irony: the love of his life had caused him the deepest sadness he'd ever experienced and yet filled his heart with happiness. The joy of seeing her was rife with the irony of losing her yet again.

Late Wednesday afternoon while Johnny headed to his apartment after his last delivery, he looked up at a tenement window to see a woman's curtained outline. Eclipsed by lamplight deep in the background, her hazy image mirrored Nora's the night he went to her apartment to show her to her father's grave. Aware of the danger of siding with a Rebel, he'd taken her a uniform to wear, so she might pass for a Brit, at least at a distance. She tucked the sleeves of the corporal's jacket tightly around her arms and shoulders, folded the sleeves above her wrists and ripped off the British flag sewn under the corporal's stripes. She set off with him like a shrunken pauper, and as fate would have it, made it to the gravesite at Arbour Hill.

A clock in the fenced window of a jewelry store told Johnny he had two hours before Esme went on stage, enough time to alter his plans and head to Rags-to-Riches to help her steer the bike to The Woebegone.

He turned onto Thirty-seventh. The severely poverty-stricken street was suspiciously alive. Black, brown, and crimson faces, curious and yet strangely matter-of-fact, peered from the curbs and the few bars they were allowed to patronize. On storefronts an endless score of colorful gangland encryption flowed, enhanced by sparkling lights. A series of car doors slammed. From a wagon situated on the far side of the street a drunk shouted out for money. Johnny had almost cleared the intersection before he realized Rages-to-Riches was just a block away.

The door to the store was locked but the mirrored lights were streaming across the main room. The manikin had retired for the day. He knocked and waited but no one came. He knocked again and when no one showed, he suspected she'd gone to the storage room for the Indy. He headed around back. The barn door was closed but the lock-post lay on the ground.

"Esme?" he called out. Footsteps approached from the other side and the door flew open. In a shaft of blue light stood a lanky man wearing enormous spectacles. His eyes, atop a foot-long neck, were closed. Smoking what smelled like turmeric and sporting a breath cured in absinth, Johnny knew the fellow had to be Lars.

He slowly opened his huge eyes, raised his arms and spread them wide. Johnny tensed worried that the guy was about to bring them down on his shoulders or worse yet, hug him. Instead, he swayed and stumbled against the door. "What do you want?" he asked clinging to the door and gumming his spittle.

"Is Esme here? I'm a friend, Johnny by name."

The muscles at the man's shoulders crowded his neck. "Who are you?" His voice had a slightly Germanic tone.

"A friend of hers. Johnny by name." The man backed into the empty room. The Indy was gone.

"The name Lars belongs to me," he said in a muddled voice. When Johnny offered his hand, Lars simply stared at him. "So, you're the Irishman, the one she trusts even though you know no Shakespeare. Well, then, I'm certain it would be all right if I shared her secret with someone who'll not be able to follow it." He removed the tainted stalk from his mouth and smiled. "She's on her way to Elsinore Castle, to rid it of the witches." The smile narrowed into seriousness. "That's what she does on Wednesday nights. She left early for she's chosen this night for her pilgrimage, a spiritual pilgrimage of sorts. Like Romeo in the Capulets' tomb seeking his beloved Juliet, she has gone into the darkness to find love. You're privileged that Esme's taken you into her confidence. She welcomes just a few, I can tell you." He pulled a small bottle from his hip and offered it to Johnny. "A bit of absinth to aid your mind?

Stuck between bemusement and annoyance, Johnny put up his hand. "I came to help her with the bike but I see she's already taken it, so, I'll be going now."

"Wait a moment." The veins on Lars' neck thickened. "You should know, Esme and I, we're friends, nothing more. I gave her a job when she arrived, realizing we both were insane. She keeps her distance and I do the same. We respect one another's distaste for what others consider righteousness." His bulging eyes looked away. He puffed on the stalk. A sly laugh tumbled out on his exhale. "Tell her something for me, if you will. Tell her I have no choice but to be her friend as I am bound by the witches on the ramp, same as she is bound by the Bard, himself. But she most likely knows that. She's knows as well that her friend will be leaving soon for my homeland."

"I'll be sure to tell her," Johnny said, having no idea what the Lars was talking about and certain he was drunk.

Lars looked up at the darkening sky. He stood motionless for a minute, staring as if he were trying to orient himself. "Look there," he said. "The moon will descend before the night is done, spreading darkness into every hole and crevasse. And on the narrow walls of Elsinore the cackling women in black will curse us. I must return forthwith and help prevent it. Gotterdammerung!"

"So long," Johnny said and hurried to the streets.

The chill burned his cheeks. He sped up to find warmth. Within a block of The Woebegone he could see the crowd gathering under the painting of Cuchulain. Most of the grown-ups had children alongside them, holding their little one's hands or rubbing their faces to keep them warm. Unable to spot Joshua and Dillon among them, Johnny felt his heart ping, hoping Joshua hadn't chosen this as the day to head south. The doors opened and the bystanders cheered and squeezed together to push inside.

The tables filled quickly. Johnny stood in the rear, gripping the railing as he searched for Joshua and Dillon. No sign of them. His worry deepened. He was about to make his way backstage when Esme appeared from behind the curtain. When she saw him, she blew him a kiss and mimed a "thank you" to which he wanted to reply, "Where are they?" but knew it would be useless. He tried to smile and tightened his grip on the railing.

Esme sang three Christmas carols, two Irish, including, "The Wexford Carol" and "Jingle Bells". When the applause died down, she called a succession of children to the stage, each with a story to tell. Every story was touching, among them one by a teenager named Toby whose home, a rickety barn out-side Kildare, had been set afire by the Tans, sealing the boy's ears forever. Esme's hands played gently before him and while silent at first, he gradually began to whisper, and soon his register rose and poured into song matching her alto.

Then, a German girl of twelve, Zoe, a victim of the War. Her family had deserted King Wilhelm and gained passage to America because she'd lost an arm to a stick of dynamite tossed into her playroom. She played a harp one-handed with Esme accompanying. Her hand wove between the notes like a raven's wings between gusts of wind. She told the audience that Esme had taught her to play the harp by stringing tight pieces of wire nailed into the floor and into the rafters in St. Raphael's church.

And to Johnny's great surprise and relief, Esme called Dillon to the stage. Joshua brought him out and sat him on the floor in front of the other children. Esme went off stage for a moment and returned with the coconut drums and positioned them between Dillon's stubs.

She began to hiss, not like a cat but like the shush of a parent to a babbling child. She put her hands together as if she were about to pray and brushed them up and down against one another. The children did the same. Together they created a gentle swishing sound. Moments later she parted her hands and began to click her fingers. Then she pointed at the children, motioning for them to separate into two sections. She directed one group to swish their hands and the other to softly click their fingers, bringing the sound of gentle rain on a tin roof.

She pointed towards Dillon and motioned for him to begin. The accompa-niment of the groups rose as he tapped the drums while sliding his fingers faster and faster over the foils on the coconuts. Within moments the composi-tion became a dance of pouring rain. Esme coaxed the kids in the front row to join her in bringing the rain to a climax so thunderous Johnny thought it would end in a bolt of lightning striking the stage. But before a crescendo, the sound unexpectedly softened, and to his amazement snowflakes began to fall from the rafters where helpers were dipping their hands into buckets and tossing handfuls of papier-mache into the air.

Dillon thumbed more gently. His fingers made their way over the drums effortlessly following his smile from side-to-side. Zoe strummed her harp more slowly. The chords combined with the flakes, allowing them to fall silently, joyfully, a gift to one and all. Johnny could sense the crowd's delight. They'd found shelter from the encroaching storm and were appreciative.

The applause rippled through the railing and sent goosebumps down Johnny's arms. Joshua ran across the stage and scooped Dillon off the floor. Everyone roared as the children bowed and turned to Dillon with cheers.

Esme patted the air to call for silence. A stagehand rushed out to give her a mike and she moved toward Dillon, stopping at the edge of the stage to look out at the audience "This young boy comes from a different place, a different time and a different set of circumstances. Neither he nor his father have seen war, at least war as we know it. But they've seen war's essence, its very core, the heart of hatred." She swept her gaze across the crowd. "Hatred far more disgusting than war itself, hatred of another kind, of one human to another because the other person happens to be of a different culture, a different background, a different color. Hatred whose only purpose is to rule over others and by doing so vaunt one's idea of one's self to the blessings of a god who they feel appreciates such things. That god's name is, of course, Beelzebub, guardian of Hell's Kitchen, known more commonly in Celtic lore as Bile."

Esme didn't let up. She returned to Dillon's story and told it thoroughly. She mentioned the town of Malville, Judge Aiken by name and the very words he'd spoken when sentencing Dillon to his fate. The audience sat horrorstruck. No one spoke. Johnny thought could see light reflecting in the stream of tears from Joshua's eyes as Dillon reached out to hold onto his pant leg.

When she finished, Esme seemed unsure of her whereabouts and surprised to find herself on stage before a packed room. Her face turned slightly red. "Forgive me," she said. "Let me tell you the good side, the far better side, maybe one that has overcome such odium. Two men, one here with us this very moment, came together to create a special Christmas gift for Dillon." She framed her mouth with her hands and called to the far side of the stage, "Fellas, bring it out!"

As the Indy came rolling onto the stage, a shimmering silver light flashed from the rafters. The bike's spokes lit up like tinsels. The light quickly became sunset and the Indy's frame turned a color Johnny wondered if he'd ever seen before, something between the frame's original orange and the gold of Esme's hair. The name of the color he was searching for was ochre. A thin Santa Claus whose age was hidden beneath a deep, sandy beard rowed the bike to center stage.

Dillon's face lit up in amazement. He slapped the floor with his hands. The children scooted back to make a path for him. The man dressed as Santa jumped out of the seat with a roaring "Ho! Ho! Ho!", snatched Dillon off the floor, slipped back onto the leather seat and snuggled him into his lap.

"Merry Christmas, young man! This is your gift. Hands around the baseball bats now, then pull them toward you one at a time."

The bike began to move slowly across stage. As they approached the edge, Santa helped Dillon lean to turn the wheel. As the audience cheered them on, they guided the Indy back to center stage.

Esme went over to Dillon. "Now go enjoy your life like never before!"

Joshua jumped to his feet and shouted, "Bless you, Esme! Bless you! Bless you! Bless you!"

Everyone stood and repeated the blessing, and like the sound of rain moments before, the words became a flowing chant that seemed to bring God to center stage. Johnny chimed into the blessing while wiping his eyes to clear the blur. Dillon drove around in circles, making three laps. Beaming and breathing hard, he came to a halt.

As everyone began to leave the stage they gave Dillon hugs and kissed Esme. Johnny closed his eyes and gratefully inhaled the smell of sage. He thought of Hailey building the Indy, how the anger drained from his face as he finished, when he'd evened the score at last.

"Johnny, someone would like to say, thank you."

Johnny opened his eyes as Joshua snatched him and hugged him so tight he could barely breathe. He glanced at Esme who winced apologetically.

"I had very little to do with it," Johnny said. "Hailey did the work. I lent a hand where I could. He wanted to be here tonight but couldn't get away."

"But without you, Johnny, there wouldn't be no Indy. Esme said you took the idea to Hailey and he built it. I could never thank you enough, not if I started this minute and went on until I left this earth. Here it is, hope on wheels. Like the Angel Gabriel. Where would we be without the messenger?" He tightened his grip on Johnny. "Gabriel's getting a little too old to be tromping around Hell's Kitchen, so God chose you this time. And don't you worry, we'll find our way down to Hailey's this Saturday and give him our thanks. You can be sure of it."

"If you and Dillon are taking it home tonight, I'd be happy to go along. It's getting crazy out there," Johnny said.

"You've already done way more than your share," Joshua said. "Besides, ain't nobody gonna mess with a seven-foot black man carrying a two-foot kid with three sets of bongo drums. They'll think we're from some African nuthouse. Get a good night's sleep, Johnny."

"Wait for me!" Dillon shouted circling the stage again while Santa stood watch. "Daddy, come get me. I want to say goodbye."

"Come with me, Johnny." Joshua said and together they rushed down the aisle and climbed up on the stage. Joshua picked Dillon up and held him over his shoulders.

Dillon reached out to Johnny and slid into his open arms. He clinched Johnny's ribs with his thighs, wrapped his arms around his neck and kissed his cheek. He leaned back slightly. His eyes searched Johnny's. "I love you," he said.

The words stabbed Johnny in the heart.

"Thank you for the Indy," Dillon said. "It's like having a racecar or maybe an airplane."

"I'm so glad you like it," Johnny said, convinced that Joshua would never threaten to go South again.

Dillon smiled and looked at his father. "Daddy, white people smell like prunes, except Esme. She smells like lilacs."

Joshua grinned. "Well then, what's us black people smell like, or maybe you shouldn't say?"

"Coconuts, Daddy. You know that. Black people smell like coconuts."

They laughed as Esme helped Dillon to his dad. "Will I see you and Dillon this Saturday?" she asked, glancing at Johnny.

"We'll be there, prunes and coconuts alike," Joshua replied.

As Joshua carried Dillon across the stage where Santa was waiting, Esme turned to Johnny. "I don't think I thanked you for coming with me to the beach. I'll never forget it."

Chapter 28

The closer to Christmas, the higher the spirits and the greater the gangland warfare. Crime and salaciousness were taking their toll in a horrendous, yet ironically festive way. The more police assigned to the Kitchen, the smaller the force became as more cops shucked their duties and joined the party mood. The area became wilder than the Wild West. Given the weakening tentacles of Prohibition, merriment combined with the age-old Christmas spirit to delay guilt and worry from surfacing.

Everyone felt free to do as they pleased: to run freezing naked along the shore, escape the cops with a dash into a forbidden alley and drink a toast to Jesus as the sound of windows being smashed incited happiness. Even the vagrants participated. They were given ale from the bars, food from the coffee houses and leftover fruit from the grocery stores. They came out of hiding, looked straight into people's eyes and occasionally laughed.

And all the while Johnny could not forget the sight of Esme's body surfacing from the water, her body brimming with azure borrowed from the strange sunset, or the moment he mistook her closeness for affection and leaned toward her only to be led into her eyes where the sun and moon rested on different horizons. Even now, days later, he had a difficult time believing it had been anything more than a parlor trick she'd learned in a bar or maybe from Lars. What was it she'd said about her eyes? "The fairest stars in all the heavens?"

And her gut-wrenching tragedy at the hands of the Tans. Not only raped but deprived of motherhood. It was a crime on the same level as murder, and yet she'd managed to move on. How had she? It couldn't have been that long ago, a few years maybe. Take Hailey and what happened to him as a boy. It had clung to him for decades and he'd only shaken it yesterday. Whatever Esme had done to save herself was truly remarkable.

Johnny wondered if, in any way, it spoke to forgiveness, and if so, where had she found it? Certainly not in His Name? After all, with war, the Almighty had taken to revenge like a mother to milk.

He stopped on a corner he didn't recognize. Trapped in the moment he searched the tenements for some hint of familiarity. A long, inseparable line of red bricks, stoops, shuttered windows and brownstone, nothing more. He was lost, lost in the strange vortex of crime and celebration, Nora and Esme, Dillon and Joshua, Jenny and a cop named Chandler. Lost in his own mixed feelings about his gun and why he'd given it up, he went too far and found himself on the East Side. It came to him that, St Brigid's, the church where Nora would be speaking had to be nearby, but he didn't have time for a visit, because he'd be late for his rum.

He was about to retrace his steps when he remembered what his mother said, "If you're flummoxed, go sit in a church and let God come to you. Church is where your father goes to clear his head when he's had too much to drink. It's where he goes to try and escape the guilt that comes from my forgiveness. He sits in the back pew, never in front because he doesn't want God to recognize him. That's what he tells me. He always goes to the Catholic Church, never with me to the Anglican, 'for Protestants haven't ascended,' he often said."

Johnny continued eastward.

The spires of St. Brigid's towered over the corner of East Eighth and Avenue B where an elongated, stained glass window, peaked and arrogant, cast its authority into the park across the street. The sharply-sloped slate roof was hemmed on both sides by a spire that soared high above the neighboring buildings. Far below on the welcoming marquee, it read: "Nora Connolly to speak here Sunday."

Compelled to see inside, he pried open the front door and slipped into the rear of the vestibule. Against the last row of seats, a long table bearing a banner labeled the *Table of the Lord* held at least a hundred candles. Only one was lit, a red votive that smelled of cinnamon and barely flickered. Above the table, swaying in the fine drafts of heated air, a second banner read, "Bring me three Sunstones and three Moonstones, and I will summon an angel for you." It bore what Johnny took to be a modern-day signature of Saint Brigid.

The heavy walls curved inward, sweeping down toward the altar like the bow of a ship. The altar was entirely dark except for a sleek, gold cross suspended from the ceiling of the vault by invisible wires. Shadows cast by the nave's arches reminded him of those suspended from the sails of *The Pestilence* when he first spotted it from the bluffs above Kinsale Bay, on that horrible day when the sky was thick and endless and the shadows lay on top of one another absorbing Nora's image as she disappeared on horseback into the woods.

The red carpet leading to the altar split the vestibule into two sections, each side with pews that might have accommodated several hundred people. Maroon carpeted aisles lined the far sides of the nave. Above the outer aisles, seated balconies stretched the length of the church. Stained glass windows galore turned the muted sunlight into a cauldron of colorful tones. But what held Johnny's eyes more than anything were the five-pointed arches behind the marble altar, the reredos. His father had taught him the Mexican word when he'd taken Johnny to the church in Cork on his eighth birthday. There, they journeyed with Christ to his death as they visited the fourteen stations of the cross. His old man had forced him to memorize all fourteen.

Johnny took a seat in the rear pew, all the while remindful of his father's desire to avoid being seen by the eyes of God. Sitting in a church during a joyous, crime-ridden Christmas season, what was he thinking? A place for rest meant contemplation, as his mother had reminded him. He leaned forward and closed his eyes.

"Rest, child." Was it his mother's voice or the one that had come to him on the bluff warning him to remain calm so he could hear the ship's foghorn calling him aboard from the Bay?

"May I help you?"

The woman's Irish brogue echoed in the vastness of the church. A nun emerged. She approached smiling, her dark habit oddly striped with stretches of white and green. The colors seemed sharpened by the paleness of her skin. Atop a head of stark white hair trimmed close to her ears, sat the square biretta of a priest. Johnny started to stand when she reached out and touched his shoulder.

"Please, stay seated. I didn't mean to alarm you," she said.

"I was just using the church as a place to rest, Sister. I probably should go elsewhere."

"Churches are for strangers as well as for the members. Otherwise the heavily laden would never come. Some vagrants come here to sleep. We permit them as they might find God in their dreams. Have you been here before? I don't recall ever seeing you."

"No, I came over from Ireland when the War for Independence ended and haven't had time to find my... my way here. My father was Catholic. We're from County Cork."

"As are many of our worshipers. This was the first refuge for those who sought shelter when they came to America to escape the Famine. We have the lineage from those who came then to those who followed soon thereafter, such as yourself. You would fit in well here."

"Now that I know the way, I won't be hesitant to return. In fact, I'll surely be here Sunday to hear Miss Connolly speak."

"She comes to us as one of God's blessed, one of His favorites, a hero, if you will. You know of her?"

Johnny did not hesitate to answer. "Only what I've heard and read in the papers. I understand she fought for the Rebels, but I didn't realize she was Catholic."

"She strayed from the order occasionally, as did her father, James, but thank the good Lord, just before he was executed, he made his way back to the faith, a stronger believer than ever. I'm told he desperately wanted to die, as he believed — as did Christ on the Cross — that his death would further a cause much greater than himself. In Connolly's case it was the cause of independence. I don't know how true it is, but there are those who believe he called out to his executioners, begging them to do their duty. God granted his request and history bequeathed the rest. Because of it, I'm sure he pours the Savior's wine to this day."

Johnny took a deep breath. "Sister, those who served on his firing squad. Are they forgiven by God?"

"If they are laden with guilt, they must forgive themselves, and if they cannot find it in their hearts to do so, I suspect the Almighty will grant them release in the hereafter because, as it turns out, they were serving His purpose."

"How do they go about forgiving themselves?"

"By returning to the scene of their wrongdoing, when God has given each enough time to tell the difference between who they were then and who they've become, understanding full well that the two are different. What we do today is not what we would do if we had to do it all over again. And yet, there are those among us who occasionally lie to ourselves in order to convince others we've changed, when we haven't. That becomes the greater sin."

Johnny was confused. We cannot do things over again. In our memories we can imagine we'd do things differently, but that makes no difference to the victim. "What about the members of Connolly's family, such as his daughter? Could she ever truly forgive those who killed her father?"

"She's coming to share her thoughts on Sinn Fein and her belief in a government whose main purpose is to feed and protect the poor, while spreading the idea of freedom. It's hard to imagine that a person so steeped in caring would possess a heart held prisoner by anger or hatred. No doubt she's managed to move well beyond her past."

It was what Johnny wanted to hear and what he didn't want to hear — move beyond her past to where… where love no longer mattered?

"We need more like her," the Sister said. "The world does, in fact, even here in America where God's invisible signature is prominent on The Declaration of Independence."

Johnny hesitated for a moment, searching for a way to change the topic. "Sister, you are a nun, are you not?"

"Why do you ask?"

"The biretta. I thought that only…"

"Priests wear them?"

"Yes, but little do I know. It may well be different in America."

"You're correct in your suspicion. I am a priestess, an abbess, if you prefer, a woman priest, and it is no different here than anywhere. We women, are not allowed to become priests — accept under very special circumstances. In my case, I was chosen and appointed during the Feast of Imbolc. I tended the eternal flame for a month at the Church of the Oak where Saint Brigid founded religious life for women and bestowed abbatial privileges upon me."

"May I ask your name?"

"I am Saint Brigid."

"*You* are Saint Brigid?"

"Her name was bestowed upon me one summer's night at St. Brigid's in Kildare at the traditional ceremony of Imbolc, where we gathered to celebrate the joy of our own spirit. I sat , by the eternal flame with men and women alike as Father Markus went against tradition. He did not seek even a cardinal's approval and took it upon himself to confer upon me the good Saint's name. Since that blessed day, I have enjoyed her legacy, one of miraculous underpinning, for it has been said she converted water into milk for Easter and by prayer stilled the wind and brought rain to barren fields. She healed a leper and, even more in the spirit of the incredible, gave a maidenhead to a woman stifled by her lack of virginity. The stories of her majesty are endless."

"Do you have those same powers?" Johnny asked.

St. Brigid smiled, spreading the colors of her habit. "I'm afraid not. My mission is of a different order. I was sent to America to help the church form a school. Saint Paul, our cardinal, governs the church along with me, and it is with his guidance that the beautiful reredos you see behind the altar have been restored. Soon we will apply his vision to the steeples and have them tapered. Their weight is bringing cracks to the rear walls of the church. Father Paul has done the calculations. Hopefully God will grant us time to raise the money we need for the restoration."

"The steeples are beautiful. How tall are they?"

"Counting from the ground up, sixty-three feet, believed to be the height of the three crosses on Golgotha when added together and multiplied by three. The multiplier stands for the sum total of the Holy Trinity."

Johnny followed the arithmetic, but beyond her storybook tales, everything she'd shared reminded him of Esme, until the reason behind his being in the church overcame it.

"Sister, I know you have other things to do, but I'm just curious. By chance were you in Ireland during the war?"

"Indeed, I was, for the first two years. Yourself?"

"Aye. May I ask you yet another question I've been unable to answer."

"Of course, but first, to whom do I have the pleasure of speaking?"

"Excuse me for not introducing myself. I'm Johnny. I didn't mean to be rude."

"Not at all. Now, Johnny, your question please."

"Can love and the need for revenge exist side-by-side between two people, or is forgiveness necessary before love is allowed to blossom?" Johnny hesitated. "Forgive me, Sister, what I meant to ask is this: *can* love or *should* love be able to overcome the desire for revenge, or maybe I should say...? Let me try again. Should love overcome the inability to forgive?" He looked at the reredos. "I'm sorry, Sister. I'm not making sense. "

"Johnny, one is reminded of what Jesus said with regard to Judas: 'Woe unto him who betrays the Son of Man. It would be better had he not been born.' Judas was neither saved nor forgiven in any way. He sold out for thirty pieces of silver with no contrition in mind, and I'm certain he doesn't sit at the right hand of God these days. Bear in mind, even though someone forgives you through the sacraments of forgiveness, there are cruelties for which Christ Himself would demand repayment. Consider Joshua and the city of Jericho. Joshua was ordered to strike the loathed Canaanites for their sins, which included incest and child sacrifice, and bring the walls down upon them, and he did so, to Christ's delight."

The name, Joshua, sent Johnny's mind hurtling down the historic question of might versus right. Did the sister's story suggest that Joshua was doing the right thing in returning to the South to kill a man? Was Nora's refusal to forgive him for serving on the firing squad the equivalent of the sins of the Canaanites? It was all too complicated, a mixture of yeas, nays and maybes, a stream of confusion based on the wanderings of those who wrote the Bible.

"Sister, thank you for that, but I've well overstayed my welcome. I must be going."

She stepped aside. "That said, if one is to be forgiven, he must ask God's forgiveness and stand firm in the belief that His forgiveness will only be bestowed if the sinner has returned to the past and come away convinced that under the same set of circumstances, he would never respond the same way again. Only then might the Father lift the burden which is too heavy for us. If one chooses to deny Him that power and let fate decide instead, as with the Canaanites, the burden shall fall where it must, upon the seeker." Her eyes questioned him. "Would you like to go to the confession booth? It's a start on the road home. I'd be happy to try and find Father Paul, or you could let your heart speak to me."

Johnny glanced at the dark booths on the far side of the church. They reminded him of coffins set on end. "You are very kind, Sister, but perhaps another time when my mind is clearer."

Saint Brigid looked toward the altar and then to Johnny. Her face was not accepting nor was it unforgiving, bathed as it was in the rainbow colors of the stained glass. She caught the trance in his eyes. "The blues and greens before you are symbols of birth and renewal, the yellows and reds those of fire and damnation. They light the stations of the Cross you see on the pillars, as they did on the last day of Christ's life. Before you leave, I would be proud to accompany you to each of them."

Johnny hesitated. "Thank you, Sister, but my father took me to the stations when I was a boy. I've never forgotten. I must go now."

She crossed herself. "May the birds and wind guide you. May the angelic faeries, the handmaidens of Christ, release your burden. Above all else, may the desire for God to accompany you reside deep in your heart. But even if you refuse Him, I hope to see you Sunday."

Out on the street, he wasn't sure he'd fully understood her or himself. And yet, despite his confusion, the holiday spirit made itself felt. As he approached the Kitchen, the smiles from the vagrants, the laughter from the afflicted and the thoughts of bones being delivered to broken families by Doolin, spread his lips awkwardly wide. He wondered if it was the smile of a loon.

Chapter 29

Johnny went to Hailey's determined to stay sober. He wanted no hangover to spoil seeing Nora — and for once he wanted to enjoy the ascendency of Esme's voice to its fullest, without the phantom weight of poteen breaking it into bits of silence. One glass of poteen. Well, he thought, maybe two and he'd leave for his flat.

He'd never seen the room so packed. Everyone was standing in a breathy closeness, except for those at the bar. Hailey had held two seats empty for Joshua and Dillon by hanging crayoned signs on the back of their stools saying, "Reserved." Time after time patrons attempted to take the seats and Johnny had to tell them they were being saved for a crippled boy and his father. Once said, everyone backed away pleasantly.

When Joshua and Dillon arrived at the garden door, Hailey shoved his way through the crowd to greet them. Joshua lifted Dillon from his shoulders and held him out toward Hailey. Immediately Dillon threw his arms around his neck and slid his nubs under his arms. Hailey held him for the longest time. With joyous eyes Dillon clung to him while Joshua looked on grinning.

As soon as Johnny felt he could greet them without interrupting, he left his stool and made his way over. Joshua had barely given Johnny a hug when Dillon slid from Hailey's arms to cling onto Johnny.

"I love my Indy! It lets me do so many things I couldn't do before!"

Johnny wished Esme had been by his side.

"There ain't no other words except, bless you and Mr. Hailey," Joshua said.

"Did you bring the Indy with you, Joshua?" Hailey asked.

"Parked it outside in the shanty."

"Safest place in Hell's Kitchen," Johnny said.

"Over to the bar," Hailey said, placing his hand on Joshua's shoulder. "We got seats for you two, and the drinks are on me if you're having one, or more." He looked at Dillon. "For this young race-driver we got Coca-Colas, and Esme brought some chocolate. She'll join us during the break. Look there, she's about to go on."

On stage, Esme waved with the mike in hand. Dillon's grin stretched to his earlobes as he returned the excitement clapping.

"Looks like we're the only black folks in here, Mister Hailey, and I don't want to cause no trouble after all you done for us," Joshua said.

"Don't you worry. If trouble comes, it's trouble that'll pay. But these people aren't like that. They're good folks just here to celebrate the holidays and toast Prohibition. Brings out the good in them. Take your seats, mates, and remember, chocolate bars and vanilla pudding go together."

Laughing, Joshua placed Dillon in his lap to give Johnny the open seat. As Esme sang, Dillon clicked his fingers and tapped on the counter. Patting the bar intermittently, on pace with the songs, he swiped his hands against one another, creating a sound like the ring of a soft instrument finding its way into the song. When she started to sing "Silent Night", Dillon began at exactly the same instant, as if he'd known the song was next in line. Closing his eyes while clicking his fingers, he slid his hands back and forth on the counter. Johnny closed his eyes imagining snow blowing in the wind over his pram.

When intermission came, Joshua placed Dillon on the counter and stood up to clap. He raised his hands high above his head, shouting, "More! More! More!"

Esme smiled and waved as Hailey climbed onto the stage to tell everyone they could rest assured she would return right after the break. Meanwhile, Hoagy Carmichael would be coming their way courtesy of RCA Victor.

Johnny dipped under the applause to lean closer to Dillon. "I love the sound you make with your hands. It's like magic even when it's just on the counter. I went off into another world."

Dillon pointed to Esme leaving the stage. "She taught me," he said. "I get a sore throat when I try to sing — from the mud that got caught in it when our house fell down, so she taught me to play hand music. And she made me a set of coconut drums. She says it brings the songs inside, like we was inside a house or a barn while outside it's raining."

"You're going to be playing in Radio City Music Hall one day," Johnny said.

"I can find my way over there now because of what you and Mister Hailey done. I know I'm supposed to call it my Indy, but sometimes I forget and call it, Fetcher, because I can fetch things I never could before. Like yesterday, I took an empty can of pancake syrup on a ride and me and Daddy fetched some falling snow and brought it home and prayed over it, thanking God for taking it out of the clouds for us. It was so much fun!"

"Sorry, to serve him first, sir," Eoin said to Joshua as he set a glass of poteen in front of Johnny, "I already knew what he wanted. Didn't have to ask. What would you like?"

"Same as him."

"That's poteen," Johnny said. "Have you ever had it before? It's powerful."

"I'll go slow. Don't forget, we're mates now. I gotta find the Irish in me."

Eoin leaned toward Dillon. "And young man, what's for you?"

"A Coke Cola, if you got one left."

Eoin clicked his fingers. "We sure do. Now let me guess, ma'am. A poteen like the older fellows here?"

They turned to find Esme standing beside them. She'd woven unseen through the crowd.

"You guessed right," she said.

"Want it in the flask or a tumbler?"

"Tumbler, please. I have to make quick work of it, and as luck would have it, my flask is full for now."

"Be back in a second," Eoin said and rushed to the end of the bar.

Esme put an arm around Joshua and Johnny. Dillon leaned in between them.

"Santa came to see me early," he said.

Johnny couldn't take his eyes off the boy. "If I had a son, he would be the exact likeness of you, young fellow."

"But can white people have black babies?" Dillon asked.

"It works out that way sometimes."

Everyone smiled, including Joshua. Johnny could see Dillon's grinning reflection in Joshua's eyes.

Eoin returned with a tumbler of poteen and a bottle of Coke. Esme emptied the tumbler and set it on the counter. Licking her lips, she shook as the drink went down. They watched as Joshua took his first sip. Instantly, his head lifted and he coughed so fiercely he had to pound his chest.

"Give it a minute to clear the tunnel and you'll be okay," Johnny said patting him on the back.

Hailey left the bar to return to the stage. Esme took a half-step back, pulling gently on Johnny's shoulder. He slipped off the stool, and she put her hand to his cheek urging him to come closer. "Now, both Hailey and Joshua have their revenge," she said. "Maybe not exactly what Joshua had in mind but enough to put it all behind him, into a different world where today means so much more than yesterday."

Joshua's cough worsened. He bent over the bar and grasped at his coat.

"You alright, daddy?" Dillon said patting his shoulder.

"Bathroom," Joshua uttered.

"Here, come with me," Johnny said, placing Dillon on his stool. "It's alright. It's the stuff he's drinking. It goes down hard if you're not used to it. I'll take him."

When they'd made it back, Joshua's dark skin looked almost cloudy, as though someone had draped a grey sheet over him.

"Daddy, you look funny. Are you okay?"

Joshua opened his mouth but no sound followed. He eased onto the stool and sighed. "I got sick to my stomach, son. That's all. I should have listened to Johnny. This Irish whisky ain't for everybody." He straightened as best he could. "We'd better get going while there's enough of our poor friends out on the streets to protect us." A pained smile stretched his pasty skin.

"I'd be happy to go with you," Johnny said.

"No, man, I'm fine. It won't be no trouble getting home. After all, we got Indy-Fetcher to speed the way." Dillon waved to Esme and she blew him a kiss.

"You're sure you don't want me to go alongside? With poteen, you never know. Just when you think it's let go of you, here it comes again."

"We're on Thirty-eight and it's straight as an arrow to get there." Joshua looked at Dillon. "Sorry, buddy, I know you'd like to stay longer."

"That's all right, Daddy You can sit me in your lap and I'll steer us home."

Hailey made his way over to say goodbye and went with them out to the garden. Lit by the reach of Christmas lights from the doorway, the snowy hill carried a descending sheen of blue and green, like the windows in St. Brigid's, Johnny thought, watching Joshua fasten Dillon into the seat.

Joshua cleared his throat. "Please tell Esme we're sorry for leaving early."

"Happens to the best Irishmen," Johnny said.

As they left, Hailey glanced at Johnny. "Wish they could have stayed but they did the right thing. Let's get inside for the finish. "O Holy Night" sends chills up my spine. If I had anything to say about it, that's all she'd sing, over and over again."

Back inside Johnny realized Esme wasn't quite yet on her closing masterpiece. Tightly wrapped around her slim body, her emerald dress seemed to bring more attention to her elevated hip, but as she moved back and forth on the stage, it was hard to tell if she was just one person whose hip simply rose at certain times or if she were, as he'd often imagined, one's top and another's bottom joined at the hip. Even though he'd seen her naked on the shore, he could barely separate the possibilities. He conceded she was probably the apparition she considered herself to be, but he couldn't say if that meant a specter whose image was simply impossible to define or a real person who just seemed to be the person she wasn't.

She was barely into "O Holy Night" when he heard Dillon's scream. He jumped off the stool and ran for the door. His heart leapt into his throat when he saw Joshua sprawled on the curb, clutching his head. The Indy lay on its side in the street. Seth along with Amos and Jacob, the keg loaders, were standing behind Dillon laughing as they attempted to belt his nubs and arms.

"Leave him alone!" Johnny shouted, running toward them.

"Celtic Stone Roll, Johnny!" Seth called out pointing to the street. "Blacks roll like chunks of coal 'cause that's what they are. We're going to take turns rolling him. One who gets him across the street wins a free keg. Want to join in?"

Johnny erupted. His fist uppercut Seth's jaw. Seth dropped to the ground clutching his face. Moaning, he straightened, rolled onto his side and grabbed for his pistol but his hand was spasming so hard the gun dropped into the snow.

Jacob stood frozen in place as Amos ran toward Seth, dropped to the ground and lunged for the pistol.

"Touch it and you're dead!"

Johnny wheeled around only to be blinded by a panel of gleaming lights. They sliced Esme's being into layers as she dashed into the garden with his Mauser.

"Esme!" Dillon shrieked.

"I'm coming, child!" She stopped to lower the gun within inches of Amos's face. "Untie him before I blow your brains out!" The pistol was shaking but her hands were still. She cut her eyes at Amos. "Did you hear me?" she shouted.

Huddled against the curb, Joshua struggled to get to his feet, then suddenly seized his forehead and fell to his knees. Johnny ran to him. "You're bleeding, mate. Here," he said whipping off his coat and pressing it against Joshua's skull. Can you hold it?"

"I got it," he muttered. "Is Dillon alright?"

"He's fine."

Esme was behind Amos, gun drawn as they untied Dillon. She made them lie face down on the ground and with her free hand carefully straightened Dillon's crimped fingers.

The fury in Johnny raged as he approached Seth. "What did you do to his dad?"

"We didn't do nothin'. He fell down and hit his head on the curb."

"He hit him with a gun!" Dillon yelled. "That man lying on the ground. He done it! I seen him! And you knocked over Fetcher!"

"You little nigger, I ought... Ahhhhh!" Seth shrieked, grabbing at his back as Johnny's kidney punch straightened his spine. He collapsed and curled, wormlike into a ball.

"Get this animal out of here," Johnny said to Amos.

"I'll have to drag him."

"Better now than when he's dead," Esme said.

A thin shadow came out from the shrubs lining the hill.

"Locust?" Johnny said. "What the hell are you doing here?"

The boy's mouth gaped open, wordless.

"Out with it!" Johnny demanded.

"Seth came down here... to kick you outta the Angels... 'cause you wouldn't carry a gun, and I came all the way from the pier ... begging him not to. He knew this is where you came on Saturday nights, to... to see the lady there. That's what he told that man... the one in the red hat... who was after you. We got here about the... same time these... these black folks came outside. He hates... you know, Negroes, but I didn't know how much. I hid in the bushes. I'm so sorry I came."

"Locust, if and when Seth opens his eyes, let him know you delivered the message and give him one from me. You tell him, if I ever see him again, I'll kill him. Now get him the hell out of here."

"But... Seth saved you... from drowning, Johnny."

"And I'm returning the favor."

With Johnny's help, Joshua struggled to his feet. "Still a little dizzy," he murmured. With a bloody hand pressing Johnny's coat against his head, he reached out for Dillon but staggered, clutching a knee to steady himself. Johnny picked Dillon up and held onto him as he hugged his father.

Dillon looked at Johnny. "When they got hold of me and Daddy, I prayed for God to let us live, and see what He done? God talked straight to you and Esme and you heard Him, didn't you?"

"I did," Johnny said. "And Esme heard the faeries call on Him for help."

Esme smiled. "Johnny's right. I did."

"And Mr. Hailey, did God say something to you?" Dillon asked.

Johnny turned to find Hailey wrapping a towel around Joshua's forehead.

"Most definitely He did. And He's speaking right now, saying you and your Daddy shouldn't go back on the streets tonight. Daddy's not fit and you both need rest, so the good Lord's suggesting I bed you both in the basement. We'll set the Indy upright. Thank the good Lord, all they did was turn it over. I'll make breakfast in the morning and if you feel up to it, then you can leave. How's that sound?"

Maybe it'll be warmer in the morning," Dillon said.

Hailey grabbed Johnny's coat from the ground and handed it to him. "Warm as toast and some Irish stew will make it more so. Off to the bed-ment," he joked. "What do you say?"

"We say, bless you," Joshua managed. "What about the Indy?"

"I'll hide it in the shed," Eoin said.

" Anger, as well as the remnants of fear, hung in the air as Esme examined the lump on Joshua's forehead. "It's a huge knot but with a lot of rest and ice, you should be alright."

"I'll fill a bowl right now," Hailey said.

When you get downstairs, before you go to sleep," Esme said, "rest your forehead on the ice. Do it every few minutes or so, until it's melted, then use what I'm about to give you to tie the towel around your head." Esme turned away from the bar to slip off her shoes and then a stocking. She draped the stocking over Joshua's shoulder. "Tie it tight, but not too tight."

Johnny guided Joshua and Dillon downstairs. Eoin brought down an even larger bowl of ice and a bunch of blankets from the storage room to soften the cement floor and cover them. When they were settled in, Johnny went back up to the bar. Hailey handed him a few blankets and suggested that he and Esme sleep under the stage where the floorboards had plenty of give and space was plentiful.

"Hailey, if you don't mind, could we maybe have one whisky here at the bar, only one, I promise, and then we'll set off for home instead?" Johnny asked.

"You two can drink until you pass out, if you like. Lord knows you've earned it. And if you do pass out, you can count on me to drag you under the stage for the night. Otherwise leave when you like and take your chances on the streets, though I wouldn't advise it. You just don't know. Nowadays, bad passes for good. Satan and righteousness are on the same side."

"Maybe just one at the bar, with your blessing," Esme said.

"Take your seats, mates."

Hailey set two tumblers and a full bottle of poteen on the counter. He uncorked the bottle and filled their glasses. "Enjoy and keep in mind you are welcome to stay if, well, if you can't find your way to the door. I'm going to bed and see if I can somehow get this night out of my mind. Johnny, I imagine you'll have to find a new gang for the rum. Unless, that is, you might like to take a job here."

"A job here?"

"Working the counter and tables with Eoin and helping me mix now and again. I'll pay a little extra if you stay up late and help me count the daily take. Give it some thought."

"I will."

"Esme," Hailey said, taking a deep swallow from the bottle. "You might prefer Johnny waiting on customers stone-sober rather than trying to make sense of your songs when his brain's drenched." He closed his eyes. When the pain hit his midsection, he winced and moaned softly before going over to soften the rafter lights and head to the loft.

As the lights dimmed the silence deepened. A calmness settled around the bar. Esme's hazy mirror image appeared much closer than the distance to the glass. An unfamiliar closeness to her removed the vacancy and replaced it with something Johnny had trouble identifying. It seemed as though she and his own spirit had somehow joined together in the stillness.

Johnny glanced at her. "I, too, owe you for saving my life in the garden."

She smiled. "I believe your former friends, if you will, the bog-badgers, wherever they might be now, are the ones who really owe me a thank-you. From the look of things, if I hadn't shown up you'd have killed all three of them."

"It crossed my mind," Johnny said, smiling. "Oh, by the way, where's my gun?"

"You mean *my* gun. It's under my skirt in a holster fastened to the curve of my leg."

"I though you said you sold it."

She took a sip of poteen and smacked her lips. "That is what I said, but I lied. And come to think of it... come to think of it... I want to ask you something."

"Sure."

"Just now, outside. Something deep inside you burst forth and justice was done. When you hit that bastard, you got your satisfaction, did you not, for what they did to Joshua and were about to do to Dillon?"

Johnny felt every word. Without a doubt, the desire for revenge surfaced the moment he realized what the bastards had done. And he had to admit, when Seth's jaw cracked, it was a reward no money could buy.

"It is deep within me as well," she said, "though thankfully the door has opened,".

"I don't follow."

"Neither do I, at times."

With a questioning brow, she kept the glass close to her lips, considering yet another, but she set the glass down. Her image in the mirror gradually disappeared. She cleared her throat.

"Johnny, what I told you about the worst day in my life was true, every word. It was what I failed to tell you that wasn't. I not only lied about your gun but what I need it for. It isn't to sell, but to have my own revenge." She halted, staring at the mirror.

Again, it came to him she might be thinking of killing herself. Maybe the idea of being denied a normal woman's birthing life had overtaken her at last. Maybe it explained why she intervened so brazenly outside, that she no longer cared if she lived or died. But how in God's name could she possibly believe suicide would bring about revenge? Is that what Joshua had thought?

"Revenge of what sort? Against...?

She leaned toward him.

"No, please don't," he said, worried she was about to jerk the gun from her leg.

"No, don't what? No, I cannot kiss you?"

Surely, she was playing a joke. He guessed she would ask him to look into her eyes to follow the sun and moon, but her eyes were closed. He smelled her fragrance and felt her warm breath just before her lips touched his. She pressed against them but only slightly, yet enough for him to feel her heartbeat or was it his own? He moved closer, hoping her lips would part, and for the briefest moment they did, but only to whisper.

"Your eyes are full of surprise, Johnny. 'Twas but a tender kiss, to say I love you as an ally in things seldom understood by most — though I must confess it's hard for me to separate such a feeling from something more. But, as you know, I've been prevented from falling in love."

Johnny had no words.

"I read your concern about the gun. It was as clear as a telegram. Let me ease your worries with the truth. The pistol's not for me to kill myself, but so I can kill another. Revenge, Johnny, that's what I've been having the hardest time admitting to you. Time doesn't heal all wounds."

He could feel the hollowness in his chest and he waited, as one who has shouted inside a cave waits for an echo.

"I didn't mean to frighten you," Johnny."

"It was just the poteen rebounding," he said, not knowing what else to say.

Her hand followed the flow of her dress along the curve of her leg. He straightened when her fingers grasped the handle of the gun. "Remember Ina, the woman who took care of me?"

"Yes," he said watching her fingers tremble as she removed them from the gun and pressed them into her thigh.

"Yesterday I received a letter from her, several pages long. Ever since I came to America I've been waiting to hear from her. Waiting... for what she might find out. I never thought I'd see the day and tried to escape thinking about revenge by helping others. But fate stepped in yesterday, or perhaps Satan, and delivered her letter. It put me back on course."

"What did it say?"

"The only thing that could have truly answered my prayers. Soon after the War, the Tan who struck me and took his pleasure, settled in a small village by Kilkenny called Shonkine. After the Treaty, I guess the Brits wouldn't allow his crazy kind to return to England. The Brits hid their identities and lodged them in the villages where they became farmers and filled bodkins for the shops and fought each other in the pig troughs when insanity rang the bell. But that's only the beginning."

"How did Ina find out?"

"The bastard confessed."

"He gave himself up to the rebels?"

"No, to the British and the irony of all times, to God. His name is Owney McGrath, one lunatic Irishman of thousands sent to the Continent to serve the Brits, but after he showed himself for the bastard he really was, they refused to let him return and sent him back to Ireland to serve with the Tans. They wouldn't let him back after he bragged to them about the torture he'd put the rebels through. Apparently, the fool confessed everything he'd done, with the mistaken idea that the more he revealed, the more likely it was the Brits would bring him home, a hero.

"Among his trove of horror stories, he told them about the gun dance, admitting he'd struck a man's 'mad daughter' with the butt of his rifle when she attacked him, and fearing her madness, he searched every crevice of her body for a weapon. They agreed to give him a stipend to stay in Ireland, but only if he would confess his sins to a priest, ask forgiveness and promise thereafter to keep his mouth shut forever, or lose the stipend."

Esme looked at Johnny with glassy eyes. "Ina was called upon to hear the priest's confession where all was revealed."

"The *priest's* confession? You mean McGrath's."

"I mean the priest's. McGrath took the Brits up on the offer and went to the local priest, Father William, who heard the confession and having searched his soul, offered forgiveness, but soon thereafter, the Father was unable to forgive himself for having done so. Because he couldn't overcome his shame, he took it to mean he'd blasphemed against the will of God. According to the Bible, to do so is an unforgiveable, mortal sin. By way of contrition, the pastor decided that the only chance he had to earn The Divine's forgiveness was to wing his way to the gates of heaven and beg entrance."

Johnny listened in complete awe.

"In the letter, Ina admitted something I never knew or even suspected, that she and the priest had been 'close' at one time, so close that without the mercy of a visiting cardinal, Father William would have lost his cloth. That aside, he called Ina to give her his version of a confession. He said that he loved her and asked her to please forgive not only what he'd done but what he was about to do, then hung up the phone. She ran through town to the vestry, but it was too late. By the time she got there, he was having convulsions. Strychnine beans, 'poison from the well', as she described them, were scattered around him. Who knows how many he'd eaten, but certainly enough, for he died the moment she put her arms around him.

"She closed with this: 'I pray this letter makes the crossing and in time you will, as well.' "

"So, you plan to avenge the priest's death by killing McGrath?"

"No, I'm avenging my Da's death and what was done to me. I've lived for the day. I've put a shelter of kindness around me, so no one would ever suspect such a thing, and when done, I'll make no effort to hide it. I'll stand up and take full credit for putting a bullet in his head. If I'm sent to the gallows, so be it."

"You've never killed anyone, have you?"

"No, Johnny, of course not."

"I have. And let me warn you, as I tried to warn Seth, it will stay with you forever. There is no way to forget the face or the voice once you've pulled the trigger."

She focused her concentration on the glass. "I'll not want to forget. I will relish the memory of sending him to Hell on the throes of agony." Her eyes glittered as she raised her glass. "If God would allow me to watch McGrath burn in Hell, I'd be willing to become a believer."

For a moment Johnny felt he'd been brutally awakened to the real person she'd been all along. He'd been a fool to allow himself to be drawn to this, this what — this apparition he'd begun to believe in, this phantom who had appeared perhaps more in his mind than in the flesh. Who else but Esme would have blessed his own insanity, justified his craziness by saying that everyone, at one time or another, was mentally bereft and should be grateful for it? He gently touched the hand that crushed Seth's face. The bones crackled but there was no pain.

Esme's fingers followed his. "It's okay, Johnny."

He let his eyes close, wondering if her mind had been hyphenated, much like her body, into two differing but compatible halves. Even so, even in his doubting her, he tried to put his worries aside, hoping her fingers would urge him toward her, but they slipped away to grasp the bottle and lift it to her mouth. She wiped her lips. "You needn't be worried, my Irish mate. My purple partner here in the bottle is going to protect me by sleeping with me under the stage, assuming I can find it."

Johnny took her arm and walked her to the stage. The fragrance of her skin drifted through the dim lights. The faint shimmering found its way through her hair to brighten the figure eight on her breast.

She climbed under the blankets Hailey had laid there and looked up at Johnny with unease in her eyes. "There's room. Will you stay with me?"

Before he could reply, her head slumped onto a tuft of blanket and she lay still. He whispered that he would stay, but she didn't answer or move.

Chapter 30

Before he could lie down beside her, Johnny thought he heard a bagpipe in the distance but discounted it by telling himself it was a memory forever implanted in his head — Florence Begley, the unshakably brave piper who led the brigade into battle many times playing his pipes on the battlefield. His size is what many rebels believed brought an initial fear into the hearts of the enemy. A widely spread rumor that he had descended directly from Cuchulain magnified the fear. The rebels fanned the myth to the extent that even they began to wonder if it was true.

But now, here, in Hell's Kitchen, Johnny realized the distant sound of a bagpipe playing, "Once in David's Royal City", wasn't a memory. He listened as the beautiful notes of the Christmas song came forth as stirringly as those that had led him into battle:

Once in royal David's city
Stood a lowly cattle shed
Where a mother laid her baby
In a manger for His bed…

"Johnny? Johnny, what's that?" Dillon's voice penetrated the piper's notes.

Johnny climbed out from under the stage and looked down the staircase to find Dillon standing at the bottom in his thick coat and wooly pants. "Is your daddy awake?" he whispered.

"He's asleep," Dillon replied. "What's that music? It's really pretty."

"Shhhh," Johnny said putting a finger to his lips. Cautiously, he headed down the steps. "It's a bagpipe, lad. Let's get you upstairs so you can hear it better. Here, onto my shoulders."

When they reached the bar the pipes were even more distinct. "It's beautiful, Johnny. How do you play it?"

"By huffing and puffing, on what's called a blow-stick, into this thing that looks like a balloon. Then you finger the holes on the stick, sort of like playing a bunch of flutes at the same time."

"Can we go see?"

Johnny could hear Joshua snoring. "Okay, but we have to be quick about it. Wrap your arms around my neck."

"What in the world are you two doing?" Hailey stared at him from the doorway to his room hidden at the end of the bar.

Even in the dim light Johnny could see the concern on the old man's face. "Dillon's never heard pipes before. I'm going to take him out where he can hear them better. We'll be right back. If Joshua wakes up, let him know everything's fine."

They hurried, following the sound to the corner of the block where a large group of vagrants had filled the curbs with candles stuck into empty rum bottles. The piper wasn't dressed in a kilt but in brogans and a ripped leather jacket. His cheeks swelled with every breath.

When he finished the memorable song, a few clapped and several lit cigarettes in the tiny flames. The piper paused to gather his breath before launching into "Amazing Grace". When hymn began, Dillon straightened and pointed to a wooden crate leaning against a phone pole.

"Johnny, can you put me over there?"

"Okay, but we can't stay long," Johnny said and sat him on the curb behind the empty crate. Dillon turned the box upside-down and clutched narrow sides with his knees. His head perked up as he moved his stubs along the sides of the crate, while swishing his hands on the wood and clicking his fingers. A woman sitting next to him began to click hers and soon a dozen or so onlookers were clicking theirs. A black youngster rolled over a five-gallon keg he'd been sitting on and squeezed in next to Dillon. His hands tapped the wood, setting a slightly faster pace to the melody, and soon someone rolled an even larger keg over, turned its top to the sky and added a basso tone.

The sound of rain accompanied the piper. As he started to march in place, the background patter blended in more and more with every step he took. "Amazing Grace" came to an end but the sound of rain continued. The piper paused to listen. Some copied the hissing sound by whispering to themselves but whispering only one continuous word unbroken by another's breath.

The piper smiled and began to play "Love's Old Sweet Song", the hand-me-down Irish ballad Begley had played by the campfire after the battle of Bandon to ease the sadness while Johnny's brigade took note of the dead and waited for the missing to return home. Johnny listened as his comrades whispered the unforgettable words:

Tho' the heart be weary, sad the day and long,
Still to us at twilight comes Love's old song...

It was the day Nora disappeared from the front line to go to the aid of a group of elders hiding inside a shattered house. Johnny, unaware she'd left, thought for certain she'd been killed. As he searched for her among the bodies, she appeared from the far side of the road, gun in hand with her eyes gaping at the number of dead.

The song went on and on as though the piper was playing in synchrony with Johnny's memory. The beauty of the song's sadness caught in the air and failed to settle even when it was over. The applause lay in the reverence. No one got up to leave when the piper went over to Dillon. "Young man, you're made of music," he said.

It was as though Begley's voice had been delivered by time. Johnny suddenly realized the piper was Doolin, Father Doolin, the bone collector he'd met in the labyrinth. He smiled at Johnny and nodded.

Dillion reached out his hand. "I'm Dillon," he said happily.

The piper beamed and shook his hand. "Dillon, a pathfinder, what a perfect name for one who loves music. And indeed, you conducted a symphony before our very ears." He put his hand on Dillon's shoulder. "Music is how the Lord delivers hope. He has you on a mission, my son. By the way, my name is Doolin, not far from Dillon when you think about it."

Johnny stared at the piper. He listened to what had become a crowd of musicians as they started again, this time adding hums and clicks of their tongues and finger snaps to bring back the gentle sound of frogs, crickets and whippoorwills that Johnny had heard often heard in the glades and bogs of Fermoy. It blended into the hovering chill, warming him.

The piper glanced over Johnny's shoulder. "Are you his father?"

"No," Johnny replied.

"I'm his father."

"Daddy!" Dillon yelled.

Johnny turned to find Joshua a few feet behind him. The lump on his forehead pushed into the towel. It was now the size of a hurling ball, but the bleeding appeared to have stopped. "Hailey told me to follow the sound of the bagpipes," Joshua said.

"Your boy is an astounding lad," Doolin said. "And it's more than his musical talent, which inhabits every bone in his body. He has the gift of inspiration. I've seldom witnessed such a thing, not even in church." Doolin glanced at Dillon and the piper's voice began to crack. "He sits with an orange crate tucked between his short legs and smiles not only with his mouth but with his eyes as well and... and those sitting here... snarling and laughing at one another before he showed up were overcome by his goodness, as was I. Overcome to the point we were drawn into the assemble."

"I didn't realize... I don't what to say," Joshua muttered.

"Again. Do it again, child!" Someone called out.

With a wide smile on his face, Dillon looked at the piper. "Can we, can we do it again?"

"Marshal your sound, young fellow, and I'll join you in a moment." Doolin turned to Joshua. "He's been given a gift bestowed only by angels. I find it remindful of the Scottish Proverb: 'Be happy while you're living, for you're a longtime dead.'"

Johnny reached into his shirt pocket, took out the crossbones and handed them to Doolin. "The bones of twins taken from the hull of *The Pestilence*, the famine ship I came over on. They were wrapped in their mother's arms."

Doolin stared at the bones, brought them to his lips and kissed them. "My children," he said in a faint, grateful voice. "Their mother was no doubt my goddess." He tucked the bones into a small pocket on the bagpipe's strap and began to play beneath the hissing and swishing of hands.

Joshua leaned toward Johnny. "I could barely hear what he just said. A Scottish Proverb?"

"An old saying which has found its way through all of Wales and Ireland," Johnny replied. 'Be happy while you're living, for you're a longtime dead.'"

"Something I'll take with me," Joshua said.

Johnny wondered if Joshua had chosen the words by mistake or as a reminder to all, that despite what everyone had done to help change his mind — from Esme and her drums, to Hailey and the Indy, and to the piper's bestowal of a virtual awareness about Dillon's remarkable talent — it wasn't enough to overcome his need for revenge.

When the song ended, Joshua rushed over to pick up Dillon. They whirled, hugged and kissed amidst the ovation.

"It was the most fun I ever had, Daddy," Dillon said, clicking his fingers softly.

Chapter 31

Once back in the basement, Joshua tucked Dillon under the blankets, laid down and snuggled the boy to his chest.

"Thank you so much, Johnny," Dillon said.

"A hundred Irish Proverbs for what you done, mate," Joshua added.

"The two of you, together, made it what it was," Johnny said. "Sleep well."

At the top of the stairs he heard Esme's deep, sleep-filled breathing. The clock above the bar read two in the morning. He so wanted to tell her about Dillon and the piper but it would have to wait until morning. The bottle of poteen was still on the counter. He sat down and struggled with an urge to drink more. He slid the bottle toward the far edge of the counter. Still within arm's reach, it was tempting, but he forced himself off the stool and headed under the stage to get some sleep.

Despite the chill in the air, Esme had removed the blanket, taken off her clothes and lay sleeping naked on her side facing away from him. The soft Christmas lights made their way through the seams in the stage floor and hovered over her, creating, as he'd seen so often, a thin veil of rainbow mist. The glow penetrated the vapor and coated her skin with what appeared to be a faint silt. Faerie dust, she would no doubt say.

His eyes followed the shape of her body to her raised hip and down along her legs, both of which were wonderfully shaped but so unlike. Her arched left thigh still bore a faint imprint of the holster. The leg had the shape of a ballerina's while her right leg with its sculpted, olive-like calf resembled that of a trim Irish footballer. A host of words went through Johnny's head as he searched for a way to describe her: twins inseparable, a myth twice told, a gorgeous work of insanity? And having run the list, he had to admit she'd best described herself: an apparition, a specter as might be found in the village of Knockbridge by the stone of Cuchulain.

Drawn into the smell of lilacs, he leaned closer. He was tempted to touch her even if she might wake up and slap him across the face. It would be worth the price just to slip his hand into the vapor and barely touch her skin. Then, he realized he wasn't being honest with himself. In truth he wanted to feel her lips against his and taste her breath. It didn't have to be sensual or lead to anything more than a brief kiss. He only wanted to feel their softness so that he could always remember them.

And for the moment did it matter that she'd lied to him and was off on a mission that meant he'd never see her again? His fingers answered by softly brushing the chimera of dust from her cheek. He lingered to smooth the fine, illusory powder. Johnny jerked his hand away as she rolled slowly onto her back and the thin rays lit the image on her breast. As she raised an arm across her forehead, her lips moved.

"The mark of infinity, Johnny, touch it gently," she whispered.

As he reached toward the emblem his hand trembled. Fighting to steady it, he traced the figure's double loop around its edges. She sighed and he circled it again. He could see and feel her heart beat. Her nipples hardened like gemstones.

"Stroke my breasts," she murmured.

He ran his fingers over them, pinching her nipples tenderly. Her skin began to moisten and her hips started to rise and fall slowly. Routed by desire Johnny slid his hand down the shallow valley between her ribs. When he crossed her navel, she shuddered. He could feel her heart throbbing as his hand sank toward her hips. He hesitated. Then, unable to control himself, he let his fingers move slowly below her waist through the ridge of soft blond hair into the moisture between her legs, where he caressed her cautiously at first. The valley became wet, his touch fast and firm.

Suddenly, she gasped and convulsed as if she were coming apart. She shoved his hand away and grabbed the blanket to cover herself. Still shaking fiercely, she stretched the blanket tight under her quivering chin. Her frightened eyes stared at the slats.

Johnny didn't know what to say or do. Her eyes were aglow with tears. He wanted to console her and apologize. He slowly backed away onto his heels. "Esme, I'm so…"

She hushed him with a quick finger to her lips. "I heard the echoes of my mother's heart as she passed away, and I thought her womb was about to cave in on me." She wiped her eyes with the edge of the blanket. "It's my fault, Johnny, I'm sorry. I shouldn't have encouraged you. That was selfish, unfair of me, but as your hand moved between my legs, my birth overcame me. I've never had it happen before and dare say, it will never happen again."

"I'm the one to blame, not you. You were honest with me…. I was far out of line."

She let the blanket settle across her throat and smiled. "I was the one out of line, misaligned, if you will."

"Your body is stunning."

Her smile faded. "You are very kind. But on Sunday you will see the love of your life, a real person, not a ghastly, incapable mystic whose body cannot respond to her wants but only to the whims of fate. Your love for Nora is to honor born, for she rejected the command of fate. She refused the use of *might* to avenge her father's death."

He remained silent for a while. "But she will never forgive me."

"Don't be too sure. You can rest assured she's forgiven herself. She earned her own forgiveness by letting you live, and now she's free to forgive you as well."

Esme's comments gripped his heart. Had Nora's words on the Bluffs, those words slated to endure for a lifetime, faded from her memory, from her past forever and thus the forgotten had become the forgiven?

"Johnny?"

He wanted to ask Esme what she thought but couldn't bring himself to face the answer. "When are you leaving, lass?" he asked, awkwardly.

"Lass?" she said, grinning. "Were I but a lass! Were I, and you a lad on the fields of Inishmore searching for the likes of Cuchulain. If only we could choose one, just one time in our lives and start anew while knowing what we'd learned thereafter? But to your question, I'll be leaving in a fortnight. I wanted to go sooner but had to wait for a ship I could afford. Lars helped me get a room aboard The Holland Line. He's donating a bushel of clothes to the maids who work on board, so I got a ticket for free, though the ship goes straight to Rotterdam and from there I must find my way home."

"Suppose McGrath leaves before you make it back?"

"He's there forever. I sent a telegram to Ina to ask where he was. She replied that his entire being is tethered to the memory of the priest. He sleeps by the Father's grave unaware his confession was rebuked. Let us say he sleeps on hollow ground."

Johnny tried to control his impulse but fate got the better of him. "Esme, would you go with me? To St. Brigid's to hear Nora speak?"

Her eyes widened. "I'm not going to ask why in heaven's name you would want me there. A port in the storm, perhaps? You really want to see the love of your life while accompanied by an apparition?" She paused, returning his stare. He thought the silence would never end.

"All right, Johnny, for all you've done for me I'll go," she answered, at last. "But Nora mustn't know we're together. That would be wrong for both of you. Now, find your way home. If ever anyone's earned a good night's sleep, 'tis you. I hope you can make it to The Woebegone Wednesday. Earlier in the day I have to try on the clothes Lars is donating for my journey and put them out for sale, but eventually I'll be there, with rags on."

She leaned over and kissed him on the cheek. It was a peck of forgiveness, he hoped, assuring him that he'd done nothing wrong.

"Will you be talking with Joshua?"

"There's nothing more I can do, except call the police. I've thought about it many times, but forcing him to stay by having him thrown in jail would be about as bad as letting him have his way."

"But there's more," he said.

"What do you mean?"

Johnny told her about Dillon and the piper. Her eyes were full of delight, until he came to Joshua's curious follow-up to the Scottish warning to be happy while we're here because we'll be a long time dead.

"Something I'll take it with me? That's what he said?" She replied. "Well, Johnny, that most likely doesn't mean what you're thinking, that he was trying to end the conversation with a token, *thank you, but no thank you,* or with a gratuitous comment, or even being sarcastic. He may have truly taken the proverb to heart."

"I have to make sure. Where's the pool hall located?"

"Johnny, no. You're way out on a limb. There's nothing you can do to make sure. All that can be done, has been done. Let it be. Please." Her stare was laden with rebuke, but her voice was tinged with understanding. "Blimey's on West Forty-third," she said. "Upstairs, behind the Elk's Lodge."

Chapter 32

Johnny set out for his apartment with the unending fog still blurring the streets. There were no signs of morning, no sight of the setting moon or the rising sun. The intersection where the piper played was barren except for an empty horse wagon and a police car with its hood smashed against a telephone pole. Johnny could make out the rails and smell the faint smoke the fast train had left in the air.

The sound of a foghorn summoned Nora's image, but it sank into the second call of the horn. For the first time, the memory failed to leave him feeling alone and deserted. Instead, he felt an odd sense of release as hope settled in his heart. He would see her on Sunday. No matter the size of the crowd or how far from the podium he sat, they would be together again, if only for the moment.

The thought captivated him, until Esme's fragrance, still in his clothes, seeped into the air around him creating a cavern so deep he couldn't feel the street beneath him. He became dizzy as he remembered touching her and caressing her dimly lit body. He'd wanted to make love to her but had known it was forbidden, as for the longest time it had been with Nora. And then it happened: in the loft of the barn her body had shuddered in that pinnacle moment when no other thought or sensation can intervene to stop or delay it. And more, that day in the woods, how she'd practically demanded it without stopping, until she scraped his butt rare against the tree and exhausted them both.

A gunshot. The bullet whistled through the air. Johnny ducked, staring around the corner. At first, he thought the Angels might be seeking revenge for pummeling Seth. Thoughts of Seth gave way to Dillon, who within an hour of their bullying brought joy to a group of street people poorer than the boy's own father. They'd borrowed from Dillon's spirit, singing and swaying in the magic of his talent. He'd stepped into the certainty of the unseen, the generosity of the unknown, the aura of the Angels lamp, giving him courage to walk into the darkness. He'd ventured far beyond the moment, paying no attention to what they'd done to him in the South.

Had Joshua seen into his son's new world or was he still determined to go back and kill the judge? Esme had let the worry go, but Johnny could not.

He stopped outside his flat. After a moment to catch his breath, he mounted the stairs, telling himself that Joshua's plight could not be left to fate, for fate had no mercy. Had Joshua really changed? Johnny could not sit by and wait for destiny to answer.

Chapter 33

Hailey moved fast, immediately ousting the Swamp Angels and arranging for the speakeasy to be protected by Five Points, the new and ferocious Italian gang now determined to take over Hell's Kitchen. Before Johnny showed up for work the next day, the gang had delivered its array of Italian liquors and demonstrated how the drinks were to be mixed. They'd brought glasses to replace tumblers. Gin and vodka were poured instead of rum and poteen. All sorts of sweet mixers waited behind the counter to flavor the minty drinks. As partial repayment for Hailey's willingness to replace the Angels with Five Points and have the Italian members deliver his whiskey, the capos agreed to station two armed guards outside the garden door. They were ordered to kill any and all identifiable Angels.

Lucky Luciano, the grizzled, yet young capo who governed the eastern part of the Kitchen, came by later in the day to explain everything to Hailey, Eoin, and Johnny. With a thick Italian accent and a suspicious tone of friendship, he told them how the Italian vagrants, comprised largely of immigrants from lower Europe, had seen tremendous opportunity with the onset of Prohibition and thus, had recently united behind the Mafia. Once a member, there was no turning back, short of death, the capo explained, an admonition that reminded Johnny of Joshua's drunken conversation with Esme when he revealed his plans.

Luciano had given Hailey a list titled, "Fees for Services Offered", which included five dollars to beat up a person, ten to break a leg or arm, thirty to torture an unfaithful husband or forty-five to kill him. Rumors had it that Five

Points required only a finger pointed by a capo and the item was quickly seen to. Their brutality exceeded even that of the Gophers, he bragged.

Because of the change in whiskeys, Hailey reluctantly moved away from Irish brew to bathtub gin and rum, though he whispered to Johnny that he need not worry because he'd hidden a ten-gallon keg of poteen in the mixing room. They had to learn to mix flavored drinks with weird names like Bees Knees and Dubonnets. There was even one called a Fallen Angel. Johnny liked the sound of that one.

While the drinks changed every day, the patrons did not, though they began to arrive earlier than before. Hailey encouraged Johnny and Eoin to mingle with them and talk up the new drinks. The patrons were ecstatic, especially the women, many of whom had had their fill of rum, ale and an occasional tumbler of poteen. The goblets changed from tumblers to dainty V-shaped glasses and the contents became colorful. Everyone was thrilled with the new additions, even though, Johnny and Eoin, while always rushed and confused, often mixed the wrong ingredients. They overloaded the alcohol, especially crème-de-menthe which they'd never offered as it was too soft a booze for the Irish patrons. With the Fallen Angel it was mandatory to get the minty flavor just right. When the mix was off, the mint was heavily overcome with the pure taste of gin, but no one complained. Infatuated with the drink's name, the guests toasted one another with the elegant glasses, holding them high and shouting for more when they ran dry.

Johnny watched the numbers swell overnight. After the first night's offering, the word of the new drinks had spread alarmingly fast. The regulars brought their friends, and they brought their friends as well. After eight o'clock, patrons could barely get in the door. Hailey had to open the basement where he placed an extra speaker. The music bopped up the steps creating an extra vibration in the dance floor. Women and men alike took off their shoes to enjoy the tingle.

Despite the later closings, Johnny enjoyed the crowds. They tipped well, often shoving dollars into his shirt pocket. In fragments of relief during the unforgiving pace, he thought about Nora. How would she respond when their eyes met? Would she stare in disbelief and forget her next line, or would she simply continue, pretending he wasn't there? Oddly, while the choices were a source of anxiety, they possessed a weird sense of excitement. Johnny realized that hope most often outweighed reality, but told himself things could be different this time.

And yet, despite the anticipation of seeing her, the enjoyment of his new job and the strange but unforgettable night with Esme, he couldn't put aside what he'd become convinced of, that Joshua had not changed his mind. By Wednesday the worry had besieged him. He asked Hailey if he could leave in the late afternoon and possibly skip work that night to spend time at The Woebegone. But his plan was not to go near The Woebegone. It was to go to Blimey's.

"Eoin and I'll survive as long as we don't have a heart attack," Hailey said. "Please give Esme a hug for me."

"Maybe I can make it back by nine or so, depending."

"Not to worry, lad. You bring light to her face. Now get!"

Johnny passed between the two Italian guards and quickened his pace. He thought about taking the new train to Forty-third, but he couldn't bear the idea of sitting down when every nerve in his body demanded he stay on the move. He walked and ran, driven by sudden jolts of fear, warning him that he could be on the verge of making a costly mistake.

Half-way up the front steps of The Lodge, he encountered a huge steel elk standing guard. In keeping with the holiday spirit, someone had painted its penis, antlers, and lips bright red. Undaunted, Johnny climbed the dingy stairwell to the pool hall, its walls lined with pictures of Yankee, Dodger and Giant stars. Each plate of glass had been smudged by years of cigarette smoke and fingerprints. Red and yellow lights creeping through the crinkled glass door at the top of the stairs coaxed the players' faces from the shadows. He came across an autographed photograph of Lefty O'Doul. The player's eerie, smiling eyes appeared to follow him up the steps.

The door opened on its own, inviting Johnny into a crowded room of pool tables, players and the clatter of billiard balls incessantly striking one another. Ragtime jazz came from a glowing Wurlitzer whose thick, arch-like structure was framed by bands of fading, and slowly recovering, yellow and red lights, reminding him of the windows at St. Brigid's.

Though pool tables filled the room, his attention was drawn to the center table where the players stood leaning on their cues watching a crimped old man struggle to chalk his cue tip. The man was scraggy, unshaven and as contorted as a skeleton on *The Pestilence*. He leaned over the edge of the table and took a rapid series of shots, leaving the table empty. When he finished the round, he took a swig from a bottle of ale, lit a cigarette and glanced fiercely around the room. At last his eyes settled.

"Get over here and rack the goddamn balls, boy!" he shouted. "This here's your table!"

Joshua rushed out to the table from deep in the room. "Sorry, Boolean," he said, frantically digging balls out of the pockets and setting them in the rack. He rearranged them until they were in order and slid the rack to the far end of the table. He positioned the rack carefully and stood back for the break.

Boolean bent over the far end of the table. Setting the cue in the wedge between his thumb and index finger, he took aim but suddenly paused to glare at Joshua. "Get away from the table, you fucking wildebeest! I can't shoot with your black-ass shadow hiding the balls!"

Johnny felt his pulse quicken as Joshua headed toward a bench by the door. "Joshua?" he called.

Joshua's eyes lit up in surprise. "Over here," he mimed, waving excitedly.

Johnny hurried over and sat down beside him. "Who's that asshole?" he asked, nodding toward the table.

"Boolean Spoil, or that's what he goes by. He took five bullets outside Paris and wouldn't let no doctors take them out because he believed that suffering through the pain was his best way of getting back at the Germans. Every time he moves he grimaces. Story has it he recuperated hobbling around a pool table in the psychiatric ward of a veteran's hospital. He mustered out of the Army a pool sharp and a crazed dope-head."

"How do you put up with him?"

"I got no choice. Anything short of doing what he says and I'll lose my job. It's all I got right now. It supports me and Dillon just barely."

"Where is Dillon?"

"Blimey lets me keep him in the back room along with the Indy. It's safe and quiet so he can do his homework and we don't have to worry about the Indy getting stolen. Sometimes Blimey helps him do his arithmetic. It took me a while to figure out the numbers on pool balls, much less add them up, but Blimey can multiply and divide."

"They say music and numbers go together."

"I knew Dillon was good at music. I just didn't know how good until the other night. The piper put it better than I ever realized. 'Remember the gift, the gift of giving,' he told Dillon. You could feel it at that intersection." Joshua's eyes turned toward the table. "They're having trouble sinking the balls, all except Boolean. Too much whisky, except for him. Gives me a minute longer. By the way, Johnny, what in the world are you doing here?"

"I wanted to ask you something, something… that has to do with Dillon."

"The boy loves you, Johnny." Joshua looked at Johnny. "Thank you for taking him to hear the piper. I never knew the things he told us. I never had the brain or wherever that kind of understanding comes from. I've never been able to get past my hatred for what that fucking judge did. If that piece of dirt walked through the door right now, I'd kill him." Joshua's hands clinched. "Sorry, Johnny, I know you didn't come all the way here to listen to my troubles."

"That *is* why I came."

"Well, now you know, my heart's full of hate." He glanced at the table again. "Seven balls left on the felt, with Boolean's turn coming up. Just enough time to go get our boy. Hold on."

Johnny watched as Boolean began to run the table. After each shot when he straightened, he grimaced in pain but smiled. Between shots he drank from his tumbler, laughed at the other players and warned them he was about to start collecting his bets. Just as the game ended, Joshua came rushing out of the back room with a delighted Dillon on his shoulders.

"Joshua!" Boolean yelled, slurring. "Get your black ass out of the slums of Jericho and set us up!"

Joshua cut to the table with Dillon. In one motion, he sat Dillon on the far end, spread the boy's thighs, grabbed the rack and slid it between them.

Boolean yelled and pointed his cue at Dillon. "Get him the fuck off the table before them nubs rip the felt to shreds!"

"Sir, he knows how to rack and his nubs are covered," Joshua said. "They won't scratch a thing. Be done in a second." In a frenzy Joshua fished the balls out of every pocket and rolled them to Dillon who set them in the rack so fast his hands were a blur. When the rack was full, Dillon looked at Boolean with pride in his eyes. Bending awkwardly, Boolean placed one hand on the felt and stared at the rack.

"You dumb monkey!" he barked. "The five and twelve balls are supposed to be in the corners!" He lurched around the corner of the table and rammed Joshua into the crowd

Boolean's astonished eyes fastened on Dillon "You were thinking what a no-good cripple I am, weren't you? That's why you messed up the rack. I saw it in your eyes, but you was afraid to say it. That makes you a coward, a god-damn lying coward as dumb as Daddy Trash over there. He weren't in the War for a minute." Boolean jerked his stick into the air.

Johnny bolted off the bench toward Dillon. "Duck!" he screamed.

The cue cut through the lights but unexpectedly stopped on the way down. Johnny looked to see Joshua towering over Boolean with the cue in his huge hand. He'd caught it in mid-air

"You crazy fuck!" Joshua shouted.

Boolean's eyes hardened in terror as Joshua yanked the cue over his head.

"No, Daddy!" Dillon yelled.

Joshua glanced at him.

"He's a cripple like me, Daddy! God won't forgive you!"

Joshua hesitated, then hurled the cue the length of the room and jerked Boolean upright. His crazed face was frozen in so much pain Johnny wondered if the bullets inside him had dislodged.

Johnny seized Joshua. "Let him go! You paid him back! Look at him, trembling like the coward he is, in plain sight of his mates. You needn't do more."

Joshua shoved Boolean toward the Wurlitzer. "If I ever see you in here again or anywhere for that matter, I'll rip those bullets out, load a gun and shoot them right up your ass!"

Boolean's legs wobbled and he sank to the floor. No one moved as he fought to his knees and started to crawl toward the door. All of a sudden, his arms gave way and his face smacked the floor.

"Somebody help him!"

"He ain't our friend, mister," said a man drenched in sweat. "He ain't nobody's friend. He got what he's been deserving for a long time."

Johnny had no idea why, but he went over to Boolean and tried to raise him. Boolean cringed. Johnny could feel the nuggets in his shoulders. Trying to lift him alone would make things worse. And then to his surprise, Joshua came to his side with Dillion on his shoulders. "I'm gonna sit you by the Wurlitzer. "Be back in a second."

"Where're you going, daddy?"

"Ahh, just to help this old fellow get moving."

They dragged Boolean to the door and forced him to his feet. He stared at Joshua. His eyes were stained with rivulets of blood.

"Weren't your dick big enough to make a baby with legs?" he said.

Johnny wanted to kick the bastard down the stairs. Joshua looked at him as if to ask if he could have the first blow. Johnny nodded at the stairway. They smiled oddly at one another and lugged him down the steps.

Outside, they straightened him up against the building. He shifted from side-to-side, moaning as the slugs scraped the bricks.

"My name ain't Boolean. It's Judas," he said, looking toward the sky. "I sold my soul for thirty pieces of silver and God planted them in my back and shoulders to get His revenge. When they cause me pain, I feel like I'm returning the favor. Now, get out of my sight."

Johnny and Joshua looked at each other as Boolean grabbed at one of his shoulders and grimaced.

"Let's let him go," Johnny said. "He's already bought himself a one-way ticket to Hell."

"As did Judas," Joshua replied, releasing him to lurch awkwardly toward the street.

Back in the pool hall, Dillon was huddled against the wall beside the Wurlitzer. Joshua picked him up and brought him to his chest. "I didn't mean to leave you, son. I love you."

"You didn't leave me. You wouldn't ever leave me, Daddy. I love you, too and I love you, Johnny."

Those words, spoken once again, the pledge they carried, the promise, the same immortal tone, the same vibrancy of eternity, but this time with a greater assurance of trust than Johnny had ever heard.

"Where's Mister Blimey, son? With all the commotion, you think he'd be out here."

"He went to get some more paint for the elk. He says it helps bring in the customers."

Slowly the chatter of the players and the clatter of striking balls reclaimed the room. Cheers for sunken shots gradually began to resonate around them.

"What are we going to do tomorrow, Daddy?"

"Tomorrow started a few minutes ago, son."

The words hovered around Johnny, threaded in the noise. He thought knew what lay beneath what he'd just heard.

The Wurlitzer joined in with Jelly Roll Morten playing the piano and singing in celebration. The piano accompanying his basso voice turned the song into a fairytale. Dillon tucked down into Joshua's arms and closed his eyes.

"Judas, if that be Boolean's real name, couldn't leave his past behind, could he, Johnny?" Joshua said. "It finally caught up with him."

"Revenge in a coffin. Sacrifice for a purpose less than himself," Johnny added.

"Short time alive, long time dead. You never realize what you have until you've destroyed it... or left it behind," Joshua said, kissing Dillon's forehead.

The room wasn't silent, but it was. Words so soulfully spoken, as if channeled from the battlefield mates Johnny had known who, after an attack, were forced to look back on their obliterated home town.

"My love for this one," Joshua said rubbing Dillon's forehead. "Until tonight, I never realized what I had. I should have known when the piper told me. I should have listened and believed. I only paid lip service to what he said. This boy knows far more than I do. He's taught me what love means." He looked at Johnny. "Have you ever lost someone you loved?"

"Yes," he said and paused, "a woman I fell in love with..."

"Did she leave you?"

"She did, or maybe it's more honest to say, I left her."

"I can't do that to Dillon."

"Were you planning to?" Johnny said, forging the question.

"Johnny, you know the answer. It's why you came here, isn't it? I know that now but an hour ago I had no idea." Joshua raised Dillon and hugged him as the boy's head slowly slipped to his shoulder. "I will never leave you again, never."

Johnny listened to Dillon breathe, watched the men moving around the tables, heard an opening break and another, shouts of victory and none of failure.

"We'll see you at The Woebegone tomorrow night," Joshua said.

This time there was no doubt in Johnny's mind that father and son would both be there.

Chapter 34

The unending mist still blurred the buildings, covering them in pallid shadows. At the intersection where Dillon and the piper had played, the orange crate was still on the curb waiting for Dillon to return.

A feeling of calm came over Johnny, a sense of peace which felt more than fleeting. The crazed Boolean had steered Joshua down his tortured road to Malville where he'd discovered, hidden like a buried treasure, what he'd come so close to losing. And he'd returned. The irony struck Johnny with its purity and simplicity. He hurried across the street down Death Avenue, walking away from the train tracks to avoid stumbling over those sleeping there. The smell of coal from the last train hung in the air as did the sweet smell of horseshit left by the Dusters.

He heard the familiar sound of a foghorn in the distance and found it strangely comforting, unlike the foghorn he'd heard while on the bluffs of Kinsale moments after Nora rode off. For the first time, the memory failed to leave him despondent and deserted. Instead of melancholy, hope swelled in his chest. He walked faster, as though the street led directly to St. Brigid's.

He wanted to shout, to thank God or whoever deserved the credit, for Nora's presence and the gift from the High Court. On Sunday she would be here, the two of them together, if only at a distance in the church's nave. Then he remembered that he'd asked Esme to go with him. What had he been thinking? And as if irony were suddenly on a mission to occupy his thoughts, he remembered the shock in Seth's eyes as Esme, gun in hand, sliced through the beams of garden light, in essence saving his life and rescuing Dillion.

It took a moment to realize he'd arrived at his apartment. Looking forward to a glass of poteen, but swearing he would limit his take to only one, he mounted the stairs, unlocked the door and rushed into the room. He swilled quickly from the bottle, washed himself, set the bottle on the table beside him and climbed into bed. Telling himself he'd not quite swilled the equivalent of a full glass, he took another swallow and lay back to wait for the burning to fade. And then took another, and another, with the knowingly false notion that each swallow would shorten the burn of the one just before.

Unrecognizable images, like those scribbled on the piers and street corners, passed through his vision. An imagined moon replaced the sun in a valley of velvety, wet grass where Nora lay nude and stretched out, her body framed by the softness of the meadow. He started toward her but halted when Esme stepped into the dream and lay down next to her. Their bodies merged as they had behind the counter at Rags-to-Riches. He heard the sound of rain in the distance and recognized Dillon's strokes upon the coconuts and his clicking, swishing fingers. As Nora and Esme's sparkling eyes became a pair, the aura it cast widened from the corners into their hair.

"Johnny, come join us."

The dual melodic voices echoed off one another and then faded. The vacancy repeated the request for Johnny to join them as their voices rose in virtual harmony. He wanted to comply with their wish but without warning, found himself shoulder deep in vines and flora, stroking his way across the rise of Esme's hip onto the plateau of Nora's tight waist. There, the black and blonde colors that dovetailed between their legs blended into a dark green thatch of tall and tightly woven shamrocks. Esme's fragrance flowed from the growth, deluging him as he fought through the brush. The flora parted and he found himself watching their conjoined breasts swell stretching the sign of infinity into circles floating, one about the other. As their glittering green eyes scanned his body they came to rest between his legs, and despite the poteen he could feel his penis stiffening.

"Forced to choose, which of us would you grant the pleasure?" she, they, asked in a voice so mischievous he sensed that their real intent had nothing to do with how he answered.

"Both," he replied. "I would choose both of you."

Inseparable, they sat up. "Only one. You may choose only one."

Fingers reached out to unbuckle his pants. They dropped to his ankles. The soft silky hand stroked him. "Make your choice, or we stop."

He stammered until, unable to hold it in, his voice broke out, "Esme!"

He lurched forward into the alarming echo of his choice. When the climax began to roll over him, he grabbed for the figure's shoulders, but his hands sank into its vagueness and grabbed his manhood. Groaning, shuddering and thrusting his hips so fiercely the bed rattled, he awoke startled, his heart throbbing and in disbelief. As his body sank into the mattress he could feel the wet splotches of semen below his hips.

"I'm sorry," he said, hoping that one of them or the other or both could hear him. "Forgive me." Instantly, he knew he was speaking to Nora. Ashamed of betraying her, if only in what he now realized had been a convoluted dream, he stumbled to the basin wondering if he'd inherited his father's lustful ways. "Not a speck above an anthill am I," the old man was fond of saying when in his cups.

Johnny sank back into the bed. Neither Nora nor Esme returned, leaving only the image of Cuchulain, the irrepressible hero, perched above The Raven's door.

Chapter 35

The next evening at The Woebegone, Johnny couldn't find Joshua or Dillon. The sage had not settled or even thinned but hovered thick as a cloud. He thought maybe they were hidden in the mist. He could feel the crowd's warmth and the excitement in the muted voices. The stage seemed like a faraway island. He wished he were closer but he'd arrived a few minutes late. Esme always started on time and he wondered what could be holding her up. A host of things, he assumed, maybe from deciding on the right dress to having a bit too much poteen.

He waited, hoping the mist would thin before she came on stage. The large minute hand on the huge wall clock skipped past the half hour mark and he began to worry. The clock continued clicking, reminding him of the clock over the door in Kilmainham that led to the Stonebreaker's Yard. As each of the signatories stood waiting for the door to open, they could not take their eyes off the minute hand. They often trembled and even more so as the appointed time approached.

By the time the memory dissolved, the mist had thinned somewhat, and to Johnny's relief and joy, he recognized Joshua and Dillon side-by-side on the edge of the stage. Johnny lifted his eyes to the ceiling and whispered, "Thank You." To whom he wasn't sure, but there were times when thanks simply had to be given, if only into the air.

The patrons' anxious voices accompanied their eyes around the room as though expecting Esme to appear magically in an aisle. Heads turned Johnny's way, maybe suspecting a surprise entrance from the rear of the theater. Just when he was about to look for one of the staff to ask if they knew why she was so late, she walked onto stage dressed in a dark blue, knee-length coat. Her hair was spread away from her face and fell in long curls over her shoulders. Joshua had been keeping the mike and handed it to Dillon to give to her. Esme bent over, took the mike and kissed him on the cheek.

"I love you," she stuttered into the mike. The words traveled around the room, echoing in tiny waves as though seeking out those who would be most touched. Silence set in, only to deepen as she approached the audience.

"I have something to tell you," she said softly. Beneath her voice lay an unmistakable tone of sadness. Johnny braced.

"Tonight will be my last performance, as I will be leaving America next Wednesday to return to Ireland where an ongoing family matter has summoned me home, so tonight... tonight I am saying goodbye. Someday I hope to return to you, for I have never been in the presence of such caring and deserving people. Please bear with me for a moment while I try to recover my regretful voice." She coughed as sadness gripped the audience.

The mike shook in her fingers. She clutched it with both hands, glanced at the rafters and gradually pulled herself together to begin her favorite, "The Wexford Carol". At first her voice refused to co-operate, emerging in a low, struggling timbre. She wobbled in her gold, high-laced shoes and for a second Johnny tensed, but a verse into the carol and she steadied, as did her voice. Johnny knew the song well, for he'd sung it as a child in church with his mother.

Esme paused just before the last verse ended and in a wrought but flowing voice, she repeated it, in tears, just before the words ran out.

Near Bethlehem did shepherds keep
Their flocks of lambs and feeding sheep;
To whom God's angels did appear,
Which put the shepherds in great fear.
'Prepare and go,' the angels said...

Her voice faded. An embarrassing hush prevailed, until Dillon started to clap hard and loud. The sound ran like a bolt of electricity throughout the room. The vibrations seemed to lift Esme's shoulders. She removed the coat to reveal a shimmering emerald-green flapper dress that fell only to her knees. Dropping the coat to the floor, she blew a thankful kiss to the audience and began to sing, "All I Want for Christmas." A beat of happiness infected the patrons and they, too, overcame their sadness and began to sing and clap.

When the song came to a close, she waved to Johnny while the patrons roared for more. She bowed in an attempt to free herself, but they wouldn't let her go. Johnny had heard her thunderous ovations before but none like this. People yelled and came to their feet and knocked into one another trying to get to the stage. As "O Holy Night" filled the room, they stopped. She hit notes so increasingly high that Johnny shivered.

He expected the room to break out into hysteria as she lowered the mike, but the theater fell quiet in a way that seemed to show more appreciation than the applause. A flock of children ran to throw their arms around her and cling to her as their parents hurried to pry them away. Engulfed by the children she couldn't move. Eventually, they loosened their grips so others could make their way to her.

The crowd dispersed, slowly backing away from the stage. The room cleared with their blessings and begging for her to come back soon. The congregation bunched together at the door, nudging and scuffling to stay for a last word of goodbye before they left. Johnny sat at an empty table and watched, no longer wondering why he'd asked her to accompany him to St. Brigid's.

Esme stood alone on the stage stuck in a bow of gratitude as Joshua and Dillon made their way up the aisle. When they stopped to say goodnight to Johnny, Dillon looked over his father's shoulder. "I don't want her to go, Daddy."

"Nobody does, son. She's blessed all of us with her gifts. Like you, my boy, she's been blessed by God."

"Do you think God knows she's leaving?" Dillon asked. "Maybe if we go home and pray, He'll let her stay."

Joshua smiled. "What do you think, Johnny?"

"I think maybe He's made up His mind."

"When's she getting down off the stage, Daddy? She looks frozen up there. I love you, Esme!" Dillon shouted.

"That's enough, son. It's time for us to go. There's no more *good* in good-bye." He looked down, shaking his head slowly but with a smile. "Bless you, Johnny. What you did for us... I'll never be able to thank you..."

"You already have, Joshua, but it's you, the father, who deserves the thanks."

"Thank you, Daddy."

"For what, son?"

"For never leaving me."

Johnny could feel Joshua trying to get his mind and heart around what Dillon just said. He knew the question of coincidence versus heavenly intervention had to be spinning through his head. Had Dillon somehow known what his father had intended to do? Or was the coincidence due to fate knowing that today's appearance of goodness would be used to pave the way for much worse to come, regardless of every indication otherwise?

The answer came from Joshua's bloodshot eyes as he hugged Dillon and glanced toward Esme with a smile of discovery on his face. His eyes held no questions or accusations, no skepticism, distrust or blame. Huge tears tumbled from his eyes. His broad mouth tried to smile but gave way to gratefulness as he again whispered a silent, "*Bless you*" to Johnny.

Johnny watched the doors close behind them. In the midst of it all he'd lost track of Esme who was standing at the end of row looking at the door.

"Thank Goodness, they were here tonight," she said. "I wish they hadn't left. I wanted to take Joshua aside and ask him again, as you suggested, but I...

"I've got something to tell you that should ease your worry."

She sat down and he next to her. As he told her what happened at Blimey's, she clasped her hands, staring at him, astonished.

"He's not going back," she whispered, the relief in her breath so intense the words seemed more a part of her soul than her vocal chords. "Why didn't you tell me sooner?"

"I wanted to wait until tonight to make sure. If they hadn't come tonight... but now we can rest assured."

She pulled up her short skirt and slipped the flask from its holster. "I could use a little of this right now." She took off the cap, lifted the flask toward the stage and handed it to Johnny.

"I, like you, could certainly use some but I'm fine for now," he said

"It's become a staple for me and a bit less for you, hasn't it, like milk for a child," she said. "I don't know what I'll do without it, but I realize I'd better cut back if I want to keep my aim straight." She took the flask and fastened the cap.

He waited for her to say something more but understood why she stayed silent. A warm sense of understanding gathered around him, and he was sure around her as well. They both accepted; they both trusted more than that — they knew Joshua's change was for real.

Johnny nodded at his intuition alone. Esme was nodding to herself as well.

"Have you gathered enough used clothes for the trip?" he asked.

"I believe it's spelled out in Luke, to wit, 'One shall spend no time gathering clothes when the church bell chimes.' Thus, today I went to church instead, to St. Brigid's."

"You went to St. Brigid's?"

"I was drawn there early in the morning, less by the chimes than by the need for likeness. One apparition drawn to another I guess you could say. We specters have it in common, you know, a sense that when we're apart we must seek one another's soul."

"Did you see the priestess or abbess, St. Brigid, as she was christened or benighted or whatever word she used?"

"Aye, I did. Bestowed is the word. She told me how she was visited by the original St. Brigid at the Church of Kildare during the Feast of Imbolcs while she sat the Flame. She said my mother's spirit was present that very night. She was enthralled by its presence. As it turns out, mother told me many times about the miracles the abbess performed, how she healed a leper and halted the wind and rain in their tracks, but I had no idea.... You're smiling," Esme paused. "The other night at the beach I showed you the sun and moon in my eyes. You seemed bewildered. Did you think it was a magician's trick, some sleight of hand?"

He searched for a way to answer. "No, I was bewildered. I wanted it to be real."

She reached across the table and placed a hand on his. "It was real. And if you doubt me, I take responsibility for your skepticism, for I have lived and told a swirl of lies while in America. My stories got me through Ellis, gave me safety, a hideaway to await my calling. It kept me hidden and protected from men. Lying never failed to give me solace, until I met you."

"I'm sorry... what did I do to change it?"

"It's not what you did. It's what you encouraged me to do. I didn't realize it, until St. Brigid helped me understand. 'God speaks to us through what we have learned,' she said, and this is what I've learned, be it God or the faeries speaking: trust is the one thing love can't exist without. As strange as it was, I trusted you since the first time we met and do this very minute. The sties in your eyes. When I touched them, they opened just long enough for me to see inside your true being. When I washed the blood from your chest and felt the cross in your pocket, it came over me in the next breath. I'd never trusted any-one before. Until that night at Hailey's, I'd never realized that I needed some-one I could trust, and unfortunately for you, you were chosen."

"Didn't it cause you to wonder, when I told you how I'd so much as lied to Nora by hiding that I'd served on the firing squad."

"I have lied to you in the very same way. And before I leave, I must confess." She handed him the flask and looked at him nervously.

"It's all right," he said. "You can trust me." He cringed, hoping she didn't think he was making fun of her.

Instead, her eyes streamed with appreciation. "What I told you about my being raped was true, but what I told you about what followed wasn't. My womanhood wasn't destroyed, though I've kept it at bay ever since. I've strangled every urge that has come to me because I feared any such feelings might lead to falling in love with someone, thereby disabling any chance to get my revenge. Not only did I turn from men but from myself as well, rejecting any and every impulse, keeping my hands in chains lest they create a desire that would rule me. I feared that if I committed one mistake that my life's mission would be over."

Johnny reached out to brush her worried face.

"Like a nun, I refused to surrender to my body's call. Until the other night under the stage when your fingers moved between my legs. I could not stop the shudder. It spread over my entire body. I felt like I was coming apart. I wanted you inside me so badly I almost cried out for you to possess me, and then fate double-backed, reminding me that Nora is the true love of your life... and afterwards... when you'd left, I realized fate had done me a huge favor. I'm happy knowing you are in love with her, for now I can share what I've been withholding, knowing there is nothing to fear, for I have forgiven myself, not only for the lies but for the truth I've withheld from you and from myself."

"Miss Esme?"

Esme flinched. A tall, wiry man resembling a grouse leaned over the railing. He wore a pair of glasses with only one lens. "My God you scared us, Stephan," she said. "I thought you were back stage with the staff."

"Sorry ma'am, I didn't mean to frighten you but I just wanted to ask if there's any chance you'll ever come back?"

She glanced at Johnny with a near-leer in her eyes. "I'm hoping to."

Their smiles contained the same anticipation. They looked at one another to make sure the other got the pun. Neither could refrain. Laughter burst first from Esme, then from Johnny. They doubled over laughing at their own laughter. Unexpectedly, Stephan joined in as if he too was in on the joke. Gradually, the laughter became mirth, the howls chortle, then happy sniffles.

Stephan settled down first and headed toward the door. Sitting straight and wiping the laughter from her eyes, Esme attempted to wave goodbye, and they rose together.

As she and Johnny approached the door, they spontaneously started laughing again, this time turning toward one another, dipping their heads, then glancing at the ceiling and repeating the moves of some weird folk dance. Back and forth they went as if prodding one another to keep exchanging some unspoken rule of laughter to exhaustion.

Johnny couldn't remember when he'd ever laughed so hard, not even in their first insane outburst the night he met her at The Woebegone. To his surprise she took his hand. She said nothing but stepped onto the sidewalk and headed him in the direction of Rags-To-Riches.

When they arrived she loosened her grip to unlock the door. Before stepping inside, she looked into his eyes and let her breath out slowly. "Tennyson said it best."

> 'Twilight and bell,
> And after that the dark
> And may there be no sadness of farewell
> When I embark.'

She ended the poem in the flicker of a smile. "I'll see you tomorrow at St. Brigid's. You're still coming, aren't you?"

Chapter 36

When he left The Woebegone it was snowing again, this time amidst a wet wind so cold, that he had to take the trolley across town. The poor on the curbs were grouped in their familiar small bunches for warmth. Occasionally, they shuffled around to swap those on the outside for those on the inside so as to exchange warmth among them. Johnny's heart went out to them. He was a veteran like many, and in a way, a vagrant as well. Why had fate spared him such a life, or had it?

He felt guilty being excited among these veterans and vagrants and so nervous that the thrill of seeing Nora bordered on fear. He'd stayed awake anticipating every possible reaction she might have, if and when she first spotted him in the audience. Gradually sorting through the reactions, he was left with two bad ones: that her eyes would seethe with hatred or fear or that she would neglect any feeling that arose, dismissing him as she might anyone on the battlefield she'd laid to rest in her memory.

But those dark possibilities gave way to the gnawing hope that her eyes might rest on his with care, that her spirit might show itself to be eternal, as Esme's seemed to be. Both she and Esme had been bestowed their spirit from afar, Esme perhaps from the faeries, as she claimed, and Nora undoubtedly from her father. As she was fond of saying, he'd launched her from his shoulders into the history of Irish freedom and watched her every move, even as he camped in the afterlife. He'd written a note bestowing on her the name, Sarosa, and he'd slipped it into Johnny's hand just before the soldiers came to escort him to his death. Nora had taken the name to mean *unyielding*.

James had gotten it right, for Nora's spirit was indestructible, whether in battle or by the campfire or in his arms. If anyone could overcome the ravages of grief, she was the person. For her the past was gone, but was *he* gone with it? Did she ever wish she'd stayed with him? Had she found a new lover? Did she regret taking the gun from his head?

When he arrived at St. Brigid's, parishioners and visitors, even those who'd become non-believers due to the conflicting horrors of war, were rushing to the church. The stone stairway to the entrance was jammed. He wedged between them and was carried into the nave, stirred by the enthusiasm. He almost panicked at the thought of not being able to find a seat and having to stand in the rear, so far away that she might not be able to recognize him. To his relief he spotted Esme seated in a middle row, her thick golden hair looping over the shoulders of the manikin's dress.

St. Brigid was seated next to her by the aisle. The abbess turned and saw Johnny. She tapped Esme on the shoulder and together they waved him down. St. Brigid squeezed into the aisle. "Saved for you, Johnny. Sorry to run but Nora's about to appear and I have the introduction. I spent time with her this morning, and I can say, without hesitation that she's determined, that one."

Johnny watched as she disappeared into those searching for a seat.

"She's remarkable," Esme said when she and Johnny sat down. "She recognized me the minute I came into the church. She introduced herself and brought me right here, saying she could feel that this is where I should be sitting."

"Did she say anything else, anything about Nora?"

"She said we float on what we call our destiny. For most people fate and destiny are one and the same, the place in life where we are inescapably bound. 'But, not on your life,' she said. Fate finds amusement at our inability to escape the worst in us. She said a perfect example was the Tan who attacked me and his confession. By confessing he thought he'd found a free and welcoming life after death. But no. There are cruelties for which Christ Himself would demand harsh repayment, such as what McGrath did to me. And the task falls to me to deprive him."

A shivering man seated in front of them turned around and put a finger to his lips. "She's about to begin."

Together, Nora and Saint Brigid mounted the altar steps and went to the podium. Johnny tensed. He could barely watch but could not escape.

Nora wore a black clerics robe with a scarf bearing the Irish tri-colors draped around her neck. Her dark hair hung free and unkempt, longer than Johnny recalled. In her father's make-shift bedroom in the Royal Castle, the first time he'd seen her, she'd also been wearing black: a black coat, a black tight-waisted dress and a body-hugging black blouse with a narrow neckline. He now realized the sensuality he so fondly remembered did not project from her as it did with Esme but stayed hidden within her body. Yet she possessed a statuesque, impenetrable beauty, one that passed along unchallenged in hand-me-down photographs and drew one's eyes into her ancestry.

Saint Brigid introduced her, backgrounding her history as a rebel, her role as a member of Sinn Fein and to Nora's smile, the skyward flight she'd taken from her father's shoulders bearing the name he'd bequeathed her, *Sarosa*.

Nora's flesh-colored lips opened in appreciation. She thanked the audience for attending and St. Brigid for inviting her. She spoke about the purpose of Sinn Fein and pleaded with the audience to contribute to the cause of independence and by asking relatives in Ireland to join the movement. "St. Brigid has received approval from the Church to donate today's offering to Sinn Fein. We desperately need your contributions and trust that the Almighty will bless your tithes."

Then she began to read the Proclamation. She read slowly, with pride, solemnly but with enthusiasm. She did not look up until the last line, which she passionately recited from memory: "In this supreme hour the Irish nation must, by its valor and discipline, and by the readiness of its children to sacrifice themselves for the common good, prove itself worthy of the august destiny to which it is called."

Johnny remembered reading the Proclamation for the first time in Buckles. The words had affected him then, but reading it himself was far different than hearing it spoken by Nora. Her voice possessed the soul of her father. He wondered if James was speaking through her, from heaven.

She leaned towards a hushed audience, nodding as though giving herself permission to continue. "We must cherish both freedom and independence, for they are what our forebears, friends and relatives died for. The authors and signatories of the Proclamation achieved their common destiny, their ultimate revenge, by dying for Ireland at the hands of the British forces. And to that end, I would like to share the story of my father's death."

The shock sent piercing barbs through Johnny's chest. Esme grabbed his hand. Though tempted to leave, he knew he'd never make it up the aisle. He was as bound to the pew as James had been to his post the day Johnny shot him. He took deep breaths and let them out slowly as Nora began.

"The night before my father was put to death, my mother, Lillie, and I were staying at a friend's house. At one o'clock in the morning a messenger came to tell us that my father was to die and that he'd asked to see his wife and eldest daughter. On the morning of the Rising his leg had been shot to pieces in the General Post Office, so mother got the idea that his injury had overtaken him at last. I knew better. His execution had been ordered. Since the day he was captured, he'd prayed to die before a British firing squad, fervently believing that his execution, along with that of the other signatories, would serve to unite Ireland behind the Rebellion.

"They drove us in an open lorry to see him. There wasn't a soul in the streets. My mother said she'd never heard such silence in Dublin. With hope in her voice, she wondered if God had given Ireland its well-deserved freedom and declared the Rising over. I said that I hoped it was so, fully knowing it wasn't but lacking the courage to say more. The air over the Quay smelled of gas and burning buildings, but there was something in the stench I couldn't identify, something neither pleasant nor foul. The next day it came to me. It was the smell of death." Nora paused and gripped the sides of the altar.

"The loving nurse outside my Da's room had always searched us before entering to make sure we weren't bringing him a gun or knife, but on that night, she said it wasn't necessary and let us pass.

"My father asked momma if she knew what this meant, and she broke down, knowing the true answer. He begged her not to cry. 'It's been a beautiful life, James,' she said. 'And it is to have a beautiful end,' he replied. Then, a British officer entered the room unannounced. 'Time is up. He's to be shot at dawn.'"

The audience sat breathless as Nora stopped to wipe her eyes.

Johnny's hands were trembling as he remembered being called to Lieutenant Danes office earlier that night and being told that Connolly was to be executed. Danes forced Johnny to select from a deck of playing cards spread on the officer's desk. If he drew either a spade or a club, he would have to serve on James' firing squad. If he drew a diamond or a heart, he'd be allowed to return to his daily duties. Johnny's hand quivered as he reached for the card. He'd drawn the jack of spades.

Filled with anguish, Nora's voice surfaced through his memory. "They took my father to the Stonebreaker's Yard, strapped him into a chair, and pinned a tiny white tag over his heart."

Johnny was hurled into the story. He was kneeling before James with his hands and arms shaking so hard he could not hold his aim, until James, though blindfolded, somehow knew and demanded that he pull the trigger.

"They fired... and sent my father into eternity," Nora said. "Then, the priest checked his heart and ordered the *coup de grace,* to be certain his soul would be available to make the crossing into heaven." She looked toward the stained-glass windows.

When her eyes returned to the audience, they locked on Johnny's. She gaped in shock. Fidgeting and tinkering nervously with the papers before her, she could not take her eyes from him. Her hands fumbled with the mike. To Johnny, the silence registered even louder than before. He was besieged with fear. Would she call him out by name? Would she point to him and shame him for all the Irish to see and declare him Judas? His legs began to shake. His boots tapped the floor. Esme let go of his hand and clutched his knee but it did little to steady him.

Nora's stare feasted on Johnny but gradually shifted from shock to her tried and true determination to overcome. She broke the stare. "So, I must ask you, my fellow Irish, are we bound to the sorrow of our memories or may we restore ourselves by avenging evil?" Her voice gained strength. "If we do not, sorrow and regret for not having done so will linger in every hallway of our past. It is like living in a house of mirrors until we right the wrong. Is that what we fought for and died for in The Rising?

"My father restored not only himself but all of Ireland by giving his life to avenge the cruelty of our suppressors. His death was the Sword of Damocles for our rulers, and while they've not been completely ousted, we are well on our way to having them gone. Once they are, we will be able to breathe deeply and give thanks for the many blessings God has bestowed on us through fate, His helper."

Fate was on God's side? Had Johnny heard right? Had she just said there was no room in her heart for forgiveness? Had she firmly stood by the idea of revenge by allowing him to live, cursed forever? Or had she not forgiven herself for letting him live? Is that what Johnny Ryan, the solicitor from the High Court, missed when Nora jerked the order from his hand, quickly gave it back and abruptly asked him to leave? Had Ryan missed Nora's disbelief, her incredulity that her mother had signed the order? Worried that Nora's mention of him was still to come, Johnny braced and squeezed edge of the pew with both hands.

"Easy, Johnny, easy," Esme whispered.

"My mother and I went to claim his body the next day but he'd been taken from the Yard to be buried. They wouldn't tell us where. Nurse Meeks didn't know either but she'd cut a lock of his hair and saved it for my mother. Only days later did I learn that he'd been buried with the other signatories, in a limestone pit in Arbour Hill Cemetery. Together, their bodies vanished as their souls rose victorious!"

The rise of passion in her voice ended in a sudden silence, letting everyone know she'd finished. The delayed applause climbed the walls of the church as St. Brigid made her way over to kiss Nora's cheeks. Together they turned to face the reredos and cross themselves. Then, St. Brigid returned to the altar and blessed her for coming. The applause rose. Nora left the podium, returning twice to the audience's demand.

St. Brigid stood beside her and brought her hands to prayer as the church quieted. "Please bow your heads in a moment of silence," she requested, "and offer thanks to our Lord for the presence of this extraordinary, strong and courageous woman who has aligned herself with God."

As Brigid took her arm and led her from the dais, Esme tugged on Johnny's jacket. "You must go to her."

Immobilized, his brain stunned, he watched them leave the stage. "Go to her?" Is that what he'd heard? What was wrapped in all the words she'd spoken? Should he go to her after what she'd said, effectively affirming there was no room in her heart for forgiveness, that she firmly stood by her revenge by letting him stay alive, thereby cursed forever? Or had she not forgiven herself for letting him live?

"Johnny, St. Brigid's here to escort you," Esme said.

St. Brigid was standing by him in the aisle. She wore a smile. "Esme's right. Nora's bags are in the temporary vestry behind the church. I'm to meet her there to say goodbye. You can see her alone but only for a few minutes. She boards the ship for Ireland early tomorrow and needs her rest."

"Go now," Esme encouraged, nudging him with her elbow. "Hurry, if it's only to... no matter, it will go far."

"Johnny, take the far door right of the altar," St. Brigid said. "Then to your left past the statue of Jesus on up the stairs. He'll be smiling as you pass. There is no door, for God prevents any bad weather from entering, but you should knock on the opening and wait for her there." She stepped back so he could pass.

"I'll wait for you out front on the steps," Esme said.

His heart raced as he found his way to the vestry, a small cabin-like structure behind the church. Planted between two huge leafless elms, it looked like the treehouse in Cork Park where he'd played as a youngster. . Trembling, he looked up at the opening, grasped the railing and climbed the ladder-like steps. He reached the doorway and knocked on the wall.

"Just a moment, my Saint."

Her intimate voice, the tone she'd used when she spoke to him in private, had not changed. Smooth and low with a natural quality of skepticism evident even in her playfulness. Suddenly she appeared in the doorway.

Aghast, she stepped back. She'd taken off the clerics and now wore an emerald green dress that seemed identical to Esme's, only tamer, longer and collared. Fine lines skimmed her face now, not those of age but the incisions of all she'd been through, lines of survival that spoke to her beauty.

Frozen between then and now, neither spoke. Her disbelieving stare would not give way to his. He was thrust back to the time he told her where her father had been buried and offered to take her there. The silence felt like the moment before she agreed to let him show her. As then, the awkwardness became unbearable.

Their simultaneously strange "hellos" hung in the air before reigniting the silence. Her lips parted. He waited for her to tell him to leave.

"Johnny," she said, hesitating but readying to say more. Her face bore no hostility, her voice no inflection of anger.

He took a step toward her and stopped. She didn't move. Her eyes darted toward the doorway. When they returned he grabbed her by the arms and pulled her to him. Her body stiffened and she tried to wrench away. Alarm filled her eyes but he kissed her anyway. She tried to break it off but he seized her face. Her mouth opened but only to bite hard into his bottom lip. As he tasted his warm blood, she drove her arms up sharply between his hands and freed herself.

He clenched his lip. The blood oozed between his fingers. She stepped toward him, seized his jacket and jerked him to her. He winced as her lips covered his and her tongue thrust between his teeth. The blood flowed between them. When they both began to cough, she released her lips, grasped the habit, and wiped her mouth. "There, I'm done," she said.

Done with what? He was afraid to ask. By kissing him after such an angry refusal, had she been trying to say she'd been wrong all along and forgiven him at last? Had her need for revenge been regretfully left on the bluffs, only partially fulfilled?

"Have you forgiven me?" he mumbled. "The High Court..."

"The Court has no admission into my heart." Her stare was impossible to decipher. The silence trembled. "But as hard as it's been to come to this, I will tell you. For serving on my father's firing squad, I have forgiven you, but it had nothing to do with the Court order.

"After the Treaty, I tracked down Lieutenant Danes who gave the order for my father's execution. I found him in the Royal Castle and begged him to tell me the truth. He was reluctant but he complied. He told me that my father did call out to you, pleading for you to focus your aim." She looked down at her hands which seemed more agitated than her voice.

"I also sought out Nurse Meeks who told me that you and my Da were quite close, that you treated him with utmost respect, if not with love, and he felt the same about you. Yes, he wanted to die. Yes, he demanded that you shoot him. I understand that now. It solidified all he taught me and all he sent me to do for the cause of independence. I guess you could say that in accepting his call for execution, a wooden bridge was replaced by iron." She met Johnny's eyes for once.

"Thank God I let you live. And furthermore, I let my discoveries be known through Sinn Fein because I was afraid someone would seek you out to settle what they thought to be the score. I let O'Neill know and asked him to tell our comrades. They heard your case in Kinsale but behind closed doors, and as you well know, the judges did not accept what you did and thus declared you a traitor. I have visited that court and presented them with the High Court's ruling, which they didn't take kindly, but they promised to abide by it."

Johnny stood locked in disbelief. He felt he could not have hoped for more. She understood at last and had not only forgiven him but tried her best to persuade others to do the same! Despite the pain in his lip, he was about to kiss her again. Then he saw her eyes harden.

"But whenever I think of the night I overheard Dahl ask you if I knew you'd been on the firing squad, it tears my heart out. I gave myself to you never knowing, never even suspecting you'd done anything of the kind." Her voice strained with her emphasis. "And all the while you... all the while you let me fall in love with you. You trapped me with an unspoken lie. If we had married, would you have kept it to yourself forever? Or did you believe that after years together you could confess and it wouldn't have mattered? Johnny, you draped a hangman's noose around our necks. If we'd married and I'd discovered what you'd done, the trap door would have sprung open."

Haunted by her vexing eyes, he could barely get the words out. "I loved you so much I couldn't bring myself to tell you. I was wrong and had I to do it over again... if I could trade who I am today with who I was then, I would have never kept it ..."

"Johnny, be honest. You would have done the same thing."

"So, you haven't forgiven me?"

"I've tried my utmost, more than that, my damnedest! Whenever your deception enters my head, I try to dismiss it by swapping it with the favor you did me the night you took me to Arbour Hill. I know it was dangerous and if the Brits had found out, you would have most likely been shot. I tell myself that in the main you were... are... a kind and caring person, though I've seen a different side of you in battle, as you have in me. We both seized every chance to take revenge. It is our fate that we do so."

"Still?"

A hint of exasperation showed beneath her tears. "Still, I haven't forgiven you... but this you should know, I love you, Johnny. I cannot deny it." She stared beyond him toward the opening. "Is there any chance that you would return to Ireland?" Her words were filled with anguish and shocking tenderness.

Where but on the bluff of Kinsale could he be? Where but on O'Brien's porch? Where but in the barn or in the woods making love to her? He saw *The Pestilence* in the harbor and heard its foghorn, saw the American flag on the mast, entered the hull with Seamus and made the crossing, received the Court's so-called blessing all the while hearing the very words Nora had just uttered. And yet, her request for him to return to Ireland, as gripping and irrepressible as it was, rode on the same incalculable risk as had his deceit. How long would it be before she awoke one morning to admit that what he'd done, or failed to do, was something she could never forgive?

And yet when she slipped her arms through his, the gesture did what words could never do. He had no idea what to make of it and kept staring at her. Maybe she and Esme and St. Brigid all understood something far beyond him, that revenge and forgiveness were interchangeable. Was his task to choose one or the other, or was leaving things up to him no more than a fool's game?

"I would kiss you but I'm afraid it would hurt," Nora said. "So here." She kissed him on the cheek. "We leave at eight in the morning from pier ninety-four. I'll have a cabin ready for you."

Chapter 37

Esme was waiting for him on the church steps. "My God," she exclaimed when she saw his swollen, purple lip. "What happened?"

She listened in bewilderment as he told her. "I'm glad she didn't kiss your arse or you'd be doing the Arab squat."

A laugh forced its way through his heart.

"So, she hasn't forgiven you?" Esme said, wiping the blood from his chin.

"No, at least not yet." He went on to recite as best he could what Nora had told him.

Esme listened with questioning eyes. "Johnny, how was it you forgave my lying to you, not only outright but unspoken for quite a while, my pretending to be other than I am, my deception? Was it just because you weren't in love with me and so it didn't matter?"

"I don't know."

"Meaning, *yes,* I take it. Well, it's for the best that you weren't, for it's time to part. You have little time to get ready for the crossing."

They started down the steps together. "Oh, I almost forgot," she said, pulling a piece of paper from inside her raincoat. "Here, a gift, as if written tomorrow, when lies can no longer be told, if such a thing can be imagined. Read it after a couple of poteens and remember me by it."

With a heavy chest he watched her walk away. He'd never known anyone like her, probably because there *was* no one like her. He slipped a finger under the seal and was about to open the envelope when a young girl's voice cried out. "Mommy, there he is! There's Johnny! He brought me back from heaven."

He saw Jenny running toward him with her mother trying to keep up.

He folded the letter and jammed it into his coat pocket just as she threw her arms around him. Her head was bandaged with a trauma cap — strips of gauze wrapped around her head and laced over her injured ear and through her reddish blonde hair. Johnny had seen replicas of the cap in the Royal Castle where wounded British soldiers were treated.

Jenny kissed him a dozen times and when her mother, with her face red in embarrassment, tried to pull her away, Jenny shrugged her off. "No, momma, this is Johnny! He saved my life with the wine Jesus drank." She stared at his lip and loosened her grip. "Did you get into a fight?"

Johnny chuckled. "No, I just bit my lip, while I was in church."

"That's where I saw you. We were late so we had to sit in the balcony. Afterward, I wanted to run down and see you, but the sister at the door saw my head and said we had to do the Fourteen Stations of the Cross before anything else."

Her mom intervened at last. "I'm so sorry, Johnny. The doctors think the wound has affected her mind a bit. But I so wanted to meet you and thank you for saving her. Thank the good Lord, the sister had us journey to the stations. Otherwise we would've been long gone by now and missed you. Did you forget something and have to circle back?"

"No, I had to —"

"It's okay to tell us that you stayed to give thanks. I've done it many times. Well, no matter, we just want to thank you from the bottom of our hearts."

"Jenny's giving me way too much credit. I was just there trying to protect her when she came out of the shock."

"No, you saved me, Johnny" the girl said. "You gave me a sip of wine and I tasted what it meant to be alive. I didn't know before I went to heaven, when

I got to see how boring it was up there. All these people like ghosts wandering through one another and not saying a word. And there wasn't any chocolate candy. They didn't need it because they didn't have tummies."

"That's enough, honey. This fine gentleman has a lot to do. Thank you for coming to her rescue. It was God's will, I'm sure. Let's be on our way, Jenny."

Johnny was about to ask where they lived but knew he was leaving and didn't want to set up room for disappointing her.

"My name is Jenny Patrick and my momma's Beachtree Patrick. We have the same last name because my daddy gave it to both of us."

Her mother chuckled. "That's enough, Jenny." She glanced at Johnny. My name is Beatrice, not Beachtree. As I said, she gets a little confused from time to time."

"How old is she?"

"Twelve."

"No, mommy, I already told you, I'll always be seven and you know why."

Beatrice smiled. "I know, because the word seven rhymes with heaven, and you don't want to get so old you have to live up there. Oh, Johnny, if you'd ever like to visit us, please do. We live on Avenue B, number seven."

Johnny hesitated. "That's very kind of you. I'd love to, but as luck would have it, I'm leaving tomorrow morning for Ireland."

"Where's that?" Jenny asked.

"Across the ocean."

"Are you going in a boat?"

Johnny smiled. "Sort of, on a ship."

"When people cross the ocean, can they ever come back?"

"If love goes with them."

"I love you, Johnny."

The words came again — from Jenny, Esme, Dillon and Nora, all in the same breath. "I love you, too, and will definitely come back to visit."

"O, goodie!" She turned to her mother. "Can I kiss him goodbye?"

"Of course."

Jenny pecked his cheek. Beatrice took her hand and they walked away. When they were almost out of sight, Jenny turned and waved.

With a lump in his throat, Johnny couldn't help but feel that maybe true love belonged only to children. Then he remembered Esme's letter.

Chapter 38

He opened the letter expecting no more than a note simply saying good-bye. When he saw how long it was, he worried that Esme had revealed yet another story of her past. Each had been far more tragic than the ones that went before. It came to him — what he'd so often felt, that she would take her own life at some point. Was this her suicide note? He was tempted to throw it in the nearest trashcan without reading it. But his eyes could not resist.

"Johnny, I'll not be able to come to the pier to see you off tomorrow. I wanted to, that I did, but decided not to. I don't think I could have stood there and waved goodbye. The sorrow would have just been too painful.

I'm not sure how to go about this. What I am about to write is the truth. I know with my checkered past there is no reason for you to believe anything I say, but please, promise me you'll at least put the letter in a drawer, to give it time to blossom into truth.

I've not been forthright about love, or about other things, and that's stating it mildly. I put forth my true beliefs in a liar's revulsion of revenge, while constantly hoping that someday revenge would be mine. It's what my life has been about since I came to America. I try to be kind, but as you now know, there's another side of me filled with hatred.

It's true, I am leaving to kill the man who murdered my father and raped me. In you, I have found love for the first time in my life and realize, as did Joshua, that it expands our vision, opens us to choices, desires and hopes that could, should, overcome any need to take revenge. Yet my heart is chained to finding redemption for my father. Call it the demand of hate or the Almighty, I am forced to take up the sword.

I love you — that's what I'm trying to say in this pitiful letter. I cannot open or close my eyes without seeing you, feeling you and wanting you in every way possible. Until now, I've kept it to myself and for this I've sinned yet again, for it is cruel to withhold love.

Even though I know of your love for Nora, how very much she means to you, and why at the epitome of irony, it is fate's wish that you two reunite, strangely, I tell myself I wish it also — only to catch myself in yet another lie!

Last night, I did something I never do. I knelt beside the bed and prayed. I'm not sure what for, and I'm not sure God knew either, but when I grew tired of searching for something to say, I got off my knees and it came to me to write this letter. Perhaps it came from Him.

When you and Nora are together in Ireland, I'm sure there will be little, if any place in your heart for me, nor should there be, but let me remain a recluse in your memory. Please let me remain and know I love you. Perhaps now, I'll get myself to a nunnery!

Promise me you'll go easy on the poteen — and a course in Shakespeare wouldn't hurt! If only we could revisit our past as those we've become while time has passed, we would do differently now. If only we could return and face the same obstacles, we would realize that we are not today who we were then and forgive ourselves for what we did. If only, our regrets would disappear, our relentless guilt vanish and our souls renew.

We, if only in the faeries' branches, Esme."

An unspeakable sadness came over Johnny. He would never forget her. He sat down on the cold steps and read the letter again. He felt the profound, hidden spirit whose confessions bore a thousand meanings. He got up, holding the letter as if it were an ancient parchment too frail to fold again. He brought it to his nose and smiled at the fragrance of lilacs. He understood why she'd used the lie to protect herself from men. He hoped she would find her way safely to the branches and find freedom from her past.

Chapter 39

Johnny awoke and glanced at his wristwatch. It was seven-thirty. The ship was scheduled to leave at eight. He threw on last night's clothes, grabbed his suitcase and rushed down the stairwell. He rammed the door guide and dashed out into the cold. Hell's Kitchen, this dreadful place, this demented, wretched place — the gangs, the fights, the murders, the ghosts of the past. How was it possible that leaving these horrors behind could lay any sense of regret upon him? His world wasn't here, and in truth it never had been, because still tethered to the bluffs of Kinsale, he'd never really left Ireland. He'd made the crossing, but in body only, not in spirit.

Even in fear of missing the launch, he thought of the bloody, fervent kiss. He was on the verge of collecting his breath to shout out that he loved her when the voice from the Bluffs spoke again, "She will accompany you across the ocean and beyond."

He ran harder for the pier. Was it because of Nora? Had fate found a reason to side with her? Had she been so severely punished by the death of her father that fate had become remorseful and was now mending his ways by vouching for love? Is that what he'd seen in Nora's eyes, as well as heard in her voice, if not tasted in the blood they'd shared in the vestry?

He saw the sun as it was rising and the moon as it was setting, each oddly in the sky together, each set on its own horizon. He heard Esme's asking if he'd ever been in love. With sunset masking her face before settling around her like a shawl, he'd answered her truthfully. Amidst flashes of lightning that seemed to rest on her eyelids, she listened and turned away to search the horizon.

He remembered the first time he saw Nora in her father's hospital room, James with his crippled leg caged in a wooden box that resembled a bear trap. He saw her on the road at Kilmichael where she'd seemingly washed the vanquished lad back to life and all the way to the Crossbarry battlefield in County Cork where he'd searched desperately for her, worried she'd been killed. He saw her moonlit body lying on the hay bales in the loft of the barn.

For a moment he felt curiously lost, but once upon Death Avenue, he spotted the ship only two blocks away and ran even faster. It was a huge, coal-fired steamer. The masts had been replaced with four slanted chimneys, stacks as they called them, each billowing a mirage of ghostly dark clouds. Something about the ship brought a sense of remorse to the clatter of his boots.

The foghorn blew again. He noticed a woman in the crowd of travelers on the top deck, waving frantically with both arms. He waved, and her arms appeared to leap out of her shoulders to wave even harder. It was Nora. It had to be! He tongued the scab on his bottom lip. She'd said he wasn't yet forgiven but in the next breath she'd asked for him to return with her.

When he veered toward the runway that led to the gangplank, he saw Esme waving from the water's end of the pier. With her were Joshua and Dillon and next to them the Indy. Johnny headed toward them for a quick goodbye, but slowed when they started shouting and pointing to the ship.

The loose chains fixed to the gangplank's banisters clinked as they tightened. Nora was waving feverishly and between the ship's blasts he thought he could hear her screaming for him to hurry. His heart pumped as though he were sprinting across a battlefield. The familiar illusion that had so often haunted him in battle — the narrowing bridge between survival and death — called out to him. The bridge was no longer an illusion.

As a blast of steam, signaling departure, burst from the stacks, the gangplank quivered and the pier began to shake. Johnny found himself at the fork in the tunnel. It wasn't father Doolin's voice that pointed the way but the gripping spirit running throughout Esme's note. "I cannot open or close my eyes without seeing you, feeling you and wanting you in every way possible. Until now, I've kept it to myself and for this I've sinned yet again, for it is cruel to withhold love."

Nor would *he* any longer. He dropped the suitcase and took off, pumping his arms furiously. His vision blurred, but he knew it didn't matter, for he'd learned that apparitions thrived in vagueness. Her aura rushed toward him. He threw his arms around her, jerking her off the quay. The familiar fragrance of lilacs swept over him. Intoxicated, he whirled her round and round. She hugged him tightly, locked her legs around his waist and shouted, "I love you, Johnny Flynn!"

It was neither Nora's voice on the Bluffs or something from their common mouth when she and Esme became one in the field of shamrocks. It was Esme's voice alone. It contained not only the thrill of the moment but of tomorrow as well.

Stumbling dizzily, he set her down. Joshua and Dillon clapped and shouted. Johnny's head reeled as the planks in the pier creaked louder. Without warning, Esme pulled away and took several steps backwards. She yanked her skirt waist-high and jerked his pistol from the holster. His heart sank. The gun trembled in her hand as she raised it toward the sky.

Just when he thought fate had returned him to the bluffs, Esme smiled, hurled the pistol into the water and ran to him. She threw her arms around him before he could return the smile. They kissed tenderly and then rested their lips upon one another's in an embrace far beyond sensuality into a moment of joyous disbelief. The groaning sound of the ship edging from the pier caused them to turn.

Nora waved enthusiastically, as if she, too, realized fate had been defeated. Esme waved back and took Johnny's arm. He enclosed her face in his hands. For a moment he pictured Grace Gifford's eyes staring at Joseph when they'd wed. He'd never seen such a look of love, until now.

"I do love you, Johnny."

It came to him from the letter she'd written and from Joshua as well, "You never realize what you have until you've destroyed it, or left it behind."

The words streamed across his eyes as though carried on the side of the ship as it pulled slowly into the Hudson. Time cartwheeled from then to now. The familiar voice from the Bluffs arrived breathless, unable to scream for Johnny to shut his mouth. In an unmistakably demanding tone, it shouted for him to place his faith in the aura of the angel's lamp and affirm what he'd been too locked into the past to admit — he'd fallen in love with Esme.

"Tell her, damn you! Tell her!"

"I love you!" Johnny shouted. "I love you!"

They listened as his words floated on the fading goodbye of the ship's horn. Esme's eyes widened. The sun and moon surfaced separately in each eye. Tears ran down her face as her fingers brushed his cheeks.

"Other than my Da, no man has ever said those words to me."

"I love you," they said together.

Who among us knows what brings us to the outburst of love, that volcanic eruption of the heart. Another's eyes, their fragrance, their fire, their gentleness? A tomorrow filled with faith in one another, freed from fate's captivity. Unconditional love, love with access to another's heart bereft of skepticism or doubt, blame or jealousy. Love that survives the maelstrom to make the crossing between Then and Now. They were free to determine their own destiny together, free to hold hands and kiss and run to the end of the pier, shouting, "I love you!"

Laughing, they jumped into the freezing water as Joshua and Dillon cheered.

Chapter 40

A week after Christmas, Esme received a letter from Ina, letting her know that McGrath had taken his own life.

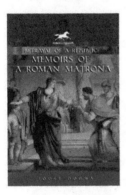

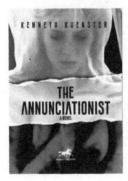

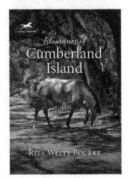